# THE KRAKEN'S QUEEN

A GRIM HOLLOW NOVEL

TATI B. ALVAREZ

ISBN:

E-book: 979-8-9893168-7-8

Paperback: 979-8-9893168-8-5

Edited By: On the Same Page Editing and Mountains Wanted

Cover Designer: Coffin Print Designs

*For those fighting silent battles and wondering if you're
strong enough. You are.*

# AUTHOR'S NOTE

This book contains elements of:

- Death of a loved one (off page)
- Explicit sexual scenes
- Domestic violence
- Panic attacks
- Anxiety
- Fantasy war
- Verbal and physical abuse

Please make sure you are protecting your mental health. If you need more information send me a message on any of my socials. Otherwise, happy reading!

Kraken Lagoon
Nephilim Land
Dragon's Keep

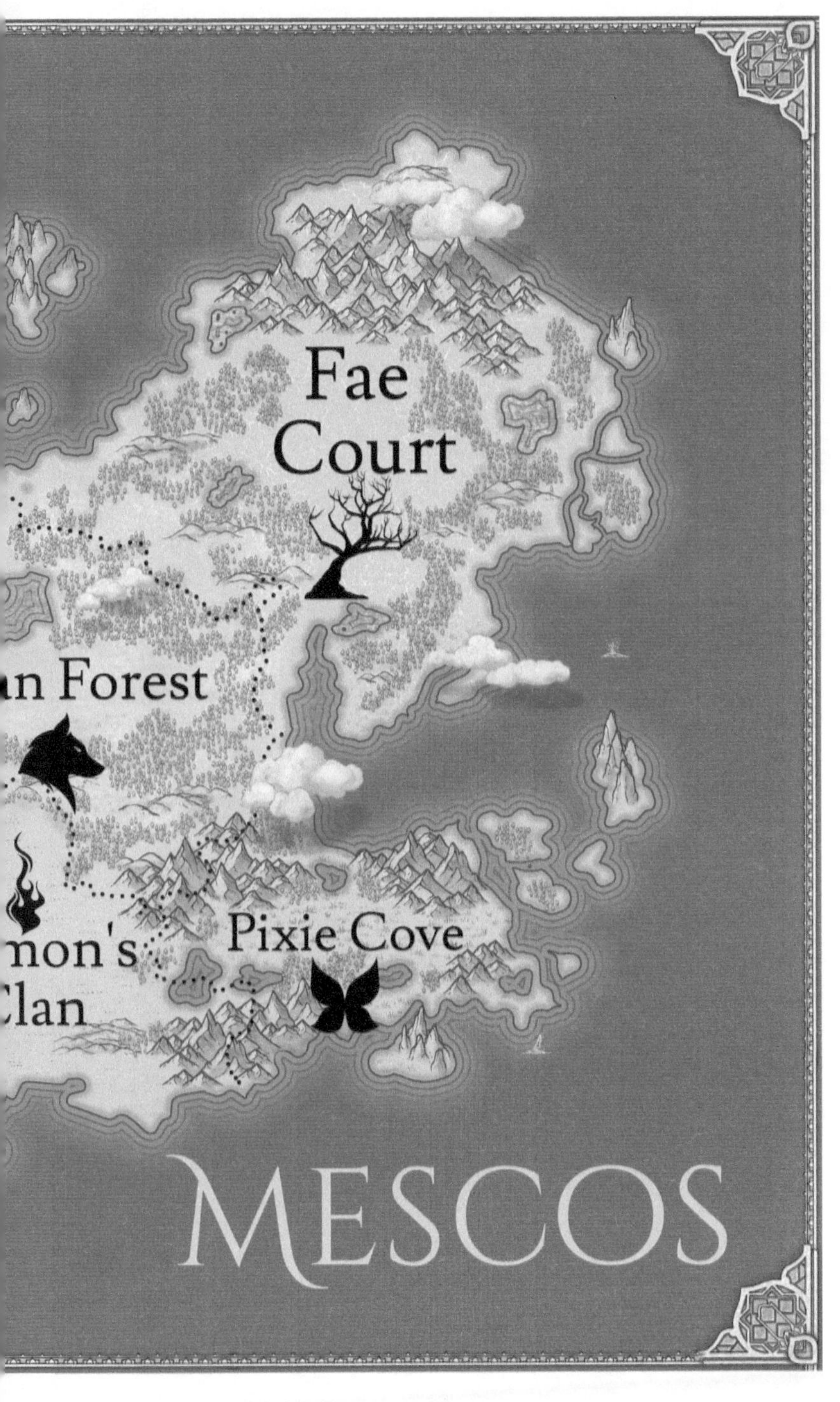

Fae Court
n Forest
non's
Clan
Pixie Cove
MESCOS

# PROLOGUE



According to historians of times before, Mescos was once a thriving country full of supernatural creatures and their human companions. In Mescos, humans held their own power, given to them by their god to ensure peace amongst the supernaturals and humans. Humans strengthened their lands and provided immense strength to the supernaturals they mated. Together, their lands, kingdoms, and people thrived.

The time for peace was short-lived, though, as a new danger emerged.

Nephilim, giant winged creatures born from greed and hatred, appeared seemingly overnight. Historians differ in opinion on how these creatures came to be. Some historians argue Nephilim were sent by angry gods, while others say Nephilim traveled from lands far from Mescos. Their origins are still unknown.

The Nephilim brought darkness to the kingdoms. Their leader, Gadreel, led the slaughter of humans to gain their magic. Thousands of humans and supernaturals died in what historians call The Great War. Each human death brought power to the hellish winged creatures.

Knowing they had very little time before the Nephilim became too powerful, the six rulers of Mescos—dragon, pixie, fae, wolf, demon, and kraken—agreed to work together in order to take down the common enemy.

The war between the rulers of Mescos and the Nephilim happened at Dragon's Keep. The rulers of Mescos, their armies, and their human mates fought countless hours against Gadreel's people. Many fell in an attempt to rid Mescos of the vile creatures.

Knowing they were unprepared to slaughter the Nephilim, the Pixie King and his human queen came together, combining their magic as one. Upon seeing this, the other rulers followed suit and, within the mountains east of Dragon's Keep, a magical prison took form.

One by one, Nephilim were captured by the magic and imprisoned within the mountains. Gadreel, knowing his army would not win this war, cursed the rulers of Mescos before he was imprisoned. He damned the kingdoms: in one hundred years, if the rulers did not find their human mates, disaster would fall upon their people, and the Nephilim would rise again.

In his final act of rebellion, Gadreel used the last bit of stolen magic he absorbed from the deaths of humans and destroyed the portal between Mescos and the human world, effectively cutting off access to their human mates.

The leaders of Mescos won that day, but it cost them everything.

Over the next hundred years, the last humans of Mescos died off. With no connection to the human world, the Nephilim rose again, escaping their prison in the mountains. Now the only hope the six new Kings of Mescos have comes from an unexpected ally known as Ender The Guardian. He alone possesses the power to travel between worlds and bring humans to their supernatural mates.

Little is known about The Guardian.

Today, the safety and future of Mescos hang in the balance. History is being written in real time. These accounts will be updated as necessary.

# CHAPTER 1
# ALLARICK

I hear the accused's pleas before I see him. The doors to the throne room fling open with a burst of bubbles. Two of my guards lead the merman inside. His teal tail swishes awkwardly, stunting his movement. The two guards wrap their tentacles tighter around the male, bruising his pale flesh as they pull him along and drop him unceremoniously in front of my throne.

My guards swim forward, presumably to draw their weapons on him, but I put my hand up, and they cease movement. They take their places behind me, golden swords drawn and at the ready. The prisoner trembles, and I sense his unease with so many powerful krakens around him.

Good. He deserves this for what he's done.

"State your name," my thunderous voice booms around us, demanding subservience.

The merman trembles and pushes himself up from the hard stone floor to gaze upon my throne made from aquamarine and pearls. It's a symbol of power. My power. And the man blubbers like a guppy.

"Kaleo, my king," he shrieks. "I'm sorry! The rumors, they are not true. I've been framed—"

"Which is it?" I interrupt him, arching a brow. The merman sputters nonsense, not understanding my question, so I repeat myself. Something I'm not fond of doing. "Which is it? Are you sorry, or have you been framed?"

"F-framed, of course, my king!"

Lie.

He smells of rotten seaweed and rum. I know these types of mermen. Men who think the law doesn't apply to them. Weak men who take advantage of women simply because they can.

"Bring her in," I say to no one in particular.

A moment later, the doors open again. Much different than before. Two females, both merwomen, swim in. One wears the steel uniform of my guards, while the other wears orange shells that match her sunset-colored tail. A band of pearls is clasped tightly around her, accentuating her waist. Her small form shakes, but an encouraging nod from Danika—the guard —has the merwoman standing taller.

The bastard on the ground tenses, face contorting into a violent rage. "You *bitch*!"

The guard nearest the merman lurches forward and brings the hilt of his sword down hard into his stomach. He doubles over, coughing and groaning in pain.

"My king," the woman says, her voice small but mighty. It takes great courage to stand up to monsters, and, as far as I'm concerned, she's the strongest one in the room. "My name is Aerwyna. I've come today to…"

Aerwyna hesitates, eyes wandering over to the male on the ground. For a brief moment, fear overtakes her features. Then Danika is at her side, providing comfort in a way only a woman who has seen the ugly ways of men can. "Go on, Aerwyna. No one here will harm you."

Aerwyna takes my guard's hand in a way that makes me wonder if this bond goes deeper than friendship.

"I'm here today to tell you the crimes of Kaleo," she continues, a new hardness to her voice. "I speak for myself, but also for the victims not ready to come forward. For the victims too traumatized by what this man has taken from us."

"And what has he taken from you, Aerwyna?" I know very well what this man did, but this is Aerwyna's chance to heal, and I shall not deny her that.

"My safety and peace of mind. He stole from me, just as he has done to several other merpeople, a gift we did not willingly give."

"It was willingly!" Kaleo shouts. "Each one came to my bed willingly and laid themselves out for me. I took what they gave."

"Silence!" I roar, and Kaleo flinches like I've slapped him. He'd be so lucky if that is the worst of what I do to him. "Keep him silent," I command, and the guard on his left tears off the tattered shirt Kaleo wears and gags him with it.

"None of us came to him willingly, King Allarick. He forced us to sleep with him, and I do not want anyone else to go through what we did. He is a danger to us all."

Aerwyna turns her attention to Kaleo, her face hardening. "You are a weak, sorry excuse for a merman. May the sea goddess rip your soul to shreds."

"Thank you for recounting the horror this man put you through. I know that wasn't easy. I will punish him with the full extent of my power. He will die so he'll never hurt anyone again."

At the proclamation of his death, Kaleo screams, though the gag muffles his cries. He thrashes against my guards when they reach for him, but they wrap their tentacles around his body and squeeze, immobilizing him.

"Thank you, King Allarick." Aerwyna bows, and Danika leads her out. She doesn't need to see what comes next, but she can trust I'll keep my word.

Once the door closes behind the merwomen, I focus back on Kaleo. My red tentacles move to his gag and rip it free. "Any last words, Kaleo?" I ask as my personal guard, Delmare, hands me his golden sword.

All color drains from Kaleo's face, and his cries start back up. If I weren't such a patient man, I would end his life now and be done with it. It's exactly what I should do...but decorum suggests I give this pathetic excuse of a man his last words.

I don't even realize I've raised my sword until Kaleo screams, "Wait! Please wait! I have information you'll want to hear!"

My attention flickers to Delmare. The older kraken frowns, crossing his arms over his chest. Something akin to curiosity sparks in his eyes. "Speak fast, felon. You try our king's patience."

"It's just whispers from the dark sea—"

"I care not for whispers." I raise my sword back up.

"It's about the Nephilim and Leviathan!" he screams, and the room goes silent. Not even a swish of a tail or tentacle can be heard.

I hate to admit it, but I'm intrigued. "Go on," I growl.

A spark of hope flashes across his face, and Kaleo quickly spills his secret. "There's talk of the Leviathan's song carrying through the walls of their prison. The Nephilim strength fuels them, and it's only a matter of time before they become powerful like the Nephilim. They will escape if someone doesn't intervene."

If Kaleo expects his news to shock me, he's sadly mistaken. This information started as a rumor one would hear whispered in a pub. Slowly, it trickled out, as gossip does, and alerted those closest to me. When rumors gain momentum, I find there is some truth to them. It's why I have been looking into this privately for the last few weeks.

My expression remains blank, and I see the moment he realizes his life will not be spared. "Please! I can help! I can—"

I don't get to hear what Kaleo claims he can do for me because I bury my sword into his neck. Crimson red stains the water. I watch the life drain from Kaleo's eyes, and I feel no remorse. Not for him. He has to answer to the sea goddess now. His fate it out of my control.

Still, Kaleo's final words ring in my ear. A reminder to not give up my quest for knowledge about these creatures known as Leviathan. "Delmare."

My guard is at my side in an instant. "I will look into

it, my king," he says without prompting. That's simply our relationship. We've been by each other's sides for decades. Delmare can read me better than anyone here. He offers me advice and has become more of a father figure than anything.

"Report back."

My order is acknowledged with a nod, and just as suddenly as he came, Delmare swims away.

"Dispose of the body. Send female guards to check in on his victims and see if they need anything. We will provide it," I tell the remaining guards. They all nod and make a quick exit. One carries Kaleo's corpse. The damn merman tracks blood throughout the room, tinting the water pink.

Finally, I'm alone and sink into my throne. It's not comfy, but it lets me take in everything that just happened.

Kaleo.

Nephilim.

Leviathan.

And it's my job to protect the merpeople and krakens under my care.

I'm not alone with my thoughts for long. A sudden noise down the hall draws my attention, and I sit up. Moments later, a grave-looking merman comes in. He bows, and I motion for him to speak. Nothing can prepare me for what he says, though.

"My king, Ender is here. He has your queen."

# CHAPTER 2
# ALLARICK

I'm hit with the smell of cedar and pine. A cool wind caresses my chest, reminding me that winter is leaving us soon. I surface on the outskirts of Lycan Forest, scanning the area for potential threats.

And Ender.

The people of the sea don't wander above water often. Some of us have the ability to shift between land legs and our true oceanic form. The world above is a mess with their own set of problems. My people feel safer within our sacred city. The water is familiar, and the land...not so much.

However, meeting Ender and my wife-to-be in my kingdom is out of the question. The human won't have the ability to breathe underwater yet, and Ender is the last person I want in my kingdom. I'm forced to take the man's help, but I still don't completely trust him like some of the other kings of Mescos do. There's something about The Guardian that doesn't sit right with me.

Something he's hiding.

The moment I reach the shore, my bright red tentacles—their natural color—change to better hide in my surroundings. Red is a dead giveaway to enemies, but I'm able to adapt and camouflage myself to blend in better. Soon, I trade my tentacles for legs. Even though I have done this hundreds of times, it always takes me a moment to gather my bearings. My body feels heavier here, and I have to reacquaint myself with my legs. One step forward. Then another.

Before leaving, I remembered to grab a pair of pants. Others may feel comfortable enough to meet their mates with their cock jutting out, but I don't want to scare her. Not when I must make this woman fall in love with me.

Love. Such a small word that carries a heavy weight. A burden and strength wrapped up in one.

"King Allarick," a deep voice calls, and my head whips up. I'm not used to being snuck up on, but Ender has a knack for doing just that. I finish pulling up my pants and move farther onto the land, leaving my ocean and home behind.

Just for a little while.

"Guardian." Ender's gray skin reminds me of a boulder. A massive, impenetrable boulder with horns. He towers over me, the largest man I've seen on land yet. I would be a fool if I felt anything other than unease around him. This man harbors secrets like a sea nymph harbors unsuspecting men: in abundance.

"The contract has been fulfilled. I come to deliver your mate." Ender is straight to the point. He isn't one for small talk, which I can appreciate.

Having been so focused on the man before me, I didn't notice the woman he carries. She's frail and limp in his arms. Her face is covered by a mane of black hair. The steady rise and fall of her chest tell me she's not conscious.

Her skin, golden brown with earthy undertones, has purple and blue bruises running up and down her arms. There are darker bruises around her neck. I can't see the rest of her body, but I'm sure more scars and bruises color her arms and thighs. A beautiful, broken disaster.

This is to be my wife?

"What happened to her?" Her wounds surely can't be inflicted by Ender taking her against her will. The Guardian is many things, but a threat to human women isn't one of them. "Does she need medical attention?"

"Her name is Erin Goodwin," Ender ignores both of my questions. Bastard. "Her story is not mine to tell. Perhaps, if you earn her trust, she will feel comfortable enough to answer your burning questions. But I will say this: Erin has been through more than any person should go through. She's free of her prison."

Again, I take Erin in. I yearn to know her story. How she received those bruises and why she agreed to be swept away from her life to be taken to Mescos. What prison did she need to escape so badly that she was willing to uproot her entire life?

A seed of anger is planted inside me. Hearing more about Erin's past will only make it grow until it consumes me. It's irrational to feel like this about a human I just met, but it's now my job to protect her. I take my jobs seriously.

"Allarick," Ender's voice takes on a somber tone, giving me pause. The Guardian isn't one for emotions, at least none that I've ever witnessed, but he stares down at Erin with a look of sorrow. I have the distinct feeling I'm not going to like what he has to say.

"Erin has been through much in her short life at Grym Hollow. This pairing between the two of you won't be easy." As soon as he says those words, dread tightens in my chest.

I didn't know what to expect when I agreed to take a human mate. All I knew was that the fate of my kingdom relied on this match. My power and the destiny of my kingdom are dependent upon a human mate. Both the Dragon King Malix and the Wolf King Rip are proof of this. The reason their people are still alive is due to the bonds the humans made with their kings. They provide their own magic unique to humans and strengthen their people.

My hope is that my human bride can provide the strength and safety my people need. But knowing my pairing with Erin will be difficult...it's a selfish thought. The woman before me is terribly hurt. Seeing her healed should be my priority right now.

"She fights her own nightmares," Ender goes on before my mind can stray further. "You will not win her heart by force, Kraken King. You must show patience, empathy, and kindness. Show her she can trust you, and then never break that trust."

My eyes narrow as unexpected anger floods my body. Who is Ender to tell me how to treat my wife? What type of kraken does he take me for?

"Erin will receive what she needs. She will be safe here. No harm will come to her."

"I hope that is the case. The two of you are destined for greatness, but the opposite is true as well. Cherish her, because any moment can be your last." Ender's voice teeters on the precipice of emotion. Like he understands lost love all too well. Perhaps he does. The Guardian is a mystery, but I find it hard to believe this stonelike man is capable of such a deep and complicated emotion.

Finally, The Guardian extends his arms, handing Erin over. The woman's head rolls to the side, her hair falling away from her face. The bruises on her neck are darker than I initially thought, and one of her eyes is almost swollen shut. Her lip is bruised, dried blood coating her bottom lip.

Who the fuck did this to her?

"Do you have somewhere on land to take her?" Ender asks as I pull Erin to my chest. The woman doesn't so much as stir.

"Yes, I'm taking her to my kingdom's emergency shelter on land." Specifically, my sister's cabin, but I don't dare give The Guardian too much information. Luckily, I had the foresight to plan a place to take my human wife before exposing her to the underwater kingdom. My sister, Atina, lives on land amongst other cabins I've set aside in case my people must flee the ocean. She graciously offered up her home, a half-mile walk from here. I could have met Ender there, since it's close to the ocean as well, but I didn't want him to see our land shelter.

Because I don't trust Ender.

"Very good. I'll be in touch, Kraken King," Ender says, and before I can say another word, The Guardian opens a shimmery white portal and steps through. It closes behind him, and I'm alone with my new wife—a broken woman I hope becomes the queen my people and I need.

# CHAPTER 3
# ERIN

The first time I ever broke a bone was during recess in fourth grade. I'd been in the middle of showing off on the monkey bars to a group of cool kids I desperately wanted to impress. I attempted to hang upside down on the bars but didn't quite manage to get my legs above me. My hands slipped, and I went crashing down to the ground as kids laughed.

I remember the distinct sound of my bone breaking, the crack and the instant pain that followed. To add insult to injury, I cried in front of the group, and they never let me forget it.

The injuries kept coming after that day. My mother used to lovingly tease me that I collected injuries like they're going out of style, that I always seemed to find the most interesting and unique ways to hurt myself. It was funny at first, something we could both laugh at.

Until it wasn't.

Until those accidents changed to rough hands on my cheek and dirty boots to my ribs. When my cries became so much more than just pain. Embarrassment and self-loathing joined the party. Pieces of me began to break, but I couldn't find ways to heal those parts of me. No amount of medical intervention could fix the scars marring my heart. Especially when I avoided doctors. They'd ask too many questions I simply couldn't answer without lying. When you're scared for your life, the truth means death.

Thoughts of James and his cruelty jolt me awake, and I gasp. It takes my eyes a moment to adjust, but when they finally do, I look up at an unfamiliar ceiling. The air is crisp, and I notice a large woolen blanket has been placed atop me. I'm in...a bed?

Not my bed. This one is much softer and smells of vanilla and coconut. I take in a deep breath and wince. My ribs hurt, like a lot. They aren't broken, though, because I can still move without being completely incapacitated.

Slowly, I pick myself up to a sitting position, leaning against the wooden headboard to survey the room. My brain is slow to fill in the gaps of my memory. James coming home in a bad mood, drinking anything he could find in the house. I was wearing makeup, which I know is stupid, but I had the urge to make myself look nice.

James got angry when he noticed and accused me of cheating. I remember the first slap, and then another... but the last thing I remember before I gave in to unconsciousness was The Guardian coming to take me away. Which means...

I'm no longer in Grym Hollow.

The room is cozy, fitting only the bed, an antique-looking vanity with a jewel-encrusted mirror, and a slightly ajar door leading to a bathroom. There's one medium-sized window that's pushed open. A salty, almost fishy, but not unpleasant, smell wafts in. Are we close to the ocean?

I'm busy trying to figure out where the hell I am when the door opens, and a large man walks in. Seeing this stranger makes me jump, and I open my mouth to scream, but a breathy whimper is the only sound that comes out. The stranger tenses and halts. He holds a hand up like one would do when approaching a timid animal.

Is that what I am now?

The man doesn't attempt to get closer, but he doesn't leave either. I grab the closest thing to me, which happens to be a pillow, and hold it in front of my body like a shield. His eyes flicker with something akin to pity.

"Erin, my name is Allarick. Ender, The Guardian, brought you here." The man's voice is low, sounding like soft velvet. There's a slight accent that I can't quite place but sounds like a cross between South African and Australian. Two accents that shouldn't go together, but on him, it's...nice.

Then his words sink in. Ender brought me here. My contract flashes in my mind, specifically the part I'm meant to uphold.

*Erin Goodwin will marry the Kraken King, Allarick Eldridge, in order to strengthen his kingdom.*

Those words meant little to me when I signed the contract. Desperate to escape and having no other option, I would have signed anything if it meant I could finally get out.

But now those words are reality, which means the man standing before me is...my husband? Or, rather, will be my husband soon enough. He doesn't look like a kraken, though I can't say I truly know what one would look like. This large, dark-skinned man with locs would not be my guess, however.

"I didn't know how long you'd be asleep," he says, oblivious to my inner turmoil. "I brought food in hopes it would rouse you. I'm going to approach you now, Erin. Just going to set the tray down."

I tighten my grip on the pillow and hold my breath as he walks forward to place a large tray of food on the bed. I brace myself, waiting for his fist to connect with my body, but he doesn't linger or try to touch me. The man—Allarick—steps back to the door, putting a respectable distance between us again.

My stomach growls at the smell of a garlicky soup. I can't remember my last proper meal, one that didn't come out of plastic packaging. Breads, fruits, and cheeses also occupy the plate. A mug of what looks like hot tea catches my attention, and I immediately grab for it, taking a sip.

The hot liquid warms my aching throat. It doesn't take away the pain, but it helps manage it.

"There are a few healing herbs crushed into the tea. Your throat—" Allarick's gaze drops to my neck, and I find myself shying away from his scrutiny. What must I look like? How visible are the scars? I haven't looked at myself in the mirror, and I'm afraid to see the reflection staring back at me.

Allarick must realize he's staring because he quickly averts his gaze, clearing his throat. "It should help soothe some of the pain you are experiencing. I'm afraid I can't do much more until my healer arrives, but they will be here shortly."

I'm half tempted to tell him not to bother, but when I open my mouth, no sound comes out. My voice is gone, at least momentarily. God, I hope it's only temporary. James has strangled me before, but never to this degree. He fucked something up inside me, temporarily taking away my ability to speak. Damn him.

No, *fuck* him.

Allarick remains by the door, and my unease coils low in my belly. He's a tall, muscular, and intimidating figure—and shirtless, which, admittedly, is distracting as hell. His body is chiseled to perfection, lean like a swimmer's. My eyes slowly travel up his umber-brown skin to his full, pouty lips. His long locs are pulled back behind his shoulders. Gold flecks catch the light and shimmer in his otherwise black hair. Honey-brown eyes meet mine, and he stares curiously upon me, studying me like I'm a new, rare species he wants to discover.

This man is gorgeous.

But from my experience, those men are some of the most dangerous. They use their beauty as a weapon.

Suddenly, the cozy room feels stifling.

I hate that I feel uneasy around a man who is obviously trying to help me. But I've lived my life in survival mode for far too long; it's not something I can turn off.

No matter how much I want to. Years of trauma, abuse, and neglect don't just go away with a kind gesture.

The truth is…those things will never leave me. They are part of my story. Part of what makes me, *me*. Maybe one day I'll be able to manage them better—god, I hope so—but I'm a long way from healing.

I almost feel bad for Allarick. I don't think he realized his future wife would be so…broken.

The silence between us grows more uncomfortable. Allarick looks like he wants to say something, but before he can, there's a knock on the door. Something a lot like relief crosses his features as he vaguely gestures to the door.

"That's my sister, Atina. I need to speak with her, so I'll leave you to your food. I'm just outside the door if you need anything." Allarick's eyes scan over me, but he says nothing as he exits the room, leaving me alone to question if I made the right decision when I signed the contract.

I didn't want to trade one monster for another. But maybe I have.

# CHAPTER 4
# ALLARICK

I close the door behind me when I leave Erin's room. There were many ways I pictured our first meeting going, but none were like this. I'm not sure what to make of the human or our current situation. Half of me wants to demand Ender come back and take Erin away. It's evident she's unsure about being here.

But on the other hand, Erin is *mine* now. I recognize my time with her won't be easy, but I've never been a man to give up. What type of king would I be if I gave up when things got too difficult?

A weak one, I imagine.

There's also another reason I don't want to let Erin go, but it doesn't quite make sense. There's a certain rightness about her presence. I feel the need to protect her and an even bigger need to make sure those who hurt her in the past can never reach her again.

My sister knocks, louder this time, before opening the front door. "I don't know why the hell I'm knocking; this is my damn house," she spits, storming inside. Atina tosses her black tricorn on the couch and runs a hand through her curly hair. I notice her bruised knuckles and do my best not to roll my eyes.

My little rebellious sister. Always looking for fights and finding them around every corner.

"So? Where is she?" Atina looks around the room as if Erin will suddenly spring up from the floorboards. "I even dressed up and everything."

"Did you bring the salve?" I ask, ignoring her questions.

"Of course I did. I don't have the memory of a goldfish." She searches the small bag slung across her shoulders. There are a few patches, hastily sewed, from random fabrics. One thing about my sister is she will use something until it disintegrates.

Which is why I'm surprised to see her in lavish clothing. Well, lavish for her, at least. She wears a flowy white tunic with a navy-blue and gold coat atop, perfectly tailored to her body. Her black breeches also fit her seamlessly and don't look like she stole them off a drunken sailor. Her freshly waxed leather boots complete the ensemble. If she's not careful, someone may mistake her for royalty.

She is, but Atina likes to pretend otherwise. Luckily, she has that ability because the throne will never be hers—only mine—and not because I wish to keep it from her, but rather because she is the product of my father's infidelity. It's not proper for a bastard to become queen. And even if was, Atina would never take it. She wasn't built for that life.

She was made to sail, sail because she never steps fin

in the ocean, even though she is part merperson. She claims there's nothing down there for her, but I believe it goes deeper than that. My sister fears very few things, but being stuck below the water is one of them.

"Just rub it in like a lotion. You should start feeling the effects immediately." Atina hands over the jar and scans my nude chest. "I don't see injuries on you."

"It's not for me."

Atina's eyes widen for a fraction of a second before they darken. "I see. Is that why she's not out here?"

I nod. "It's bad. I was even afraid to carry her here. Every part of her body is covered with bruises. Her neck is the worst, though. I think someone strangled her so severely that they injured her vocal cords. Unfortunately, I don't know what happened."

"Fuck. Does she understand the deal she made with Ender to be here?" Atina knows about my contract with Ender. She was the first person I approached when I originally contemplated it.

"I don't know. Ender seemed to think she did."

"Do you have everything the human needs? Clothes? Feminine products?"

Luckily, I had things arranged before Erin got here. King Malix, the Dragon King, was the first to get his human mate. He graciously agreed to provide me with items for my human wife after I spoke with him during our meeting with the six kings of Mescos.

"I have that covered. Anything else she needs, I will retrieve."

"Always so gallant, Kraken." She sighs dramatically before falling onto the couch, spreading her body across it. "So, other than your new wife-to-be, any news from down under?"

"I've heard an interesting story from a man I sentenced to death," I say, remembering back to Kaleo's sentencing. His words still replay in my head, and although they very well could be the musings of a man facing death, there could also be some truth in them as well.

"Yeah? What did he say?" Atina prompts.

"He brought up the Leviathan again. What do you know of them?" If there is a creature to be discovered or known, my sister is my fountain of knowledge. She hears and sees things I can't by spending her time on the surface. My knowledge of these creatures is minimal at best.

"Seriously? Did they teach you anything in those posh lessons of yours as a child?" She laughs humorlessly. Our childhood is always a sore subject. Our experiences were vastly different. My father was a good man, but he had his faults. Infidelity was one of them, and Atina is a walking reminder of that.

"I was a little preoccupied with learning how to run an entire ocean," I growl. "I remember whispers of them, warnings, but that's all I recall."

Atina waves away my comment. "The Leviathan are the closest cousins to the Nephilim. Or so we assume, since we don't know the origins. You know of the Nephilim, don't you?"

I scowl at her taunting tone. Even if I lived under a clam, I would still know what and who the Nephilim are. They are the whole reason Mescos is fighting for their territories. We grew up learning about The Great War. I often wondered how these creatures would endanger my people, but I think I'm beginning to understand.

"Are they working with the Nephilim? Are they more dangerous?"

Atina sighs like she is feigning patience for a guppy who isn't understanding their lesson. "I've been tracking the Nephilim since the meeting with the six kings, as you requested. Wolf territory was hit, but they managed to come out victorious. They've split up, but the majority of the Nephilim are headed to Demon's Clan and Fae Court. Want to hear my theory?"

"Obviously, Guppy."

"One, don't fucking call me a guppy. Just because I'm younger and smaller than you doesn't mean I won't kick your ass. King or not. And two, my theory. I think the Nephilim are trying to surround Pixie Cove. Fae Court and Demon's Clan will provide them entry from both sides, an entry point through land and the other through water. The water access is dependent upon the Leviathan..." she trails off, and I fill in the blanks.

If the Nephilim are able to access land and sea because of the Leviathan's help...our world and people will fall.

My mind is still fixated on the idea of these creatures surrounding Pixie Cove. It makes sense, though. Pixie Cove houses the majority of Mescos magic, the magic we use to heal, shift, make enchantments, and many other things that would debilitate us if we lost it.

Already, the Nephilim are powerful. But with access

to a nearly endless supply of magic? I shudder to think of a world where that happens.

"I don't need to tell you how disastrous it would be if the Nephilim gained access to Pixie Cove." Atina shudders, not from the crisp air, but rather the grim reality of the potential future we face.

"For now, your concern should be the Leviathan. I would argue they are just as dangerous, if not more, than their cousins. Because, if the Leviathan take charge of the sea, the Nephilim have safe passage into any port within Mescos. What did this man say exactly?"

"He mentioned their song can be heard outside their prison. That it's faint but grows stronger. I don't have any verification of this yet. Delmare is—"

"Ugh, Delmare's about as useful as a turtle without its shell."

"Delmare is a good man and an even better guard. He's served our family well over the past decades," I say sternly. I won't let anyone speak badly about my faithful guards, especially ones I consider friends. Not even my sister.

"'Decades' being the key word." She rolls her eyes. "Listen, let me and my crew look into this too. Delmare can only get you so much information. I can provide you more."

Well, she's not wrong. Not only is my sister an expert explorer, but her true talents lie in digging up information people believe to be buried.

"Very well. Take time to investigate Kaleo's claim and report back with anything you find. Anything that needs my immediate attention, call for the merpeople. They will deliver the news."

"I'll deliver the news personally on land." She picks herself off the couch. "I better be going, then. No time like the present, or some shit like that. Make sure you give that salve to your human mate." Atina does her exaggerated bow that would be an insult coming from anyone else, but since it comes from my sister, I find it amusing.

"Safe travels, Guppy."

"Shut it, Kraken," she growls before grabbing her hat and leaving the house as suddenly as she came.

Once again, I'm faced with the reality of my wife-to-be. And no one, not even my sister, can advise me on this decision.

Erin is mine to deal with alone.

# CHAPTER 5
# ERIN

I don't touch any of the food Allarick brings me. Part of me feels bad since he obviously went through the trouble of getting it together. But my stomach is still in knots, and the thought of eating makes me want to gag. Not to mention my throat can barely stand swallowing right now.

My entire body aches; James caused more harm than I originally thought. A person can only withstand so much damage before there's nothing more to give. I was prepared for death, even wished for it, until I sought out Ender.

Finding him was fate, of that I'm certain. James had just gotten off a grueling day of work and was too tired to pay me much mind. He went to bed immediately, and I went out to do a few errands since the car was back.

It was my last stop of the day, grocery shopping, when I overheard a familiar voice speaking loudly to her companion. I turned my head to see Sister Tammy and a poor woman she had cornered. Sister Tammy is Grym

Hollow's nun, taxi service, and the biggest gossip in town. I don't make it a priority to listen to other conversations, but I overheard familiar names.

"—another one. Can you believe that? First Rose, bless her heart, and now that troubled girl, Hettie, followed. That's two in the last month! The Guardian should be ashamed of splitting up families—"

"Did you say The Guardian?" All heads swiveled in my direction. I hadn't meant to speak, but there was no taking it back once it was out. The woman offered me a thankful smile as she slipped away from Sister Tammy while her attention was on me.

"I did, but I don't think I should tell you. Don't want you to get the wrong impression, Erin," the woman said, though I saw how desperately she wanted to talk about it. And I was the only audience she had.

"Have you seen him recently?" I asked.

The Guardian is Grym Hollow's protector, or at least that's what the town says. He's a recluse who monitors all who enter and exit Grym Hollow. But no one ever leaves—until recently—because they claim this town has everything they could ever need. I beg to differ, but leaving isn't easy. It never is, especially when you have nothing and no support.

That's what narcissists do. They alienate you from everyone else until you have no one but them. By the time you realize what they did, it's already too late. You've burned too many bridges, and there's no coming back from that.

"Well, I haven't seen him per se," she said, and I instantly deflated. She sensed my disappointment and hurried on, "But I've taken Rose and Hettie both to see him. Do you know those girls? Lovely things, though they have a lot of baggage. Probably why they left."

"Where did they go?" I tried my best to hide my rising curiosity, but Sister Tammy caught on.

"I hope you're not thinking of following in their footsteps. I can't tell you where they went because I don't know. I guess the strange Guardian did something to them, but that's none of my business," she said as if she hadn't spent the last ten minutes speaking about this in a grocery store for all to hear.

I don't know what possessed me to say the next words, but maybe it was years of pent-up anger and fear finally bursting through, needing something to change. "Can you take me to him?"

Sister Tammy hadn't been happy, but after I promised to go to church—a promise I didn't expect to uphold—she reluctantly gave me his address.

That was how I ended up at The Guardian's house. Except he wasn't there when I walked up and knocked on the door. I remember the bitter taste of loss, being so close to something but having it not work out in my favor. I knocked again, hoping he would come eventually.

Except he never did.

I was just about to turn around when something caught my attention. Off to my right was a small, decorative table with a folder on top. A manila folder with nothing but the words *Erin Goodwin* in fancy script written across the front. It should have frightened me knowing The Guardian knew me and that I would come.

But it didn't. It felt like my ticket to freedom. I snatched it up quickly and read through the pages.

I read about a world not like my own. A world where supernatural beings live and rule freely. It was so impossible to comprehend a world like that existed. The Guardian could take me away from this life, but only if I agreed to marry a man I'd never met, who also happened to be a kraken—whatever that is.

It was a testament to how badly I wanted away from James that I signed that contract without second thought. An unknown monster is better than the monster I knew. I wouldn't survive James much longer, but the contract gave me a chance of survival.

The door opens back up, pulling me away from the past and back to the unfamiliar bedroom. Allarick, the giant of a man who looks nothing like a sea monster, peers in. He offers me a smile, but when he sees my untouched food, it quickly turns into a frown. I have the bizarre urge to apologize to him, even though I didn't do anything wrong. Years of always having to be the one to beg for forgiveness don't go away after a few days.

"Can I come in?" he keeps his voice gentle and low.

Allarick waits for me to nod before he walks in. I take note of the way he bends his head to get through the door, his locs nearly scraping the top of the doorframe. He approaches the side of my bed and holds out a jar, expecting me to take it.

I do but tentatively, not sure what I'm holding.

He sees the confusion written across my face. "It's a salve. Rub it into your skin like lotion, and it should help with your injuries. At least until the healer is able to get here." He seems annoyed that the healer hasn't arrived yet. I don't mind though. Enough people have witnessed my shame; I'm not eager for another.

Allarick is still staring at me expectantly, so I unscrew the lid. I'm hit with the smell of chamomile and lavender. It reminds me of my late mother's garden in the springtime. She firmly believed plants and flowers had healing properties and would often concoct her own remedies.

I dip my fingers into the cool salve and start massaging the cream into my skin. Already I feel a soothing effect, and I'm grateful. I go to say as much, but only a pained whisper comes out.

"You didn't eat any of your food," Allarick says after a moment of silence. We both glance at my untouched meal, and I just shrug.

"Not hungry?" Another shrug. Allarick frowns. "Your body needs to heal. Nutrients will help that process."

I sigh, not sure why this man cares so much about my eating habits. He gestures to the bruising around my neck. I shake my head, hoping he understands me.

Realization dawns, and he almost looks angry. But for some reason, I don't think his anger is geared toward me. I hope not, at least. Still, my body goes into survival mode, and I curl in on myself, ready to protect my head if needed.

"It hurts when you swallow?" he asks.

I nod, relieved he doesn't push the matter or come any closer. Instead, he grabs my tray but leaves my cup of tea, placing it on the bedside table. "At least try to drink this. It'll help. In the meantime, I'll fix a broth."

I nod again, pulling the blankets tighter around me. I don't mean for this to be a signal for Allarick to leave, but he sees the movement and steps back.

"I'll let you rest. I'm right down the hall if you need me," he says then hesitates. For a moment, I think he's going to say more, but the moment passes, and he gives me a tight-lipped smile.

Then Allarick is gone.

Again.

With nothing else to do, and the events of the past few days finally catching up to me, I lay my head down on the pillow and fall into a deep, dreamless sleep.

# ERIN

*Pathetic. Stupid. Worthless.*

These words play like a mantra in my mind, over and over again until every other quality about me fades away. I'm not Erin, the classically trained musician. I'm not Erin, the woman who graduated from college early. I'm not Erin, the bubbly, vibrant woman with loving friends.

Those core pieces of my identity are stripped away until nothing but rubble is left. I started to believe James's lies and took them for the truth. Only a pathetic woman feels fear throughout the entire day. Only a stupid woman stays in a toxic relationship. Only a worthless woman would let others treat her with no respect.

*Pathetic. Stupid. Worthless.*

I've only ever had one real boyfriend. We met in high school and became high school sweethearts. Those two years we were together in high school were perfect. *He* was perfect. Or at least that was what I was led to believe.

My parents adopted me very late in life, so by the time I graduated high school, they were well into their seventies and eighties. When I lost them, it felt like a part of me died with them. Like a crater-size hole was left in my heart by their absence, and it would never be filled. The only thing that kept me going was the love and support from my boyfriend, James.

It wasn't until my parents died when I turned twenty-four that things began to change, and I started to notice red flags. Suddenly, he was checking my location more often, commenting on how often I hung out with my friends. I started to limit my time with them, but it was never enough. Eventually, we just drifted apart because of how often I would cancel and make excuses.

Then it was comments about my outfits and how they would be "too sexy" to wear out in public. Even when I felt covered up or modest, James would always have a problem with what I wore. He started to accuse me of cheating, no matter how many times I assured him I wasn't.

That should have been enough for me to leave. But I didn't...because when we weren't fighting, he made me feel special. And he was all I had left.

Even thinking his name fills me with equal amounts of rage and fear. Our last fight replays in my head like a horror movie. His smug face fills my vision, teeth bared and smelling of alcohol. He's not a particularly large man, but he hovers a few inches taller than me. His frame is bigger too, eclipsing me in his shadow.

Everything happened so fast. One minute the room was calm, albeit strained, and the next, he's yelling and hurling insults because I stupidly decided to wear makeup. He took that as a sign of cheating. I barely had time to get off the couch before pain exploded in my cheek.

And then it kept coming.

And coming.

It was too much. Too painful. I screamed. Or maybe he did. My voice was raw as I pleaded for him to stop. Begged him to let me go, but his hold grew tighter around my neck.

I remember thinking the last thing I would see in this world was the face of a monster. Then everything became a blur after that. My brain was desperately trying to protect me.

Men like James take power by breaking people down until they are mere shadows of themselves. Every time I close my eyes, I see him, the way he snarls when I do something he doesn't like, or the look of hatred radiating off him when we argue. Not even in my dreams am I free from him.

The healer came shortly after Allarick left me during our last meeting, waking me up from a nap. She was an older, grandmotherly figure with gentle hands. She didn't speak much, which I appreciated, so I smiled each time she caught me watching her. She rubbed strange but pretty-smelling substances on my bruises and made me drink a purple, tasteless liquid.

The treatment from the healer has me feeling almost back to normal. Nothing hurts, though my body is still slightly sore, and my throat irritates me when I swallow. When I finally force myself out of bed, every bone in my body pops.

Fuck, that felt good.

I glance around the room, stopping at the neatly folded clothes sitting atop the dresser. I don't remember them being here before, which means Allarick left them. He was in my room while I slept? I'm not sure how I feel about that. On one hand, I'm a guest in this house, so he is perfectly within his rights to come and go as he pleases, but I still feel uneasy.

I don't know Allarick. I don't know what he's capable of. He hasn't made me feel uncomfortable or raised his voice at me, but, as I've determined, I'm not the best judge of character. Leaving clothes for me to change into is a nice gesture, admittedly. I'm dying to get out of my jeans and t-shirt. I smell like shit, and I'm certain my hair is a matted mess. Plus, I want to get out of the clothes my abuser touched me in last and burn them.

I grab the clothes on the dresser and head into the bathroom. It's small, on the verge of feeling claustrophobic. The shower is another beast entirely. There are so many pipes leading up the wall and two shower heads pointing in opposite directions. Once I figure out how to turn on the faucet, I shriek as ice-cold water falls on my head.

Perfect. Just fucking perfect.

It's pathetic, but I start to cry. When does the feeling of being nothing go away?

It takes entirely too long for the shower to heat up to a respectable level, and I peel myself out of my grimy clothes, making a mental note to burn them later. The water hits my body, eliciting a moan from my lips. It's been so long since I've been able to enjoy a shower without looking over my shoulder for James. The feeling is...refreshing.

There aren't many products in the bathroom, and none I've heard of, so I make do with what I have. I scrub at my skin, needing to clean off the last of James. I don't need another reminder of him, and by the time I'm done, my skin is red from the pressure.

In total, I spent over an hour in the shower, and I can't bring myself to feel guilty about it. It's a small luxury that I'm telling myself I deserve. I find towels tucked behind the sink and wrap one around my body.

One look in the mirror shows a nearly unmarked face. I have to do a double-take because the woman in the mirror is not the same woman from a few days ago, thanks to the healer. Looking at me, no one would guess I was injured. There's only slight bruising around my throat. I hum, letting the vibrations rumble through me.

"Erin," I test my own name carefully. The voice that comes from my throat is a little raspy but almost back to normal. I need to rest my voice just a little longer, only because I'm not ready to talk about certain things yet. It gives me time to think about what I will say to Allarick when he demands to know what happened to me. Because he will. I see the question in his eyes now, but he keeps it to himself. I won't delude myself that he'll keep quiet for much longer.

We will also need to discuss the entire reason I'm here. To marry the kraken king. That part of the deal hasn't eluded me, but since Allarick hasn't made any attempts to bring it up, neither will I. Even if I have many questions about the arrangement, I'm not quite brave enough to ask him yet. Maybe I'm waiting for him to show me his true colors so I have a reason to hate him and keep my distance.

With that sobering thought, I leave the bathroom to dress in the bedroom. I contemplate staying in this room, but admittedly, I'm getting stir-crazy. I need to walk and stretch my legs, even if it just means moving out of this room. It'll be enough. A slight change from the new normal. Small changes are all I'm capable of right now.

Once I pull the dress over my head and flatten out the wrinkles, I take a deep breath, gather what little courage I have, and walk out of my room to take on the day. And maybe learn a little more about the man I'm going to marry.

That is my intention, at least, except when I reach for the door, something out the window catches my eye. Curiosity gets the best of me, and I move closer to the window. A small figure is crouched down by the water, several yards away. Allarick? From this vantage point, it looks like Allarick is hovering over the water, but when I get closer to the window, I see he's actually standing on a small pier.

Allarick's head is tilted down, arms crossed over his chest. He's engaged in a heated conversation with someone, but I don't see another person around. Great, just what I need. A man who talks to imaginary friends.

Just as that thought crosses my mind, something splashes in the water. At first I think it's a dolphin or some other sea animal. Then I see a flash of skin, and my eyes widen as an older man in a shiny breastplate appears. His salt-and-pepper hair is tied back in a knot atop his head. Allarick and this man are engaged in an intense conversation I can't hear.

After a moment, the older man moves in the water right before a tentacle reaches out. I gasp, clapping my hand over my mouth. At first, I think an octopus has found the man in the water and wrapped its tentacles around him. Allarick just stares, making no move to help him. I want to shout and scream for him to do something. Anything!

However, my fear is quickly replaced with astonishment as the man moves farther out of the water. While the top half of him is strictly man, the bottom half differs. Where legs should be, there are dark purple tentacles that look like they could wrap around a person's skull and crush it without any effort.

Before I can dwell on that sobering thought any longer, the man disappears under water, and Allarick walks back. I back up from the window and away from view. My mind is whirling with what I just saw, and I can't help but question everything.

Was the man I just saw a kraken?

And, more importantly, is that what Allarick will look like?

# CHAPTER 7
# ALLARICK

Erin stays in bed for two days. The healer came —finally—shortly after I left her that first night. I did my best to keep my ire in check and not dwell on the fact my healer showed up late to treat her future queen. My people hate coming to the surface, so I try to be understanding, but her lack of urgency prolonged Erin's pain.

I wouldn't consider myself a violent man. I have killed, sentenced people to death, and done things the average merperson has never dreamed of doing, but never with malice in my heart. It was out of duty. Duty to my kingdom, my people, and my throne.

However, my healer tested my patience that night.

From what I could understand of her assessment of Erin, she had a mild concussion, bruised ribs, and damage to her vocal cords. She treated all of her injuries, but it will take time for Erin to fully recover. Humans are more fragile and delicate than merpeople and krakens.

The medicine the healer gave her would make her sleep. It was the only way to keep her from constant pain.

So, for two days, I wait, checking on her every hour. She rarely moves, and if it wasn't for the slow rise and fall of her chest, I would have thought Erin was no longer part of the living. I notice the bruising around her face, neck, and shoulders has gone down tremendously. Whatever my healer did is clearly working, and a part of me is glad I didn't punish her for tardiness. Only marginally, though.

I've heard nothing from my sister yet, but I don't expect to for a few more days. It takes time to explore the ocean on a ship, and although my sister is one of the best sailors I know, she can still only move so fast above the water.

On the late afternoon of the second day, I meet with Delmare. He's my eyes in the ocean while I'm away. As much as it pains me to be away from my people, I will not subject Erin to the ocean until she's ready and healed. At the very least, I need her to talk to me.

I meet Delmare on the pier, leaving Erin in the house. It's close enough for me to still feel confident in her safety. As always, Delmare is methodical as he goes through his reports. A family has reported their grandmother missing, while another family reports hearing strange noises. He has little to report on Kaleo's claims, though. I clench my jaw, knowing things will get worse before they can get better. If my attention wasn't split between...

No. I will not blame Erin for this. Not when she could be the key to our survival.

Delmare finishes up by promising he'll gain more insight for me. Before he leaves, he hands over the water-resistant books I asked him to bring, and I head back inside.

I come to an abrupt halt when I open the door and see Erin standing only a few feet away.

Her hazel eyes widen, and her pretty pink lips form a perfect "O." She is not the same broken thing I saw when Ender brought her to me. Her hair is damp, probably meaning she figured out the shower. She's out of the dirty clothes Ender brought her in and has changed into the new set I left on the dresser, a simple pink dress that's fitted in the bodice and flares out around her hips. It was something Malix's men brought, but as soon as we are back in my kingdom, I'll make sure she has the proper attire.

Just a few days in my presence, and Erin has already unwound me.

She rocks on the balls of her feet, and I realize I've been staring at her for far longer than appropriate. I clear my throat, trying to dissolve the awkwardness between us. "Erin, I'm glad to see you're awake. How are you feeling?"

It takes a moment for her to respond, like she's trying to remember how to use her voice. "I saw...you outside," she says instead of answering my question. Her voice hasn't completely healed yet, but it's a start. Even though it's a mere ghost of what I imagine her normal talking voice will be, it's beautiful. Velvet and soft and makes me eager to hear her when she's completely healed.

"I needed to speak with my captain of the guards. He's reporting back on our kingdom." There's no sense in hiding anything from her. She will be queen soon enough, and there are things I want to show my future queen before she becomes part of my world.

"Tentacles," is all she says.

Ah, yes. Those. I can't help but smile. "Yeah, I suppose that would be daunting for a human to see. Not all my people have tentacles. Some have tails. You'll get used to it soon." Or at least I hope she will.

I will ease her into my own tentacles later, but for now, my only concern is feeding her. "Are you hungry?"

I expect her to shake her head no and prepare to argue. She's been asleep for two days, which is two days without meals. Who knows when she ate last before that? But my reasoning is not needed because Erin nods, staring at me expectantly.

I entertain the idea of reaching for her hand to guide her to the table, but I'm not sure she'd appreciate being touched yet. Instead, I gesture for her to follow and lead her to the table. As she gets situated, I mull over what to make. Something fast that doesn't require a lot of skill. I know many things, but cooking is not a skill set I possess. At least not well.

I settle on a tuna sandwich with a seaweed salad, both of which I noticed in my sister's fridge earlier. Both are soft, something I hope won't agitate her throat any further. I pray to the sea goddess Erin is a fan of fish. If not, this pairing just became more complicated since the majority of our dishes involve fish. I suppose we'll find out now.

A few moments later, I place a poorly made sandwich and seaweed salad in front of her. Erin doesn't even hesitate as she picks up the sandwich to take a small tester bite. She's slow to swallow, but I think it's more to do with her throat rather than the taste. My hunch is confirmed when she smiles and holds up two thumbs. I'm not certain what that means, but I'll take it as a positive gesture.

We sit in companionable silence, both eating a much-needed dinner. Admittedly, food is the last thing on my mind as I sit with Delmare's discoveries and Erin's wellbeing.

I sent word with the merpeople shortly after Erin arrived for Delmare to bring history books with him upon his visit with me. These books are magically protected in water and detail the history of Tetria, or, as the people of the land call us, Kraken Lagoon. I never corrected the people of the land when they called Tetria such a simple, idiotic name. The less they know about my world, the better. Knowledge is power, and even if my relationship with the other kings of Mescos is amicable, they are still outsiders I keep at arm's length.

"There's something I want to show you," I say after a moment, producing one of our history books from the chair next to me. Erin watches me curiously, eyeing what I have in my hands.

The book smells of the sea, handbound in leather. It's in perfect condition—thanks to the magic keeping it safe from the water—and holds pictures and history of Tetria. Very few people have access to the original copies, just me, a few trustworthy guards, and the scholars of

Tetria. As future queen, Erin has access to all the original books and scrolls of our history.

When I place the book in front of Erin, she reaches out and fingers the golden script on the cover. "Tetria," I explain. "That's the name of my kingdom—our kingdom." At my use of "our," Erin tenses, but only for a second. Her brown cheeks darken in a blush.

There's so much we need to discuss and put into motion, but I can't in good conscience force her into a life she knows nothing about. So, I'm willing to take it slow. At least until she's more comfortable around me. My people aren't in immediate danger, and with Delmare and Atina searching for answers, my time can be spent getting Erin acquainted with me and my kingdom.

She opens the first page to a castle made from white pillars and stone, adorned with jewels of the sea, pearls, diamonds, peridot, and serpentine. The castle stands high above the rest of the city, shining like a beacon in a vast ocean. It's a symbol of our power and perseverance. I can't help but feel a sense of pride each time I see it.

"This is our home."

Something like admiration crosses her features as she takes the image in. Just like the title, she touches the page, running the pads of her fingertips along the outlines of the castle. My chest tightens for reasons I can't explain. I've ruled alone for so long, and now that I get the chance to show Tetria off to someone else, it feels...good.

"Do you want to know more?" I ask.

Erin nods with more vigor than I've seen her capable of. Her curls bounce with the movement.

So, I try my best to describe our people, the warriors all the way down to the smallest of guppies. How each person plays a pivotal role in our community. I share our values of loyalty, trust, and family. Of celebrations Tetria has throughout the year. But my words and stories don't do Tetria justice. I can't capture the feeling of complete peace or the sheer vastness of my world. I can't describe the humility it brings, knowing you are but a small part of our goddess's ocean.

You can't bottle that feeling. It's something you can only experience within her depths.

Erin takes in all the information, curiously flipping through the pages of the book. She pauses when she reaches a darkened figure depicted on the page and points to it. My blood runs cold when I notice what she found.

The Nephilim.

Erin peers up at me expectantly. I can't lie or shield her from these creatures. They are the reason she's here. "Those are Nephilim." I point to the distorted creature with broken wings on the page. "They are creatures of chaos and destruction. They roam the land, set on ruling Mescos.

"They are a danger to us, but the more prominent danger are creatures called the Leviathan," I say, searching her face. She's giving little away, and I don't know if my words are scaring her. I don't mean for them to frighten her, but she still has a right to know what we are up against.

"In a lot of ways, Leviathan are like the Nephilim, but we know even less about these creatures. Right now, they are locked away in an underwater prison. There have been rumors, though, that the prison is weakening." A weakening prison means freedom for the Leviathan—the beginning of the end for the ocean and our safety.

But Erin is trying to heal and doesn't need to burden herself by learning all about these hellish creatures. I certainly don't want to make her recovery any more difficult than it has to be. We can talk more about them at some other time, but for now, she knows the basics.

Before we can go any further down this dark path, I turn the page and show her more of the beautiful history and landscapes of Tetria. Thankfully, Erin doesn't seem to mind—or notice—I've skipped over the Leviathan and Nephilim.

I speak for what feels like hours. The sun makes its descent, and soon night will come. Erin's eyes start to droop, and I know she's hit her limit for today. It's more than I could have hoped for.

"We should get some rest," I suggest and reach for the book. Erin pulls away, clutching the book to her chest. It's the first move of rebellion against me. A glimpse of the fire behind her sad eyes. After a moment, shame colors her features.

"Sorry," she croaks, raspy and low. The simple word costs her because she winces. It must still be painful. Erin reaches out and tries to hand me the book, but I don't accept it and push it back toward her.

"No, keep it. It's yours to read and look through." I try to keep my voice even, but inside I swell with pride. Erin wants to know more about Tetria. More about *us*. It's a damn good feeling.

Erin cradles the book once again. I watch as she leaves the table and walks back to her room, closing the door behind her. Was there a new lightness to her step?

My human surprises me. She's full of layers I want to peel back and expose until she stands bare in front of me. I want to know her secrets. Her fears. Her desires.

More importantly, I want to watch as she puts her broken pieces back together again and finds her strength.

# CHAPTER 8
## ALLARICK

Over the next few days, I try to engage with Erin as much as she will allow. Some days are better than others. There are times when she stays in her room for most of the day reading the book I lent her and occasionally coming out to point at a section she doesn't understand. I'm happy to go over the history of our people.

Sometimes I hear her crying, and sometimes I hear nothing at all. I don't know if her silence or cries are worse.

I hate her cries, though. They strike a chord deep within me, but what am I to do? Comfort her? I'm not sure she will allow me to get that close. Although she seems comfortable when we take lunch together, she still remains a good distance away. When she thinks I'm too close, Erin shies away.

The person who harmed her did more than physical damage. It's the emotional abuse that will linger with her for a long time. The thought makes me murderous on her behalf.

When I hear Erin moving around in her room this morning, I make the decision to get out of this damn house. We've spent the last four—or was it five?—days here, and the walls feel like they are caving in on me. I refused to leave in case she needed me. I'm used to the vastness of the ocean, and I'm missing the feeling of being surrounded by water. Erin still isn't ready to come to Tetria, but she is ready to meet some of my people.

Erin comes out wearing another flowy dress from the Dragon King, her arms and legs bare. Her golden-brown skin is on full display, and I'm pleased to see no remains of the bruising. Even her neck is almost free of her injuries. I'm desperate to hear her speak more, but I won't push her. Ender's words replay in my mind. *Show her kindness and patience.* My wants don't matter at the moment. Forcing Erin to speak before she's ready might make her retreat, and that's the last thing I want.

A mixture of fruits, hot tea, and bread sit on the table. She's been eating more and finishing her tea, both of which I take as good signs. Today Erin helps herself to dragon fruit, one of my personal favorites. It's not until she sits down that I tell her my idea for today.

"How would you like to get out of this house, Erin?"

She taps her slender fingers on the table, seeming to consider my request. Her eyes dart back to her room, and for a moment, I'm filled with an unspeakable amount of disappointment. If Erin doesn't want to go, I can't force her. Goddess knows she's been through enough.

Erin's slow to nod her agreement. It's not an enthusiastic yes, but it's still a yes. I'll take what I can get. For now. I have a few places in mind I want to show Erin to get her comfortable with the sea and her people.

By the time Erin finishes her tea, I'm full of pent-up energy. I feel like a guppy on their birthday, waiting for the excitement to begin. I open the front door of the cabin, gesture for her to follow, and take my first step out.

We're immediately hit by warm sunrays and the faint breeze that carries the smell of the salty ocean, making me long to be home. Even from all the way up here, I can hear the songs of the whales and excited clicks of eager dolphins as they race through the water. It's just a taste of the ocean, but it's enough to get me by for now.

"This way." I step out into the gray area between my territory and Lycan territory. The wolves hopefully won't be patrolling this far out today. I don't need them to scare Erin. "I want to show you something."

Erin shows little emotion as she wraps her arms around herself, almost like a form of protection. Physically, she's next to me, but her mind is still miles away. If I were a weaker man, I might be offended by her lack of interest in me and the world around us. But I've never been one to step down from a challenge, even if that challenge is in the form of a deeply scarred woman who needs to come into her own power.

I lead Erin to a dock Atina frequently uses when she comes back home. The water there is clear and full of schools of fish and vibrant coral. The deck is large enough for two people to walk side by side, but I hover close. Just in case she stumbles.

When we reach the end of the dock, I crouch down and dip my hand into the water, allowing it to float across the surface. It's the perfect temperature. Perhaps a little on the colder side, but that's never bothered me. I send out a silent call, one that only creatures of the ocean can hear. A curious blue guppy swims to the surface under my fingers, and I reach out to stroke his side. Happy bubbles leave the guppy as he swims through my spread fingers like his own personal obstacle course.

From the corner of my eye, I see Erin kneel, looking down curiously. Her shoulder brushes mine, sending a wave of heat through my body. I do my best to ignore it and click my tongue twice, sending out a message to sea creatures nearby. It only takes a couple of minutes before I see my first visitor. A small head peeks up out of the water and makes a slow descent toward us.

Next to me, Erin gasps as the three-foot sea turtle swims to my hand. "Hello there, old friend." I smile, rubbing my hand along his shell. I may not know this turtle personally, but he's part of the sea I swore to defend and rule fairly under the law of the goddess.

Erin doesn't make a move to touch the creatures, but she smiles. A real, genuine smile. Serenity colors her features, and her body relaxes. She's not tense or rigid like normal. Her body's natural state is fight, ready to act at a moment's notice. When was the last time she simply got to be?

I would be a fool not to notice Erin's beauty. Even when Ender brought her to me for the first time, I saw the beautiful woman underneath the bruises. But Erin at peace? She's breathtaking. A goddess in her own right. The air around her is filled with strength and tranquility.

Erin must sense my eyes on her. She tilts her head to the side, warm eyes boring into mine. I expect her to shy away, or at the very least move away from me. I wonder if she even realizes our shoulders are pressed together. Visions of her in a crown, sitting atop a throne next to mine fill my mind. I see it perfectly, as if it were a memory and not some distant fantasy.

I wish she'd speak to me, more than just a couple of words. She doesn't know I've listened outside her door, hearing the soft raspiness to her voice as she tests out her vocal cords. I want to know what she's thinking and feeling. I need to know her story and ask her who she's trying to escape from. More importantly, I need to know what makes her feel safe, so I can protect her from her nightmares.

"I've heard your world has creatures like these. Is that true?" I don't know much about the human world. I was a boy when the last of our human companions passed on to our goddess. But stories of the human world still linger within Tetria.

Erin nods but offers nothing more than that. I should be satisfied with what she is giving me, but I want more. And I think I have an idea of what might get a bigger reaction out of her.

"Would you like to see merpeople?"

At that, Erin's eyes widen. Her curiosity gets the best of her. "Yes," she rasps.

I take it as a personal victory.

"Follow me." It's time she learned about the people she will rule over.

# CHAPTER 9
# ERIN

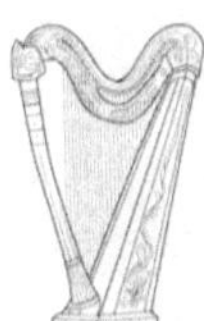

"*Would you like to see merpeople?*" is not a question I would have ever dreamed of hearing before arriving in Mescos. There are many things I believed were simply fairy tales before Mescos, and I can't believe this is my new normal.

Mermaids.

Fucking mermaids!

Allarick takes the lead, moving us away from his fish friends and the friendly turtle I regret not petting. I have a feeling I'll get the opportunity again, though.

We walk through the rocky terrain until we reach beautiful white sand. I pause and take it in because I've never seen a beach before. Grym Hollow is landlocked. The most we had around town were lakes that were either too dirty to swim in or private property that could only be rented in advance.

My father said he once lived by the ocean when he was a young boy. His family would spend their weekends on the beach, soaking up the sun and riding the waves.

The appeal to him went away after his younger sister nearly drowned in rough waters. It scared my father so much that he refused to go back to the ocean. As soon as he was able, he moved away and wound up in Grym Hollow.

Needless to say, he wasn't keen on visiting an ocean again.

So, all I had were movies, books, and pictures of the ocean. All of them pale in comparison to the real thing. Cool sand slides between my toes through my sandals. I stop walking and kick off my shoes, feeling the full effect of the sand on my feet. The bizarre, childish urge to build sandcastles with a moat washes over me. It feels like a rite of passage for the beach, no matter how old you are.

Allarick notices I've stopped and turns to see what I'm doing. Warmth floods my cheeks, and I wait for him to yell at me to hurry up or patronize me for my childish antics. It's what James would have done. Any enjoyment I had, he found ways to smother until I started believing I was a fool for my thoughts.

"Have you ever seen sand before?" Allarick asks.

Shame colors my cheeks, and I shake my head no. He probably thinks I'm a recluse who never left the house. The sad part is that he would be right. But it wasn't by choice. James controlled everything, down to when I left the house and when I could even sit outside to feel the sun on my face. I escaped occasionally when he passed out and I needed to get groceries, but that was as much as I did.

"It feels good, doesn't it? Between your toes and the way you feel like you're sinking into the ground." Allarick smiles, kicking up a bit of sand. The wind picks it up, carrying it back to the ocean.

"Good..." I murmur, voice scratchy. It's no longer painful, but I still sound like the most dehydrated person in the world.

Despite me sounding like sandpaper feels, Allarick smiles. His handsome face lights up, giving him a boyish charm. It would be so easy to give myself over to him... but I'm not ready to open my heart up for more torment. Not now, maybe not ever.

"Here, this way. We are almost there." Allarick beckons me forward, and I follow him through the sand. It's not the easiest thing to walk through, but I don't complain. I'm enjoying being on a beach too much.

Allarick leads me to a secluded part of the beach. Large, mossy brown boulders surround this area. Above us is a cliff overlooking the water. A brave soul would easily jump from the top and into the water, but an accident-prone person like me is content with my feet on the ground.

I nearly run into Allarick's back, too busy paying attention to the cliff above us that I don't realize he's stopped. Tentatively, I peer around him and freeze. My brain is having a hard time registering what I'm seeing. Allarick said he wanted to take me to meet mermaids, but a part of me was still in disbelief. Mermaids are a fantasy tale, nothing more.

Except in Mescos, they are real.

Four heads bob in the water. Allarick steps forward, submerging his feet. "Come," he speaks like a man used to being obeyed. Whereas a lesser man may sound arrogant, Allarick speaks with the confidence of a man who commands respect. "Thank you for being here."

The way he speaks to others is not something I'm accustomed to. He balances power with respect. I didn't know it could work that way.

The four people in the water move forward, bowing when they reach Allarick. "My king," a black-haired woman says. Her thick hair hangs down her shoulders, flaring out in the water. She wears a jeweled top that covers her breasts and a golden vest over it that almost looks like metal. Where her feet should be, an opal tail swishes back and forth under the clear water.

A real, true mermaid.

I'm a little starstruck.

"Oh my god," I blurt, momentarily forgetting I sound like a heavy smoker. Four sets of eyes turn to me with varying degrees of confusion on their faces. I don't have the chance to feel embarrassed because I can't be held responsible for my words or actions when in the presence of real-life mermaids.

The raven-haired mermaid breaks away from the other three and approaches Allarick. "It's good to see you again, my king. The waters are quiet without you."

"You flatter me, Danika." Allarick chuckles, a deep rumbly sound I feel throughout my body.

Danika smiles, and I find myself not liking that a single bit. It's irrational and stupid, but I don't like the way she looks at Allarick with familiarity that only comes with time and friendship.

Another woman with an orange-and-red ombre tail swims up next to Danika. She reaches for the other woman's hand under the water, and Danika smiles at her. There's so much love in that expression that I almost look away from what seems like a private moment. I feel guilty about my jealous thoughts before. I've never been a jealous woman, especially when it comes to men. I don't know why Allarick brings it out.

"Danika, this is Erin Goodwin," Allarick introduces me, something akin to pride in his voice. I tell myself I'm just imagining it because I've done nothing to warrant it. "And Aerwyna. Both amazing merwomen in their own right."

Danika doesn't seem surprised in the slightest I'm here. She extends the same greeting to me as she did to Allarick. "Pleasure to meet you, my queen."

*My queen.*

Those words don't seem real, and they most certainly don't apply to me. Feeling uncomfortable with the title, I move closer to Allarick, shielding myself from the four sets of eyes studying me. None of them look disgusted by what they see, but I'm also not keen on looking too deeply to figure it out.

My lack of response doesn't go unnoticed. Danika seems to realize I'm not going to respond and turns her attention back to Allarick. "Tetria is in good hands, my king. Waters are calm for now. When will you be returning?"

"Soon." Allarick's answer unsettles me. How soon? What happens when he goes home? Do I go with him? Stay at the house? There's still so much that needs to be discussed, and it's my fault we haven't been able to get into the details of the contract. I'm nervous about making any more decisions right now.

"Thank you for coming. We will take our leave now. Please inform Delmare to check in with me at his earliest convenience," Allarick instructs.

Danika and the other mermaids say their goodbyes and dip back into the ocean. Blue, orange-red, black, and pink tails all swish in unison. I track them as they swim farther and farther away until I can no longer make out their colors.

Allarick and I are alone once again.

Despite my hesitance, I'm still in awe over what I just experienced. Straight out of a whimsical fantasy novel my mother used to read to me before bed when I was little. If she could only see me now...

"Thank you." The words are barely more than a whisper and "*thank*" sounds more like "*ank.*" It doesn't begin to cover my feelings about the surreal experience, but he needs to know that I appreciated his efforts to show me his world little by little.

"You're welcome, Erin. There's nothing to fear in the water. You'll be safe there when the time comes," Allarick says.

For a moment, I allow myself to forget about the practicality of me living in the water and my ability to trust the wrong types of men. I think about safety and freedom. What would it be like to not have to constantly look over my shoulder or hope today won't be the day he takes it too far?

I would kill for that feeling.

All too soon, the feeling vanishes when Allarick

reaches out for me. Flashbacks of violent hands on my body flash in my mind, and I jerk away from him, scampering back. There's no longer Allarick. Only James.

Only pain. Hands on my body. Hurting me. I beg him to stop. I plead. He doesn't listen. Only grows angrier. Calls me weak. Calls me pathetic. I'm reduced to pain and tears.

Then my nightmares overtake me.

# CHAPTER 10

# ERIN

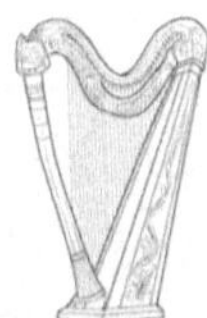

My heart races out of my chest. The world around me begins to spin, and no matter how hard I try, I can't catch my breath. My body trembles, unsure how to hold in these big emotions whirling inside of me.

I've had panic attacks before, but I usually have clues before they start. Sweating palms. Snappy moods. Even a buildup of anxiety. This one came over me suddenly. All I see is James. All I feel is James. I'm no longer in Mescos but back in Grym Hollow.

Tears blur my vision, and I think I'm screaming.

What if I'm not rid of James?

What if I'll only know pain and lies?

What if...

What if...

Hands rub up and down my shoulder. Soft words I barely hear.

"You're okay. I'm here. It's okay." The words repeat over and over again, but they aren't calming me down. I think I cry harder even, though I try to stop. I'm just a fuck-up. If I were different, maybe James would have loved me. Maybe Allarick would get a strong queen.

Maybe...

Maybe...

My body is pulled forward. Gentle hands lead me. If it weren't for those same hands holding me up, I would be little more than a puddle on the ground.

"I'm sorry. I'm sorry. I'm sorry." I hiccup, chanting the words over and over again because Allarick needs to know that this isn't the woman I want to be. This isn't a woman who has the capabilities to lead an underwater kingdom. James told me repeatedly how worthless and stupid I was. I'm starting to fear that maybe he's right.

"Shh, it's okay," he repeats. Allarick is still moving me, but I'm so disoriented, I can't tell where he's taking me. Not until I feel my feet submerged in warm water. It's enough of a shock to give me a moment of clarity.

"What—"

"Trust me, Erin. Let me help you." Allarick's voice is in my ear; his breath tickles my neck. I shiver at his proximity but don't pull away. I couldn't even if I wanted to. Allarick is supporting all my weight.

An embarrassing whimper leaves my lips, and I nod. Or at least I think I do.

Then we are moving forward again.

Warm water submerges my body. Feet first. Then legs. Then thighs. All the way up to my torso. It should feel awkward to be completely clothed in the ocean, but it feels like an extra layer of protection. Soft but callused hands wrap around my shoulders, gently stroking my back. Each slow caress grounds me.

My eyes flutter, my accelerated heart slows, and my breathing evens out. My brain slowly releases me from my mental prison as I remind myself James has no power over me here. There's no way that man will ever be able to hurt me. Not in Mescos.

I take a deep breath in before releasing it. Allarick still rubs my back, whispering that everything is okay. Something wraps around my arms and midsection. At first I think it's seaweed and try to shake free of it, but it doesn't budge. If anything, it wraps more firmly around my wrist. Not in a painful way but definitely secure.

My eyes snap open, and that's when I notice Allarick has brought me to a secluded part of the ocean. We're surrounded by jagged rocks and boulders twice the size of me. It feels like a small ocean next to the bigger ocean. The wind blowing between the rocks makes a sweet whistling sound.

My gaze dips down to the clear ocean water in attempts to pick off the seaweed. Except it isn't seaweed. "Oh my god!" I shout, splashing in the water, which proves fruitless. Allarick is the one holding me up.

"Erin, it's okay. It's just me. I won't harm you," Allarick says, but I barely register his words. No, my mind is strictly focused on the fucking red tentacles wrapped around my body. They curl around my arms and torso, feeling like a gentle hug. There's nothing threatening in the way they wrap around my body, but it's still shocking all the same.

"Is that…you?" I squeak, not sure if I could handle a

literal octopus around me after a rather grueling panic attack.

"It's me," he assures, and sure enough, when I look down, I don't see Allarick's legs. From the waist up, he's still very human. All man. But where his legs should be? Powerful-looking tentacles roughly six or seven feet long sway in the ocean. Three of them snake around my body in what I think is a gentle embrace.

The thought of any man's hands on me after James is frightening and unwanted. But Allarick's tentacles? They shouldn't feel as good as they do, but in his grip, I feel... safe. Which is a new feeling for me.

"How are you feeling, Erin?" Allarick asks. He continues to rub my shoulders—with his hands, not tentacles—and I realize this is how touch should feel. Gentle. Compassionate.

"Tired. Foolish."

"You aren't foolish. It's okay to have feelings. You can't control when panic will overtake you."

I still hate it. The crash after a panic attack is the worst. There's nothing more I want to do than fall into my bed and sleep. Except, right now, reality is more interesting than dreams because I have a kraken helping me through this episode. Perhaps I should have more of a reaction, but that would take energy. I'm all out of that.

"Why?" I ask, my voice raspier with prolonged use. Seems like an odd place to take someone during a panic attack.

"The water calms me," Allarick admits. "It's peaceful. The soft waves, the smell, and the sound of the ocean creatures. It lets me relax and stop thinking. I hoped it would do the same for you.

"When I was younger, my mother would wrap me up in her embrace after a particularly difficult tantrum or meltdown," Allarick continues. "I remember being held by her and feeling safe. It felt like I could just rest in her arms and let someone carry me through the rough patches."

My chest tightens. I didn't expect his answer to be this sweet. Is Allarick even real? Because men this sweet and sensitive don't exist. But...Allarick isn't a man, is he? Not really, at least. He's the king kraken, which is far more than any man could dream of being.

I wish I was better with words to convey just how touching and moving his actions are. How he didn't sneer at the sight of my panic attack or tell me to "calm down." So, I say the only thing I can: "Thank you, Allarick."

"Whatever you need, Erin."

Whatever I need.

My mind grows foggy, and suddenly, I'm having a hard time keeping my eyes open. What I need is sleep. Allarick seems to sense that at the same time I do, because he starts wading back to the surface.

"Sleep, my queen. I'll get you home."

With no energy left in me after my panic attack, I close my eyes. For the first time, I fall asleep knowing I'm completely safe.

# CHAPTER II

# ALLARICK

The walk home is silent but beautiful. Erin sleeps soundlessly in my arms. I'm amazed at the trust she's giving me, and I don't plan on ruining it. Today went better than I anticipated—even with her panic attack. Seeing her open up in small ways made me feel like I was making some progress with her. Like the genuine smile that lit up her face when the turtle came for a visit. Or the look of pure wonder upon seeing the mermaids.

When I reached out to touch Erin, I had planned to guide her back toward the cabin. But it triggered her, and she violently started crying and shuddering. I did the only thing I knew how to do to calm her. I had to touch her again, but I hoped she would see it as friendly rather than threatening.

Her entire demeanor changed the moment I got her in the ocean. Her body needed to feel the water, and she needed to hear the sound of the ocean creatures to bring her back to reality. It made me unbelievably proud that my queen connected with the ocean so quickly.

Back at the cabin, I carry Erin to bed. She's still in her clothes from earlier—dry, thankfully—but I wish I could make her more comfortable in the sleeping clothes I've provided her. I won't wake her to change, and I'm definitely not going to change her myself while she's asleep. So, these clothes will have to do for now.

Pulling the blankets up around her, I take my spot on the chair. Sleep will not come for me tonight as I plan to watch over her, but I'm resigned to my fate. I grab a spare blanket folded at the end of the bed and pull it up around my shoulders.

I'm in and out of consciousness, the smallest sounds wake me, and my instinct is to check on Erin each time. She clutches a pillow close to her chest, murmuring something unintelligible in her sleep. It's not the peaceful sleep I hoped she would have tonight, but she doesn't appear to be suffering from a nightmare.

Or so I thought.

Not even ten minutes later, Erin screams. A high-pitched, bloodcurdling scream that has me jumping off my chair and springing into action. I expect to see an intruder, perhaps one of King Alpha Rip's wolves who let their curiosity get the best of them and wandered too far from the pack.

But there's nothing in the darkness. I strain my ear, hoping to pick up on the sounds of footfalls or breathing, but all that comes to me are Erin's screams of pure, unadulterated terror.

"Allarick!" she screams. For a moment, I'm frozen to

the spot, unable to do more than gape. Erin thrashes in bed and soon pushes herself up. Her eyes are wide, full of terror as she desperately searches the room. It's nearly pitch-black in here, and she can't see me. "Allarick!" she calls again, choking back a sob.

Hearing her broken cry breaks the hold she has over me, and I don't think. I just act. I close the distance between us and wrap my arms around her. Erin screams and tries to push me off, because of course she does. She can't fucking see me, and I haven't made my presence known.

"Sweet girl, it's me. It's Allarick. I'm here." I repeat those words over and over again. "I'm here. I'm not going anywhere. I'll protect you."

After a few minutes of strangled breathing and a racing heart, Erin goes limp in my arms, her head falling to my chest. "Allarick?" she asks softly, as if scared of the answer. Or scared that I'm not actually next to her.

"I'm here," I say again, keeping my hold around her. I don't have my tentacles this time, but she either doesn't mind or doesn't realize what's happening. She shudders against me and reaches up to feel my face.

Her hand moves down to my neck before moving on to my locs and fingering one gently. "Allarick." This time when she says my name, it's not a question but rather a confirmation of what she needed to know. She needed to feel me to know I'm real.

"I'm sorry," she says after a long pause. Her voice wavers, and a single tear rolls down her already tear-stained cheeks.

"No, Erin. I'm sorry." My own voice is deep and full of

emotions I can't keep to myself anymore. "I'm sorry you can't feel safe in your own dreams. I'm sorry someone hurt a beautiful, smart, and confident girl until she felt unworthy of love. I'm sorry I can't do more, but understand this..."

Erin hasn't moved since I began speaking. She remains tense in my arms, and I try to soothe her by rubbing her back gently.

"Know that you are wanted here. That you will never have to be fearful of me. I will do all I can to help you heal, even if that means comforting you every night because you had a bad dream. Here, you are a queen and will be treated with nothing but the respect and kindness you deserve."

I can't fix Erin. I can't reach into her soul and mend the broken pieces instantly, no matter how badly I want to take away her pain. This human I have only known for a short time has become one of the most important people in my life. I can be there as she heals and regains the part of her that someone broke. Even if that takes one hundred years.

"Thank you," she says, but before I can answer, she goes on, "for everything. Both for comforting me during the panic attack and the nightmare."

"You don't need to thank me." She doesn't. I don't comfort her to get her gratitude. I comfort her because she deserves it.

"Still. No one has ever done that for me. Not since I was a little girl, at least." Her voice cracks from use. I don't think I've heard her talk this much to me. One day I'll learn more of Erin's story, but it is a discussion for later. We still have a few hours until morning, and she needs sleep after purging her emotions.

Erin yawns and gently removes herself from my embrace. I feel her absence instantly but let her go. She lies back down on the bed, but before she does, she snatches up the blanket I was using earlier. I can't hide the grin on my face, even if she can't see it.

She wants a piece of me. Or maybe she's just really cold, but I prefer to think Erin wants the blanket because it smells of me. And hopefully my scent brings her a semblance of comfort.

After all, it was *me* she called for in the midst of panic. I don't take that lightly.

She curls up on her side, bringing the blanket to her chest. I know she's tired because her eyelids keep drooping, and her breathing evens out. Just when I think she's asleep, Erin's small voice breaks through the silence: "I'm safe."

It sounds like more of a reminder, both to herself and me. A fragile trust blossoms between us, barely there but taking root.

"You're safe," I agree, but Erin's already fallen back to sleep with my blanket for comfort.

I smile for a long time after that until my cheeks hurt. This feels a lot like progress.

I DIDN'T SLEEP much that night, consumed with making sure Erin was still sleeping well. She jolted in her sleep numerous times throughout the night, as if she were running from someone. I wanted to take those nightmares and lock them away in a place she'd never have to deal with again. I was helpless to do much other than watch her and be there if she woke up.

Eventually, I gave up on sleeping and got up to make breakfast. She hasn't complained once about my food, even though I know it's terrible. She's polite and doesn't comment, but she also doesn't eat much.

As I flip the egg, the front door to the house opens up. I drop the spatula and turn around to see Atina waltz through the door. "Brother mine," she says dramatically, shrugging off her black coat. "Did you miss me?"

Atina strolls into the kitchen and eyes my sorry attempt at breakfast. Too-runny eggs and burned salmon. She tsks. "I don't know how you managed to keep your wife alive if this is the food you've been serving. I bet you're missing that fancy kitchen staff you have right about now, huh?"

"Have you always been this insufferable, or have the land dwellers rubbed off on you?" I frown, which earns me a rag to the face. Atina barrels past me to toss my attempts at breakfast and start anew.

"I hope you have information."

"Oh, do I ever." Atina gestures to the cupboard. "Hand me a few plates and join me for breakfast. Then I'll tell you, but I need food first."

Ten minutes and three plates of food later, Atina and I sit in her living room. I take the couch, leaving the extra plate of food next to me in case Erin wakes up and wanders out here. Atina makes herself comfortable in her chair, kicking her feet up to rest on the coffee table.

"Well," she says after taking a bite of her egg salmon sandwich. "Whoever gave you that information about the singing coming from the deep ocean was, unfortunately, correct."

"You heard it? Where? Delmare hasn't made much progress."

"Of course he hasn't," she scoffs. "I told you, this surpasses Delmare's expertise. He might be a good guard, but he's a shit explorer."

I hate to admit it, but she's right. Delmare is a great guard and will lay down his life for me and my people, but this is bigger than what he can handle. Hell, it might be bigger than what I can handle alone.

"We stopped at different ports and hung out at the local pubs there. Drunk people like to talk. There have been whispers about voices coming from the water, but no one could tell us much more than that. Not until we started to intercept ships at sea—"

"Please tell me you didn't kill these people." I know my sister and her lack of patience for answers. The people who live their lives on boats are usually the sons and daughters of merpeople and land people. They are technically mine to protect.

Atina rolled her eyes. "Please. And get blood on my favorite boots? Not even you are worth that, Brother." There's a wicked gleam in her eyes as she smirks.

"Fine, fine. Go on. What did you find?" I chuckle but instantly get serious again at her next words.

"Most of the ships we stopped admitted to feeling

uncomfortable or sick around this area." Atina removes her feet from the table and rolls out her map. She points to a spot in the ocean nestled between Lycan Forest and Fae Court, marked with a large X.

"We sailed here to see if the stories we heard were correct and..." Atina trails off. If I didn't know my sister better, I would have thought she looked nervous. But Atina Eldridge rarely gets nervous, only even.

"Go on," I urge, discarding my mostly untouched breakfast.

"There was a sound. Almost like singing, but like no siren song I've heard before. This was deeper and mournful. It affected everyone on my crew. It almost felt like invisible hands around our bodies, wanting to pull us down to join them.

"But the song was weak and only lasted a few minutes at a time," she goes on. "Easy to ignore for a crew like mine, experienced with sea creatures. For a lesser crew?" Atina shakes her head. "I'm not certain they would have been able to ignore it."

My stomach churns. A simple tale from a dying man holds more merit that I originally suspected. "And you believe this to be the Leviathan?"

"I have no other explanation." Atina shrugs. "If these are those creatures, then I think they are trying to follow in the footsteps of their cousins, the Nephilim, and break out from whatever prison they're rotting in. They are, unfortunately, succeeding."

A threat is in my ocean, and I'm not there to defend my people. I had hoped to make more progress with Erin so I could be back by now, but I'm not certain she is completely comfortable around me yet. Throwing her into a situation where she'd be completely reliant upon me sounds disastrous.

But I also can't sit on my ass and do nothing while I know about the Leviathan. Truth of the matter is that I can't stay on land any longer, not after the information Atina has brought me. I need to check on my kingdom and look into anything I can find in our libraries about the Leviathan and their alliances with the Nephilim.

"Atina, I need you to do me a favor."

"You usually do," she sighs, with no real malice behind her words. "What is it this time?"

There are very few people I would entrust Erin with. My sister happens to be one of those people. She will make sure Erin is safe and be the one to get her out of here if things go south. She knows how Erin arrived, all bruised and broken, but I haven't gone into detail of her past, mostly because I know very little. It's also her story, not mine, to tell. Atina's smart though. She can guess at the horrors Erin went through.

"I need you to stay here with Erin while I go back to Tetria. I don't know for how long yet, but I need to check on things. Catch up with Delmare and speak with the scholars." There are many other things I need to do too, but these are the most pressing matters.

I know my sister doesn't like staying in one place for too long. She has this home out of necessity, but her true home is aboard her ship, sailing the open sea. She isn't pleased by my request but nods all the same.

She's a far better sister than I deserve.

I stand, itching to leave. The sooner I leave, the

sooner I'll be back with Erin. "Good. Thank you, Atina. I will be back just as soon as I can. I'll leave now—"

"Please don't leave me."

Atina and I both turn toward the new voice. One I didn't realize was listening in on the conversation.

Standing in the bedroom doorway, dressed in a new outfit, is Erin.

And she looks terrified.

# CHAPTER 12

# ERIN

I'm up early the following morning. Sleep wasn't restful. Thoughts of James plagued my dreams, but also thoughts of Allarick. His smile. His gentle nature. And the way he was able to calm me down by sharing a part of himself with me. Still, I couldn't help but feel bad that James still has this power over me.

This would be so much easier if James hadn't ruined me for any other man. I might have physically escaped him, but he still haunts me. His voice plays in my head in every decision and conversation I have. It's exhausting.

I hear movement outside my door. I'm not the only one who wasn't able to sleep. Allarick is moving about—probably making breakfast, but the poor guy is a terrible chef. I don't mind though. It's sweet to have someone else cook for me for a change.

I'm determined to make today a better day with Allarick. Despite my lack of sleep, I woke up feeling the best I've felt since I arrived. No aches or pains. I feel much more like myself.

I put on another dress Allarick has supplied me. Either this man loves his women in dresses, or he has no idea how to shop for women's apparel, and this is the best he can do. Either way, it's nice that he tried. He also left me a few toiletries, for which I am thankful.

I disappear into the bathroom to brush my teeth. The humidity in the air is no friend to me, constantly making my hair frizzy. I do my best to put it into a slicked-back bun to get my hair off my neck. Luckily, there are no bruises I'm trying to hide behind my hair, and that's such a fucking great feeling.

By the time I'm finished in the bathroom and head back into the bedroom, a new voice joins Allarick from the living room. A feminine voice. My body freezes, but this time not in fear. This feeling is different and leaves a bitter taste on my tongue. Unexplained anger leaves me immobile, but only for a second.

Jealousy.

I don't like it.

Slowly, I creep to the door. I shouldn't be listening to a private conversation, but my curiosity is getting the best of me. Their voices are muffled, but I hear a few things the feminine voice says. Words like "Nephilim" and "Leviathan" are said in hushed whispers. They make little sense to me, and I almost tune them out until I hear Allarick's voice.

"I need you to stay here with Erin while I go back to Tetria. I don't know for how long yet, but I need to check on things. Catch up with Delmare and speak with the scholars."

My whole body freezes, breaths coming out ragged.

My body is teetering on panic once again. He's leaving? And asking a stranger to stay with me? He can't leave. No, not when I'm just starting to feel comfortable with him. Is he leaving because he's mad about yesterday? Mad that I'm still the weak girl he met that night with The Guardian?

I'm not even thinking. If I was, I wouldn't be rushing out of the room, out to where Allarick is talking to a beautiful pirate-looking woman. They are both standing, Allarick's back to me. Neither one of them notices me yet.

The words tumble out: "Please don't leave me."

I have no right to ask him. No right to keep him here if he's upset with me. But he's the only thing I know here. The only person I'm coming to trust. A better woman would never be this selfish, but in this I'm going to be. Allarick can't leave. At least not without me.

Allarick turns, his handsome face a mixture of confusion and...hope? "Erin...how did you—"

"You can't leave," I say, and for the first time, I realize my voice is completely my own again. No more rasp—whatever the healer gave me worked quickly. I don't even have the chance to be excited about it, though, because I'm terrified about what's going to happen next.

"Please don't go," I repeat again, stepping closer. Having him not immediately turn me away gives me the confidence I desperately need. The couch separates us, but I reach for him. Allarick's eyes widen as I grab his hand, holding it. His hands are soft, and when he squeezes mine, it's gentle. I've seen Allarick smile before, but never like this: full, white teeth on display, eyes squinted, and muscles relaxed. It's beautiful.

He's beautiful.

"I won't go." His words alleviate the tension in my body, and my stiff muscles relax. "Your voice is beautiful."

Heat rushes to my cheeks, and I drop my gaze down to our clasped hands. "The medicine really helped. Thank you."

Unlike with James, I don't feel the need to pull away. His touch doesn't make me feel dirty or disgusted. I don't fear his temper will flare, and I'll be his closest punching bag. This feeling of comfort makes me feel worse for pulling away from him yesterday. It wasn't him, really. Just his touch reminding me of something sinister.

"Not to be the one to break up *this*," the woman speaks up, gesturing between Allarick and me, "but not going back to your kingdom isn't really an option right now, Brother."

*Brother.*

Allarick has a sister.

Oh.

My earlier jealousy seems so silly now. They share the same honey-brown eyes. Their lips both curl upwards at the edges, and they both have beautiful black locs hanging down past their shoulders.

Allarick doesn't move or respond to his sister. He continues to hold my hand, looking at me as if he's seeing me for the first time. "Atina, perhaps one more day—"

"No, Allarick," his sister—Atina—growls. "You've been away from your kingdom long enough. A king needs to be with his people. That's your job, and although I don't envy you for it, I also can't in good conscience allow you to remain here."

Her words are a reality check. This man standing before me is no man at all. He's a king with responsibilities to his people. I can't say I know what that means or what trouble he's up against, but I know the threat is severe, or else I wouldn't be here. Ender's contract said I'm to help the kraken king save his kingdom, but he didn't go into specifics on the how or from what.

I can't be selfish. Not in this, at least. I have to let him go.

But he doesn't have to go alone.

"You should go to your people." My words shock Allarick, and he drops my hand. I immediately miss his warmth. He opens his mouth to argue with me, but I'm faster. "And take me with you."

Even Atina seems surprised by my request. Hell, *I'm* surprised by what I said, even more so that I mean it. I *want* to go. The alternative is staying here away from Allarick. And though his sister appears decent enough, she's not Allarick.

"I'm here to be part of your kingdom, right?" I look between the siblings, waiting for them to contradict me. But of course they don't. I have a duty here, and it's about time I start fulfilling it. "Then I think it's time we go. I'm healed now and—"

*I'm comfortable around you,* but of course I don't say that last part. The words are on the tip of my tongue, but they aren't yet ready to come out. It feels too fragile, and one wrong move will shatter what little progress we have created.

"If we go down to Tetria, I'll have to guide you the entire way. Meaning I'm going to have to touch you," Allarick warns.

Heat pools low in my core. The words aren't said suggestively, but my brain supplies an image of Allarick's hands all over me, running down my—

Nope. Definitely not going to think about that right now with his sister here.

"It's fine. I can handle it." I'm happy to find no hesitation in my voice.

"Well, there you have it. Your wife wants to join you," Atina says, and I bristle at the word "wife." I'm willing to go with him, but accepting the role of his wife is something different entirely. Not that it sounds bad… It's just too new.

Allarick must notice because he's quick to respond, "This is Erin. We're not married yet."

Atina just waves his words away. "Not yet, but it's inevitable." The woman then pushes past her brother, knocking her shoulder against his. Allarick scowls in her direction, and I have a hunch few people touch their king, let alone shove right past him. Sister perks, I suppose.

Atina extends her hand. Her wrists and fingers are adorned with gold jewelry that would look gaudy on anyone else but somehow looks regal on her. I shake her hand. Her grip is firm and confident, something I desperately want to be. "Nice to meet you, Erin. I'm Atina, Allarick's way more attractive sister." She winks.

"You needed something going for you," Allarick teases easily, and I stifle a giggle. Their easy banter lightens the mood, giving me a glimpse into their sibling relationship. As an only child, I have always wondered what it would be like to grow up with another person.

"If you're going down to Tetria, you need magical aid. Brother, I assume you have what you need to take her safely underwater?" Atina asks Allarick, raising a brow.

"I do, but it will take time to work its way through her system. We will need to leave tomorrow morning."

Although Atina doesn't look thrilled, she nods her acquiescence.

Allarick disappears into the kitchen and comes back out a moment later. He's carrying a clear jar with a blue liquid. It sloshes around as he hands it to me. "This is going to give you the ability to breathe and survive under the sea. It might make you tired, but that's a normal side effect."

I don't usually accept strange liquids from men, but I find myself reaching for it just as Allarick says, "You'll need to drink all of that. I've been told the taste is a little salty but palatable."

"You'll want to eat something afterwards too," Atina adds.

The siblings watch me expectantly, so I unscrew the jar. No foul odor greets me, which I take as a good sign. This is it. Drinking this liquid feels like the point of no return. I only hesitate for a moment with the watchful eyes of Allarick and Atina on me. But then I put the jar to my lips, throw my head back, and drink.

Allarick is correct in his assessment of the salty taste. I feel like I'm drinking ocean water, but I somehow manage to keep it all down. The taste doesn't last long, though. Atina ushers me into the kitchen to eat and drink juice. It does wonders to hide the taste.

I don't feel any different. Neither a tail or gills grow, which, admittedly, I thought might. I still feel like myself. Allarick and Atina don't seem disappointed though, so I take it as a good sign.

"I guess I'll leave you to it. I'll be back in the morning to see you off. Enjoy my house. I have a cute barmaid needing my attention." Atina does a strange salute-like gesture and struts out of the room.

"I like her," I say once the front door closes and Atina is gone. "She's nice."

Allarick bites out a laugh, but not a cruel one. "Nice is not something anyone has ever called my sister. But she's loyal as hell for those she considers family. I think she'll take a liking to you."

"You've both been very kind." Allarick has done everything in his power to make sure I feel safe and cared for, even when I have been reluctant or shut him out.

It's my turn to return the favor.

"Allarick. We need to talk."

# ALLARICK

I'm intrigued by her request to talk—such simple words, but they could mean anything. Judging by the distress written across her features and the way her body trembles, this isn't going to be an easy conversation.

"What would you like to talk about, Erin?" I keep my voice even, trying not to show too much emotion so I don't scare her away from speaking to me. I yearn to hear more of her story. More of her lovely voice speaking to me.

Erin rubs her hands against her thighs, looking anywhere but at me. "Did Ender tell you why I accepted the deal to come here?"

Besides the fact that she is key to my kingdom's survival? No. That's my reason, but what's hers? I know nothing about the woman who sits before me besides her resilience and her adaptability.

"Ender speaks very little, as you well know. He says

you have a story, but it wasn't one he could tell. He said you would tell me when you're ready."

Erin nods. A single tear rolls down from her eyes, and she laughs bitterly. "Fuck, I swore I wasn't going to cry."

"Erin, you don't have to say anything if you aren't ready. And never apologize for crying. It's an emotion I don't shy away from." I keep my voice soft, hoping it makes her feel more comfortable.

She gives me a tentative smile and then shakes her head emphatically. "No. I don't want to start a new life in your kingdom without fully purging myself of James."

"Who's James?" My voice comes out in a growl. If she senses my anger, Erin doesn't comment. She's lost in her own nightmare, but it's one she is finally allowing herself to work through. It's not lost on me, the significance of Erin choosing me to help carry her burden.

"James is someone I met as a teenager in school. We started out being friends, but that eventually turned into more. At the start of our relationship, things were…not great, but they were good. We had fights, but nothing that would raise any concerns. For the most part, I was happy. Plus, he was my first love, so I didn't have anything to compare it to.

"It was after my parents died that he showed his true colors." Erin takes a shuddering breath. I know telling this story costs her. As much as I want to alleviate her pain and tell her she doesn't need to share this with me, I would be doing her a disservice. She was strong enough to live through these events; I can be strong enough to hear them.

"What did he do to you, Erin?" My body acts of its

own accord, and I reach for her. She tenses, but only for a second before she lifts her head, red-rimmed eyes softening at my touch.

"It started out as an argument. I don't even remember what for, but something stupid, I'm sure. He got so mad so quickly. I didn't even see his hand move until it was too late. He backhanded me across the face. The pain didn't register at first. I think I was in shock. It felt like time paused. Even James paused, equally shocked over his actions. He promised me it would never happen again. He begged me to forgive him and not to tell anyone. The pathetic thing? I believed him. I actually believed him."

Anger is a familiar emotion. During my reign as king, I have been angry over outcomes not in my favor, a criminal committing heinous crimes, and overall annoyance for close-minded councilmen. But never an anger so potent that only blood will ease the storm raging inside me. There's no weaker man than one who uses violence to be heard. That is no man at all.

"Of course it happened again," Erin says, and I move closer to her. It could be my mind creating something that's not there, but I swear she leans toward me.

"At this point, he effectively isolated me from all of my friends. And since my parents were dead, I felt like I had nowhere to go. I kept telling myself that this time would be the last time. It became so easy to lie to myself. The beatings hurt, but the shame I felt was unbearable."

"You have nothing to be ashamed about," I say vehemently. My anger threatens to boil over, but I do my best to suppress it. Anger is not the response Erin needs to see right now, even if it's not directed at her. She's experienced enough anger in her life.

"Logically, I suppose I know that. But I still feel like it's my fault. That maybe if I did this or acted a certain way, he wouldn't have treated me like he did. It's fucking terrible to think that way, and I've been working really hard to come to terms with what happened, knowing none of it was my fault. It was his. But I'm a work in progress."

Erin shifts in her seat uncomfortably, and with her free hand, she rubs her shoulder. "We dated for eight years, but only the last three years were pure hell. It got so bad, I feared if I didn't get out, I would die. That's why I went to Ender. He found me after a horrible fight that left me...well, you saw how it left me."

I did. It is an image I'll never get out of my head. He left his dirty mark all over her body. Took her voice from her and left her feeling like she had no other choice. He's lucky he's in the human world and not Mescos. I would love to show him the same treatment he showed Erin.

I squeeze Erin's hand gently. "Thank you for telling me. No one should have to live through what you did. I will keep you safe, Erin." It's a steep promise, but one I intend to keep. If Erin never had someone willing to fight for her, then I'll happily take up that position.

I want her safe.

I want her happy.

I want *her.*

Erin has shared so much with me, more than I could have hoped for. It is only right that she has a piece of me too. "Can I tell you something?"

At my question, Erin perks up, intrigued. "Of course."

"I never wanted to share my throne with anyone," I say. "Not because I don't think another person is deserving, but the burdens that come with the throne eat away at you. I didn't want to be responsible for another's light extinguishing from their eyes. This job hardens you. Makes you do things you didn't know you were capable of. At times, it can be downright scary.

"I saw firsthand how it changed my father," I continue. "People flock to you when you're a king. He met so many different people and unfortunately took it too far one night. Atina? She's only my half-sister," I say.

Erin's eyes widen, understanding the implication.

"It was the first and only time my father cheated on my mother. But it was enough because the mermaid got pregnant. It was my mother who told my father to step up and raise the child after Atina was born and her biological mother wanted nothing to do with her. My parents never fully recovered after that."

Erin's hand squeezes mine, providing comfort. "I suppose I don't want to make the same mistakes as my parents. Hurt the one I love the most in the world." I won't be unfaithful to Erin, but I fear the burdens of the throne could change us in ways we never expect.

I've never voiced my fears of being king, but they always linger not too far from the surface. Erin deserves to know what she is getting into before she becomes part of my world. I don't mean to scare her off, but I also can't have her clueless.

"My duty will be to my kingdom and to you," I say. "I meant it when I said you are safe with me, Erin. I will do as much as I can to shield you from the burdens of royalty, but there are things not even I can control. I don't wish to frighten you—"

"You aren't frightening me, Allarick," Erin says gently, as if consoling me now. "I've known fear before, and this does not fill me with fear. Apprehension and nervousness? Most certainly. But if Tetria is half as good as their king, I don't think I have anything to worry about."

I search her face to catch her lie, but I don't find one. Yearning grows deep in my chest as I play back her words over and over again until they are imprinted on my heart. There's a lot I want to say, but the words don't come. Instead, I say, "The Guardian knew I needed you."

A faint smile crosses Erin's lips, and her posture relaxes. "Is it crazy that I trust you?"

"Is it crazy that I want you to trust me?" I ask as warmth spreads through my chest. Erin trusts me. It's not something I take lightly, and it's something I vow to never break. Her trust is the most precious gift I've ever received.

"I guess that means we're stuck together?" She laughs but only to hide the nerves I see she's trying to conceal.

"I suppose it does, my queen." At the mention of her title, she blushes. It's going to take her some time to get used to it. I felt the same way the day I became king. She'll see she belongs with the sea tomorrow. When I'm finally able to take her home.

Erin's eyes start to droop, and she suppresses a yawn.

One of the side effects of the earlier elixir. "We should get you to bed."

"Bed...I'm not tir—" Her words are cut off by another yawn. The elixir is working fast, and I suspect Erin will be asleep within minutes. I chuckle softly and stand up.

"Bedtime."

Erin sticks out her lip in an adorable pout. "Fine. Bossy," she murmurs and stands up. She sways on her feet, but I catch her before she can cause herself any harm.

"Kings are meant to be bossy. Now, I'm going to pick you up and carry you to bed. Okay?" I warn. I don't trust her walking by herself. As it is, she's hardly holding herself up. Still, I wait for her consent.

"Okay," she murmurs. It's all I need to pick Erin up in my arms and carry her to the bedroom. We aren't even in her room before she falls asleep.

# CHAPTER 14

# ERIN

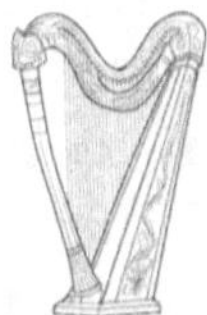

I don't remember going to bed or lying down. I definitely don't remember sleeping the day away. I do remember pouring my heart out to Allarick and him accepting all my baggage involving James. I thought I would regret sharing with him, but I'm actually relieved. Someone else finally knows my story.

When I finally come to, I'm back in my room. Only this time, I'm not alone. Stuffed into a small chair is Allarick's sleeping form. His large frame is contorted into what cannot be a comfortable position. Meanwhile, I have a large bed all to myself, but Allarick didn't join me. He respected my space.

I melt a little bit.

I shift in bed, causing it to creak. Allarick is alerted immediately, and his eyes snap open as he takes me in. When he sees I'm fine, his tense posture relaxes a fraction. "Hey, how are you feeling?" His rich baritone voice is raspy with sleep.

"I don't feel any different than I did yesterday. Did it

not work?" What would it mean if I can't go down to Tetria with Allarick? Does that make me useless to his cause?

Before I can spiral any more, Allarick sits up. "It worked. You aren't supposed to feel different until we are in the water. I just wanted to make sure you didn't have a bad reaction to the serum. It's rare, but I didn't want to take the chance."

That explains why he's in here. "You watched me while I slept?"

"Yeah." Allarick's chin dips down, averting his gaze. "I'm sorry I didn't ask. You were asleep, and I thought risking your anger was better than risking your life."

"I'm not angry," I quickly reassure. "Though you didn't have to sleep in the chair. I'm a big girl. I could have handled you sleeping on the other side of the bed." Even as I say the words, I wonder how true they are. I don't know how I would have reacted if I saw Allarick in bed with me. In theory, it sounds nice, appealing even, but the shock might have triggered a reaction I'd rather keep hidden.

"We should get going, Erin," Allarick says after a moment of silence. "Atina has left clothes for you that are better suited to the ocean. When you're done, meet me outside."

THE SUN IS out by the time I make it outside. The black spandex pants Atina left me make it almost hot outside.

The top is simple, similar to a bikini top. It covers what it needs to cover but little else. I've never been a prude when it comes to showing off skin, but the fabric is almost translucent. My nipples are on full display for anyone who looks hard enough.

"You look good, land dweller," Atina says once I reach her. She's in the same outfit from yesterday but without her tricorn. Her long, beaded braids are pulled back into a high ponytail. This woman is not only fierce but beautiful too. She radiates confidence and elegance. Everything I wish I had. I would be lying if I said I don't have a slight girl crush on her.

"You don't think the top is a little revealing?"

Atina just laughs. "Be thankful you have a top. Not everyone will down below."

Well, okay then.

"Come, Allarick is at the docks waiting for you. Are you ready, Erin? If you aren't comfortable going down to Tetria, let me know now. I would never send a woman into a situation she doesn't want to be in." Her intensity stuns me, plus the implication she would go against her brother if I asked. She's known me for all of a day but is already looking out for me.

I give her a reassuring smile. "Thank you. Truly. But I'm here to help Allarick save his kingdom. I know what I signed up for. I'm ready to see my new home."

Atina considers my words but must find them acceptable because she nods. "Let's go then. Allarick is already in the water."

Hearing that Allarick is in the water, probably in kraken form, sends a certain thrill through me. I have only seen him like that once, but I didn't get to properly enjoy him since I was too busy coming down from my panic attack. This time I'm going to take in my fill.

"Will you be joining us?" I ask Atina. Her legs are longer than mine, and I have to jog to keep up with her. But at my question, she slows down, laughing.

"Absolutely not. I don't go below the water. My place is above on my ship." She stares fondly out to where I see a black ship bobbing in the distance. "That's the *Stone Heart* up there. My ship since I've been sailing. She's served me and my crew well over these years."

"You seem really fond of her."

"Aye. She's my home. My crew is my family. We all have the heart of an explorer. Maybe someday I'll tell you about our adventures."

"I would love that," I say honestly, wondering what type of life Atina leads. It's easy to see how much like Allarick she is. Both are passionate for the ocean, just in different ways. I hope to capture an essence of their love for the ocean when I live there. Seeing the ocean through Allarick's eyes will be memorable.

"Ah, there he is. Show-off." Atina rolls her eyes, though a slight smile tugs at her lips. I follow her gaze and spot Allarick lounging by the dock. He's shirtless, and for the first time, I notice markings on his chest I missed before. A large triton takes up his left pectoral, encased in waves. His locs flow freely around him, and small gold rings adorn his strands, flickering in the sun.

Below the waist is what catches my attention next. Eight dark red tentacles move underneath the water. Each tentacle is thick, like the size of a boa constrictor.

They look like weapons that could easily harm or kill an enemy.

But I've felt the softness of them too. The gentle hold and caress on my body while they chase away my inner demons.

Allarick sees me staring and grins. Heat rushes to my cheeks at being caught staring at my soon-to-be husband. He laughs like a male who knows he's attractive. Which he is. Very much so.

"Erin, you look beautiful," Allarick says, taking his time to study me. I have the urge to cover my nipples, but I fight it. His gaze doesn't linger on my chest for long, because he's proven already he's a gentleman. Still, I don't think I would have minded him staring at my chest for a *little* longer.

"She's ready to go below. I'll wait here until I know everything has gone okay," Atina says.

Allarick moves closer to the pier. "Aw, worried about me, Guppy?"

"I don't give a shit about you, Brother. I'm here in case Erin can't stand your annoying ass," Atina says with no real anger behind her words. I think their relationship is throwing insults to show their love. Not having a sibling myself, I can't say if this is normal. From shows and movies I've seen, though, I think it is.

"Are you ready to go, my queen?" Allarick asks, and the same warm, fuzzy feeling fills my chest at the sound of his new nickname for me.

Before I go to him, I turn to Atina. I have the strange urge to hug her, so I do. Atina tenses before awkwardly bringing her hand up to pat my back.

"Thank you," I say, though I'm not sure what I'm thanking her for.

The clothes.

Making me feel better.

Agreeing I should go with Allarick.

Allowing us to take over her house.

"Erm, you're welcome," she says as I pull back. "Now, let's get you into the water."

Atina moves her hand to the center of my back, giving me a gentle push forward. My legs are slow to move, but soon I'm walking to the edge of the pier. Allarick waits below, hands outstretched. Two tentacles also snake out, providing me with extra support if I need it.

I lower myself on the pier, letting my legs dangle over. Allarick swims closer, a kind smile on his features. "You ready, my queen?" He reaches for me, and I flinch.

Allarick catches this and immediately pulls back, a stricken look on his face.

"Sorry," I murmur, hating that I made him feel bad. Again. "No hands. But maybe your tentacles?" I ask, looking at the powerful appendages surrounding him. How funny that I'm scared of the gentlest part of him while feeling comforted by the deadliest part of him.

"Good idea." Two red tentacles reach out toward me. I let them wrap gently around my waist, feeling like a silky caress. Absentmindedly, I reach out to stroke the tentacle, mesmerized by the silky feeling. I swear I hear Allarick groan, and then Atina coughs.

"Yeah, want to keep the heavy petting to yourself?" she asks, and I jerk my hand away.

My face flames. "Did I do something wrong?"

"Yes."

"No."

Atina and Allarick speak at the same time. Allarick shoots his sister a glare. Atina rolls her eyes, placing a hand on her hip. "Listen, as your sister, I want to gouge my eyes out before I watch...that."

"Watch what? Please tell me what I did wrong." Since clearly Allarick isn't going to.

"Touching his tentacle like this is the equivalent of stroking his co—"

"It's not!" Allarick growls, pulling me into the water. I shiver at the sudden rush of cold. Or maybe at the fact I was getting handsy with my almost-husband and didn't even realize it.

The terror on my face softens Allarick. "It can mean that," he admits but quickly goes on, "Typically, touching another's tail or tentacles is an intimate act reserved for partners. It's not inherently sexual unless we were...engaging in sexual acts."

Oh.

*Oh.*

"Right, now that's out of the way, you should go. I'll keep searching for more information about the mysterious singing. We'll check in soon." Atina tilts her head down in a goodbye gesture. "Enjoy Tetria, Your Majesties."

"Wait, how am I supposed to breathe underwater? I know you gave me the potion, but I don't feel any different," I say to the siblings.

"Your gills will form as soon as I take you under

water," Allarick answers like I'm supposed to know what that means.

"My...gills?"

Allarick doesn't respond this time. His hold around me tightens, and he says goodbye to his sister. Without any further warning, he plunges us into the water.

# ALLARICK

rin flails as soon as we get under water, which is expected. As a human, she's used to not being able to breathe or speak underwater. It doesn't come naturally for them. Her natural reaction is to try to save herself and swim to the surface. That would be necessary if it wasn't for the drink she consumed.

While Erin desperately tries to swim to the surface, I keep my hold on her. "Erin, sweet girl, you're fine. You can breathe and speak," I say gently.

Erin stops struggling. Her cheeks are fat with the breath she's holding, but she tentatively breathes out. I check her neck and am pleased to see her gills have formed, allowing her to come and go in the water as she pleases. I was assured by the pixie I got the potion from that it would work. However, it has been so long since we've taken in a human, I couldn't say for certain and needed to be ready to swim her to safety if they didn't form.

I watch as Erin's chest begins to rise and fall in a

steady rhythm as she discovers her ability to breathe. A hesitant smile crosses her lips. "How long will this work for?"

"Until death."

"Oh."

I touch my throat where my own gills are. "These will stay with you while you're under the water. But when you surface, you'll go back to breathing normally. It's all part of the magic from the potion," I explain.

For all the changes Erin has seen in the last few days, she takes this in stride. Any normal person would have broken long ago, but not Erin. She's stronger than she gives herself credit for.

"Are you ready to go, sweet girl?" I try to hide my eagerness to get back to my kingdom, not wanting to sway her. My eagerness comes from checking in on my people, yes, but there's more to it than that. Showing Erin Tetria and watching her—hopefully—fall in love with what she sees is ultimately the real prize here.

"Will you hold me while we swim there? You know, so I don't get lost? I'm also not a strong swimmer." Her cheeks turn an adorable shade of red, and if I were a betting kraken, I'd guess she liked her nickname. Perhaps even likes being praised.

Interesting. Noted.

"Would you be more comfortable with my hand, or is my tentacle around you okay?" I ask, though I suspect I know the answer. My hands remind her too much of the man she's trying to forget.

As if to prove my point, Erin caresses my tentacle again, and I do everything in my power not to groan. It feels damn good to have her touching me. Part of me thought she'd be repulsed by what she saw. "Tentacle please. They're soft," she hums.

I keep one secured around her waist, and another I dangle in front of her in case she wants to hold on to it. She does, reaching out with her small hand to wrap it around me. "Ready."

Immediately, I take off. We aren't far from Tetria, but it is still a complicated route for those who aren't familiar with it. It's one of the ways I can assure the safety of my people, by making the entrance a labyrinth.

The waters are calm. The occasional fish swims past, paying us little mind. Erin's shocked scream has me turning my head. It takes me a moment to figure out what startled her until I see him. The nearly translucent sea wyrm, roughly the size of a large shark, scary-looking creatures with horns protruding from their skulls and webbed wings on their back, but actually quite friendly if they deem you worthy enough.

"Don't be alarmed. The sea wyrm will not harm you if you do not harm it."

"Wasn't planning on it," she mutters, unable to take her eyes off the creature.

"I gather the sea wrym is an animal you don't have back in Grym Hollow?" I ask.

Erin laughs and shakes her head. "We don't have any sea animals in Grym Hollow. No ocean. There's a lake though. But, no, at least to my knowledge, we do not have a creature like that. We don't have krakens or mermaids either. We have water snakes and frogs."

"What about sirens? They're like mermaids, but their voices hold power."

"Definitely none of those," she says.

I don't say it, but her home sounds miserable. Living above the sea sounds like my own personal hell. I can survive on land if I have to, but my first preference will always be Tetria. This is where Atina and I are different. I'll never understand her desire to be on land, and she won't ever understand my love for living in the sea.

I swim further down until I see the underwater cave. It's easy to miss if you aren't looking for it, which is precisely why it's the best entrance to Tetria. Erin kicks her feet, swimming closer to me. Despite her disdain for human hands, I feel her hand slip into mine.

"It's so dark," she whispers by way of explanation.

I forgot that human eyesight is weak. Even taking the potion, Erin won't be able to see as well as sea people. "I can see just fine," I assure and slowly take her through the cave. It's spacious, large enough for two people to swim side by side.

Erin curls into my side, and I preen. She's leaning on me for comfort. I'm thankful she can't see the boyish smile on my lips, which widens once the first sounds of voice and music from Tetria filter in. My chest fills with longing. I haven't been gone terribly long, but I'm still homesick.

When we reach the exit of the cave, instead of looking at my home, my attention is trained on Erin. I watch the emotions run across her face upon seeing Tetria for the first time. Awe, wonder, curiosity, and excitement. What would my home look like through her eyes? I find I envy her for experiencing the beauty of Tetria for the first time.

We are at the edge of my kingdom, just outside the main city. My crystal palace rises above all other structures, shining in the ocean light. The castle's exterior shimmers in the depths like a ghostly apparition, constructed from materials that glow internally. The walls are made of coral and pearlescent shells, each formation shaped with deliberate artistry, giving the appearance of delicate filigree and intricate mosaics.

The castle towers rise like jagged spires. Glass-like crystal formations sprout from the walls, the phosphorescent glow of deep-sea creatures. The entire structure feels alive, as if it is grown from the sea itself, pulsating with the rhythm of the ocean. Vines of glowing seaweed snake around the columns and archways.

Erin tears her eyes away from the impressive castle to the other buildings that make up the city. Most are made from a mixture of crystal, coral, and stone. The structures stand about three stories tall. The bottom floor is typically a restaurant or shop, while the other two stories house families.

It's mid-afternoon, so the waters are full of merpeople swimming in and out of brightly colored buildings. A young siren child scrambles for her mother, who picks her up before the current can pull her child farther away.

Some sunlight reaches down here, but not much. Although we are able to see in little light, it doesn't mean we don't appreciate it. Thankfully, bioluminescent jellyfish linger above our city, providing light to our skies.

The guppies of our kingdom appreciate it the most since their sight doesn't fully develop until they hit maturity. It also makes for a majestic waterline.

A few merpeople glance in our direction, and shock colors their features. They freeze before remembering protocol and attempt to bow in greeting, though very few pay much attention to me with Erin here. She's gorgeous, sure, but that's not why my people are staring. Many of them have never seen a human before. Only a few elders remember a time when humans swam freely beside us, marrying into our kingdom. Their offspring are still here with their own families, but they are creatures of the sea. Not pure human.

Next to me, I hear Erin move around. With her mouth slightly agape, she stares at Tetria and all she has to offer. "I imagine this is overwhelming, but—"

"It's beautiful," Erin cuts me off, awestruck. My heart skips a beat at her words. "Overwhelming, yes, but so beautiful." She wiggles out of my hold, but I'm hesitant to let her go. None of my people would be foolish enough to hurt her, but I don't want to take chances when it comes to our queen. She also doesn't know her way around my kingdom yet, and I can't have her getting lost.

I let her out of my grasp, though I swim right behind her. She tilts her head and points to the jellyfish. "You have jellyfish to light up your city?"

"It's not a formal job, but they live here too." I smile, but Erin is already on to the next thing. She asks about the multicolored coral that makes up most of the buildings, the fish and other sea creatures that roam freely amongst the merpeople. A turtle passes by, and I beckon it forward. The creature swims in our direction then around Erin.

She giggles. "Can I touch it?"

"Him. And yes." I smile.

Erin reaches out and gently strokes the hard shell. The turtle nudges his head against her hand, and she smiles as she scratches the top of his head.

"Do you want to swim through the city?" It's the fastest route to the palace, but if it would be too over-stimulating for her, we can easily swim around.

"Oh, I would very much like to go through the city," she says, her voice slightly higher-pitched with excitement. However, a moment later, she deflates. "But...will you wrap one of your tentacles back around me? It... makes me feel safe."

*Makes me feel safe.*

No sweeter words have ever been said, and never to me.

I had once thought Erin would be afraid of my kraken side, but who knew she would fear the man more than the monster? Probably because a monster has never hurt her, but a man has.

"Whatever you wish, sweet girl." I wrap my tentacle around her waist. She relaxes in my grip, melting my damn heart. How is it possible for one human to play with my emotions so easily?

"Thank you, Allarick. You're a good kraken," she says, patting me. If it were anyone else petting me like a household pet, I might take offense. But this is Erin, and I welcome all touch she is willing to give me.

Erin says goodbye to the turtle, and I start to lead us

into the city. Colorful pebbled rocks mark the floor, creating swimming pathways. The first place we pass is the Royal Blacksmith shop. Small oceanic volcanoes heat the shop, providing exactly what Eckles—our resident blacksmith—needs to forge spears and household decorations.

Erin peers through the window, watching Eckles forge a blade. Even from here, I feel the heat wafting out of his store. I don't know how Eckles stands being so close to molten heat day in and day out. He claims it's comforting because the rest of the waters are "too damn cold; they'll shrivel my tail."

"What are those?" Erin's question has me turning to see what she's looking at. She points to floating domes, held in place by seaweed rope. About ten of these floating orbs surround the city, but there once were many more.

"Those are homes many humans used to occupy. They're water-free," I explain.

"What? Really? How is that possible? There are places here with air pockets? Are all people like you, able to shift between legs and tails...or tentacles, in your case?" Erin asks excitedly.

I can't help but chuckle at her rapid stream of questions and do my best to answer them all. "The homes have an entry chamber. Once closed, the water drains back into the ocean, allowing the person to walk freely inside their home. The palace has places with air, though that's set up a little differently. I'll explain that more when you see it. We set these up as sort of a comfort and familiarity for humans who wanted some time out of the water.

"And no. Not everyone can switch forms. There is an extensive training merpeople have to go through to get the magic to gain their land legs. Some people don't want to put in the effort because they have no reason to go up on land. But those who do can live in those bubble homes if they choose. All my guards are required to have their land legs so they can move freely between land and sea."

"That makes sense about your guards," Erin says, mostly to herself. She hasn't stopped taking everything in. To be fair, there's a lot to see. She's like a guppy on her birthday, excitedly taking in everything. I want to show her everything Tetria has to offer. A queen should know her kingdom and people. There's a lot Erin needs to learn, but those things can come in time. Right now, I just need her to be comfortable in the water.

"King Allarick," a voice bellows from behind.

Erin whirls around, and recognition colors her features. "I've seen you before."

The captain of my guard halts, clearly caught off guard by Erin's words. Unexplainable anger ignites in my chest, almost violent in nature. I've never been this angry with Delmare before, but how does my wife know him?

Erin chuckles nervously, absentmindedly stroking my tentacle. It's incredibly distracting and sexy. "I saw Allarick talking to you on the pier," she addresses Delmare then turns to me. "I might have been...spying isn't the word but watching. At first, I thought you were speaking to yourself, but then I saw him." She points at Delmare.

My anger overrode my rational thinking. I remember Erin saying she saw me talking to a man while she had locked herself away in Atina's room for days to heal and come to terms with her new life. I never sensed her watching us, but it explains why she didn't completely freak out the first time she saw me as a kraken.

"Then I suppose it's time to formally introduce you to the captain of my guard, Delmare."

The older kraken bows low, giving his queen the proper respect she deserves. "It's a pleasure to meet you, my queen."

"Oh, you can just call me Erin," she says hurriedly. It's clear she's not comfortable with the title, but it belongs to her.

"He'll call you his queen, sweet girl. It's custom," I explain gently.

Erin purses her lips but relents. Part of me wanted to see her fight back, but now isn't the time.

"I don't mean to interrupt, but I heard you were back. Word travels fast around here, and there are urgent matters to discuss. You are needed at the palace." Delmare seems apologetic as he gives me the news.

I can only guess what urgent matters he's referring to, but I don't want them discussed publicly at this time. No use in causing alarm yet.

"Can I come too? Or is this something I shouldn't know?" Erin asks cautiously.

"You are privy to any and all information." My answer comes out brisker than I intended, so I gentle my voice. "I would be honored if my queen joined me for the meeting."

Erin smiles bashfully. She asked for what she wanted, and that makes me proud of her. It's a small step, but progress nonetheless. Maybe here she can finally heal and take back what was taken from her.

"Make sure my queen has a spot next to me during the meeting," I say to Delmare. My guard nods, and I trust he'll carry out my order.

When Delmare bows and leaves, I face Erin. "If it becomes too much, place your hand on my shoulder. The meeting can pause while I escort you to our room."

"I appreciate that, Allarick. I think I'll be okay. Let's go. I'm eager to see our palace." She smiles.

*Our palace.* I love the sound of that. Tightening my tentacle around her waist, I swim toward home.

# CHAPTER 16

# ALLARICK

My meeting room is busy by the time Erin and I make it back to the palace. I had wanted to give Erin a tour of her new home, but it will have to wait now. Delmare looked forlorn while breaking the news earlier. His mood matches the atmosphere of the room. It's tense with a foreboding cloud hanging over us.

A few of my personal guards are here, along with the merperson and siren advisors. There's another figure I don't see as often, sitting at the round, silver table. Nori catches my eye and nods in my direction.

"My sister let you free?" I tease the merman, one of my sister's crewmembers. It's been a long time since I've seen him with a tail and gills; he usually prefers two legs and the surface. Still, he agrees to be a liaison between my sister and me. How Delmare got him here on such short notice, I'll never know. The old kraken is just damn good at his job, despite my sister's reservations about him.

"She has a heart, occasionally," Nori muses.

Doors close behind us as soon as Erin and I swim in. Two jeweled chairs sit together on one side of the table. I lead Erin over to her seat, but she just looks at it and then back at me, confused.

"Uhm...how do I sit?" she whispers, angling her body away from the others in the room. Her cheeks tint red with embarrassment.

I mentally scold myself for not realizing she's new to this world and doesn't understand how it works in comparison to her own. "I'll guide you." I pull out her chair and move her toward it. My tentacle glides underneath the chair and up to grab Erin. I pull her down, securing her to the chair with my limbs so her body won't try to float. In time, she'll learn to sit and move her body in the water.

"Thank you," she mouths once I take my spot next to her.

Curious expressions meet my gaze before darting over to Erin. She happens to be the most interesting person at the table right now. It has been decades since the last human set foot in the palace. The significance of this moment isn't lost on me. Humans have always been the strength and magic for their mates. They can start and end wars.

Erin doesn't know she's the most powerful person at this table. She'll see in time.

"Before we get started, I would like to introduce everyone to my betrothed, your future queen, Erin."

Erin doesn't wilt under their scrutiny like one would expect. She smiles and addresses everyone in the room,

"It's nice to meet you all." Her words are greeted with pleasantries and polite curiosity. Before they can ask any question that will take away from why we're here, I start the meeting.

"What urgent matters gather us here today? I can assume it has to do with the claims of mesmerizing singing in the deep ocean and more disappearances?" From the corner of my eye, I notice Erin furrow her brow.

"You'd be correct, my king," the mermaid—Kiera—says. "We have a total of four mermaid disappearances. All the family's stories are the same. Their loved ones were acting unusual, nervous even, and by the end of the day, they were gone."

"Similar to us," Bastian, the siren advisor, says. They frown and tap their webbed fingers on the table. "More reports of an unfamiliar song. Sirens aren't—or rather, shouldn't be—affected by songs, but three of my sirens have disappeared without a trace."

"That goes along with what we've been hearing above," Nori interjects. "We're picking up sound in the North Sea, about two hundred miles from shore."

"You've heard the song?" Bastian leans forward, their silver hair falling over their shoulder. As a nervous habit, they start to twist it.

"Aye, but it was faint above the sea. Still, to a less trained ear, it would have been disastrous. Nothing some cotton in the ear can't fix, but we have to consider the possibility of the songs growing louder and more power-ful," Nori says.

"Do we know who is making this sound?" Kiera asks the group, and all eyes fall on me.

"A prisoner, right before we executed him, mentioned the awakening of creatures known as the Leviathan," I say slowly, and I'm promptly interrupted.

"Leviathan? It can't be! They are locked away in their sea cave and have been for decades, if not centuries!" Kiera argues.

"So were the Nephilim," Bastian reminds the mermaid. "And they managed to get out. You don't think their cousins are capable of the same thing? They could be working with the Nephilim."

"One rules the sea while the other rules the land," Nori says grimly. "It was assumed by many sea people that the current war raging above the surface would not entirely affect us. That is no longer the case."

In truth, it never was the case. Danger on the land would eventually trickle down to the seas, but I didn't expect it to be this way. Foolish of me to think otherwise, but now we have a problem on our hands, and I have no solutions. Yet.

"What course of action are we to take?" Bastian asks the group. They stiffen in their seats. "We have to be proactive."

Kiera nods. "I agree, we should tell our people—"

"No," I interject. "Not yet. We can't cause mass hysteria."

"So we leave the people clueless? All while their loved ones go missing?" Kiera sneers. "My king, this isn't the way."

"I can see what the king is getting at. We don't know enough to answer all the questions that will undoubtedly come," Nori says.

The table erupts in chaos. Bastian and Kiera speak in raised voices to Nori and Delmare. No one has the right answer. Is there a right answer? Not when it comes to war. There are better outcomes, but which one would provide the best outcome to my people? Telling them and potentially risking mass hysteria or leaving them in the dark for now?

The cacophony of voices and my own inner thoughts nearly make me miss the gentle hand on my arm. When I turn, Erin is looking up at me. She tucks a strand of hair behind her ear, apprehension on her face as she averts her eyes.

"I'm not sure if my opinion matters here..."

Before she can go on, I gently place my finger under her chin to dip her head back. There's terror in her eyes, and that breaks my damn heart. She doesn't need to fear me or anyone at this table. "Your opinion is incredibly important to me. You are free to speak your mind. I value any input you are willing to give."

Under my touch, Erin softens. The rest of the table is still arguing, paying us little mind. Good. "What do you think, sweet girl? What would be best for our people?"

"Well," Erin starts. She's gathering her courage, so I wait patiently until she's ready. I would wait a lifetime if she needed. After a few seconds, though, she continues, "As someone who has gone through deeply troubling and terrifying experiences, the worst part of it all was the unknown. Never knowing what would happen day to day and whether I'd live through the week. I understand this situation is very different, but if it were me...I would want to know, so I can prepare. I feel like not telling your

—our—people will create more panic and possibly diminish their trust in you down the road."

Erin has a unique perspective, one I don't have because I've never been through what she had to endure. She knows pain, suffering, and fear. I know a life of politics, war, and solitude. I'm not so far gone that I can't consider the wise words of my future queen.

I smile at her, hoping it conveys not only my thankfulness for her words, but the pride I feel, knowing it's hard to speak her mind freely when placed in new situations. "Thank you, Erin."

I tear my gaze away from Erin's shy smile and back to the other members at my table. When I clear my throat, they cease conversation and swivel their attention back to me. "Erin and I have spoken. She's shown me it will be in our best interest to stress caution to our people. Bastian, Kiera"—I angle my body toward the two—"to the best of your ability, inform the merpeople and sirens about the potential dangers. I will have more guards patrolling the lands. Keep people informed to keep them safe.

"Nori, tell my sister about what we discussed today. Report back on what you find above shore. Those are your orders, and if there are no more questions, you are free to go."

Nori is the first to leave, bowing to both Erin and me before making his way out. Kiera leaves next, but Bastian lingers behind. "Thank you," they say once everyone else has left. It takes me a moment to realize they aren't speaking to me.

Erin seems shocked by the merperson's words and

even more so that they are directed toward her. "Oh, uhm, you're welcome."

"It will be a pleasure to serve under you, my queen." With that, Bastian turns toward the door and swims out.

"You survived your first meeting." I grin once they leave. "I didn't fare as well as you for my first meeting."

"You didn't? I find that hard to believe," she says, and I shrug.

"I wasn't always this benevolent and confident ruler."

Erin rolls her eyes, and the corners of her lips twitch up, barely concealing her smile. "Oh, wise ruler, however did your people deal without you?"

"We call those the Dark Ages."

She laughs, a genuine, real laugh. I've never seen anyone or anything more beautiful than her at this moment. I want to capture this image and save it to look back on forever.

"How are you doing?" I ask after a moment. My question sobers her up quickly.

"This was a lot to take in all at once. I'm not really sure what to think other than Tetria is more beautiful than history books made it out to be," she says.

"I want to show you more of it." In truth, I want to show her everything. Want to see her reaction. What she likes. What she would want changed.

"And I want to see all of it, but I'm really tired. I need a break. I'm not sure I can take in anything more," she says, almost sad.

"Of course. The rest of the tour can wait. Let me show you to our suite."

"Our suite?"

I pause, trying to choose my words carefully, so as not to frighten her. I hadn't considered that she'd be against sharing a room, but it was foolish of me not to. "Well, yes. However, I don't need to be in it while you are. Let me just show you."

Erin nods and reaches for me. I let my tentacles drop from securing her down to the chair so she can float next to me.

"Alright, Mr. King. Take me to the bedroom."

So, I do.

# CHAPTER 17

# ERIN

"Do you remember those bubble houses in town? The ones filled with air?" Allarick asks me as we swim down the hall. I silently thank my mother for putting me in swim lessons at a young age, because Allarick moves fast. Embarrassingly, my breathing becomes labored.

"Yeah," I say, trying not to sound as breathless as I feel.

Doesn't work.

Allarick slows, casting me an apologetic glance as he waits for me to catch up. I elected to swim without the assistance of his tentacles, so, really, it's on me. I didn't realize I needed to train as an Olympic swimmer in order to become part of this kingdom.

"The part of the castle we're headed toward is filled with air," he explains.

It takes a moment for his words to sink in, but when they do, they bring more questions. "But how is that possible?"

Allarick simply smiles. He looks almost boyish and incredibly handsome when he does that. I would be lying if I said I wasn't attracted to him. But attraction doesn't equate to love. And my judgment is all skewed.

"The same way it's possible for you to breathe down here, sweet girl. Magic comes in abundance in Mescos. You'll see that the longer you're here. Now come, follow me." Allarick starts to swim away, but this time one of his tentacles snakes around my waist and pulls me along. I'm more than happy to let him pull me around; it's something a girl could get used to.

We swim down a hallway decorated with statues of mermaids, krakens, and various other ocean creatures. It amazes me how all of this could be down here and feel so different than what I'm used to, but also familiar. There's art, beautiful infrastructure, diverse ocean people, and much more. These people are strangers, but I'm eager to learn all I can about them.

Allarick swims up. At first I think he's swimming us into the ceiling, but he takes an abrupt turn before we crash against the stone. "What—?" Before I can say more, we break through the water surface and into... something.

It feels like Allarick and I have just resurfaced from a pool, rather than an underwater castle. There are steps to lead us out of the water and onto shiny white tile. The walls are made from glass, completely see-through. Coral buildings stand tall in the distance while merpeople swim over and around us. But not just merpeople. Jellyfish, turtles, stingrays, and other beautiful creatures. Some I recognize, and some I've never seen before.

"This is amazing," I say breathlessly, feeling like Alice in Wonderland, but instead of falling through a rabbit hole, I've emerged into an ocean of mermaids.

"Most of the castle is constructed like this," Allarick says from behind me. "Our people wanted to make this castle accessible to humans. This entire upper level has bedrooms, office and meeting spaces, a dining area, and more. It doesn't get used much anymore since many of our people like to spend their time in the water."

"And you sleep here?" I can't help but think he's doing this for my comfort.

Allarick shrugs. "Sometimes. I also have a room on the first floor. I spend very little time in the bedroom. I sleep very little."

"You can do more than sleep in a bedroom." The words are out of my mouth before I can stop them. Allarick's brow rises, and my cheeks burn with embarrassment.

"Is that so, sweet girl? What else can I do in the bedroom, pray tell?" There's a playfulness to his words. They almost sound flirty, and I desperately want to be bold. To be the woman who flirts so easily, I don't even have to think about it...but I'm not.

"You know, escape everyone. It's like your own little safe haven away from people," I lamely say instead.

"I suppose you're right. It'll be our safe haven now." He places his hand on my back, gently leading me to the stairs and out of the water. Something along my neck tingles, and I reach up. Where gills were moments before is now smooth skin. Damn, it's going to take a while to get used to all of this.

At the top is an open cabinet with several white fluffy towels. I'm surprised to find them warm as I grab one and wrap it around my body. The water sloshes behind me, and I turn just in time to see Allarick walking up the stairs. He's traded his tentacles for legs. He's not naked, but may as well be for as little as his tight red shorts cover. They look more like boxer briefs and cling to him like a second skin.

I see *all* of him.

Every inch. And there are a lot of inches to see.

James has been my only sexual partner. He isn't small, but he definitely doesn't come close to what Allarick is packing. My mouth waters, and heat rushes to my core. I can't remember the last time the thought of a cock excited me. Never? Definitely never.

"Sweet girl?"

My head snaps up at Allarick's voice, and his dark eyes bore into me. Butterflies explode in my belly. I feel completely naked under his scrutiny, but instead of feeling embarrassed, I...like it.

"You're beautiful," he says, stunning me. I'm dripping wet. My hair is plastered to my face. And my nose is more than likely running. I feel anything but beautiful, but the way Allarick looks at me tells a different story.

We stay locked in silence, his eyes roaming my body and mine dipping low every so often. The urge to reach out and touch him is strong, but instead I ruin the moment by blurting out, "How are you not naked?"

My words take Allarick by surprise as he looks down

at the indecently tiny shorts he's wearing. "Specific clothes can transform with our bodies. As long as they are magically touched."

Oh. Sure, magic. Must have been a lack of normal-sized pants the day he got his magically enhanced.

"Let me show you to the room." He absentmindedly reaches for my hand. His fingers brush against my arm before he realizes his mistake and jerks his hand away as if my skin burns him. Allarick curses. "I'm sorry, Erin. I wasn't thinking."

I wait for the slimy, dirty feeling to overtake me. For the panic to set in and for me to recoil from him. But I don't pull back. No horrid memories of James resurface. My anxiety doesn't overwhelm me, immobilizing me with darkness.

It actually felt nice.

"It's okay," I say gently, surprising Allarick. Hell, surprising myself. Before I can second-guess myself, I gently reach for his arm. My hand rests around his biceps...his hard, solid biceps. Is this man even real? I think I squeeze his arm, judging by the low hum Allarick emits.

"Is this okay?"

"It's perfect." His voice is gruff, a deeper tenor than normal. If I didn't know any better, I would think he's just as flustered. Allarick clears his throat and says, "Right this way."

He leads me out of the large atrium area and down a hallway lined with portraits of who I assume are former kings and queens. We pass what looks like a dining room and another room filled with bookcases and something that eerily resembles a piano. Do they have instruments down here? I make a mental note to check that room out later.

We reach a set of white double doors with intricate oceanic imagery carved into the wood. The handles are a shiny blue that reminds me of water. Allarick pushes open the door, exposing his—our—room.

The moment we step in, my breath hitches. Like the bubble houses in the city, the room is circular and made entirely of glass walls. Not the best for privacy, but the view is worth it. It's easy to forget that I'm under the sea until I see a whale and its calf swim above our head, a sight many people would kill to see. I think of lying in bed and watching the ocean all day.

Speaking of which, a large king-sized bed sits centered near the domed wall opposite us. White chiffon bedding and pale green pillows adorn it. I don't know what I imagined a bed down here to look like, but this reminds me of one you would find in a luxury hotel.

Next to the bed is a bedside table with candles on top. The only other piece of furniture is a light-colored couch, sitting opposite the bed with a gray coffee table in front. It doesn't look like it belongs in the room, almost as if it were brought in here as an afterthought.

"The washroom is through that door. All glass windows are meant to see out, but not see in. It's completely private." Allarick points to an arched door I missed in my initial assessment of the room. "I have toiletries I thought you might need. If there is anything else you require, let me or a maid know, and I'll make sure to get it for you. Through the washroom is also the closet. I've supplied clothes, but once again, if they are not to your liking, we can purchase new ones. I'm afraid any clothes you brought with us from your world will not fare well here. The ocean water isn't kind to fabrics made above land."

I didn't bring anything from home. I hadn't exactly planned to leave so abruptly and unconsciously, but even if I did pack things, it wouldn't have been much. Allarick has provided me with everything I need.

I give his arm a gentle squeeze. "Thank you. This is very kind of you."

"It's nothing," he says.

"It's not nothing," I say, maybe a little too forcefully. "Your kindness and attentiveness are not nothing, Allarick. They're everything. You are a busy king, yet you still went out of your way to make sure your home felt like mine too. Thank you. Not just for the room accommodations but everything."

Allarick's face softens. For a moment, he hesitates before leaning forward. My heart starts to beat faster in my chest. I'm torn between leaning back and staying put, but my body is frozen in place. His soft lips brush my forehead. It's a whisper of a kiss but still leaves me breathless. This man makes me feel things I haven't felt in so long. Maybe ever.

"You're welcome," he murmurs as he pulls away. I'm instantly filled with disappointment, but for what? More gentle kisses? More...something else?

Oblivious to—or overlooking—my despondency, Allarick gestures to the washroom door. "There should be sleeping attire in there for you. I'll wait out here while you get ready for bed."

Reluctantly, I pull away from his grasp and disappear into the washroom. A small vanity and a glass tub make up the room. There's a toilet in an alcove and an opening I gather is the closet. Clean pajamas await me on the vanity, a silky lavender set with shorts and a camisole. A mixture of soaps, lotions, combs, and other hygiene products clutter the vanity, and I take my time preparing myself for bed.

By the time I'm finished in the bathroom, I smell of eucalyptus and rosemary. My legs and arms are soft to the touch, and I may have doused my neck and arms in perfume. Totally for me and not for the kraken awaiting me in the bedroom. When I walk out, I'm sad to see Allarick in long pants instead of the skintight shorts he had on earlier. He's lounging on the couch, a pillow propping his head up and a blanket draped half over him and half over the back of the couch.

Allarick hears me exit the bathroom and turns to look at me, smiling, eyes scanning over my body. "Those look nice on you. Do you like them?" he asks, genuinely curious.

"I do. They are so soft. Did you pick them out?"

Allarick laughs. "I wish I could take credit, sweet girl, but no. I sought help from the Dragon King and his wife."

"Did you just say Dragon King?" As if my reality wasn't just flipped on its axis. There's so much more to Mescos than I thought, and I have so much more to learn.

Allarick nods. "I did. There are wolves, demons,

pixies, and fae too. I'll tell you all about them another day."

"I'll keep you to that," I say before climbing into bed.

"Please do." Allarick adjusts himself on the couch. It's not particularly big, and his large frame is constricted. His feet hang off one end of the couch. That can't be comfortable.

Meanwhile, I have a bed that could easily accommodate four people plus myself. "You should have taken the bed, Allarick. I fit on the couch better than you can."

"I'm not letting the future queen of Tetria sleep on the couch the first night she's here—or any night. No, Erin, I'll take the couch. I'm fine." He pulls the blanket up around him for emphasis.

"Yeah, see, that would be way more convincing if half your body wasn't dangling off the couch. Why don't you just lie in bed with me?" My cheeks redden, but that's only because the thought of Allarick in bed with me is... well, appealing.

"I wanted to give you your space. You don't need to feel obligated to share a bed with me," he says, but his voice has gone all gruff again. I realize he does that when he gets flustered.

"I don't feel obligated. It's a big bed, Allarick. And, honestly, you bring me comfort. I think I'll sleep better knowing you're close and not trying to stuff yourself into a couch you clearly don't fit on. No offense."

Allarick chuckles. "None taken." He sits up but doesn't stand right away, almost as if he's waiting on me to change my mind. For all my faults, and I have many, I don't fear sharing a bed with another person. It's always been natural to me to have someone else in bed. I don't like being alone, and I've felt that way for so long. James's presence in bed wasn't comforting, but I also hated being alone. It made little sense, but my body craved the warmth of another person.

When Allarick realizes I'm not backing down, he finally gets up and approaches the opposite side of the bed. The whole time, his attention is on me, even as he gets under the covers and lies down, body angled toward me. There's still a good amount of space between us, but I feel better knowing he's here. I've slept alone far too much here. This feels right.

"Thank you," I whisper, sliding my arm under the pillow to get comfortable. My body realizes how tired I am, and I yawn, even though it's not that late. Maybe the drink I had earlier really took it out of me.

"Sleep, sweet girl. There's so much more I wish to show you in the morning," Allarick whispers as my eyelids droop closed.

"You'll be here when I wake up?"

"Of course," he assures.

That's all I need to let my body relax and give in to sleep willingly.

# CHAPTER 18
# ERIN

I wake to the sound of whistles and clicks. My eyes flutter open just in time to see a group of dolphins swim over our bedroom. Never did I think I would have a view like this when waking up in the morning. A small, curious dolphin comes to the glass and inspects it before returning to the rest of the group.

"It's beautiful, isn't it?" a groggy voice next to me says.

Allarick, always the gentleman, stayed on his side of the bed all night. It was only mildly disappointing that I didn't wake up with my kraken's arms around me, but I appreciated his presence regardless.

"You get to wake up to this every day."

It wasn't a question, but he nods anyway. "And now so do you."

What a crazy, beautiful life.

Allarick rises to stretch. I get a good look at his muscular chest. His dark skin is a stark contrast to the vibrant colors of the ocean, but no less beautiful. If anything, his beauty supersedes everything else.

"Are you up to more exploring today?" he asks, and I begrudgingly tear my gaze away from his chest.

"Yes, actually... Did I see a music room yesterday?"

"You probably did. We have two. One on the lower floor for parties and one up here. Did you want to see the room?"

"I do...if you don't mind. I know you're busy with meetings and such—"

Allarick braces his arms on the bed, lowering his head until he's eye level with me. "My only duties today are with you, sweet girl. I assure you, I have everything else under control."

Well, then.

Shortly after that, I pick myself up out of bed and head into the bathroom to take care of my morning routine. I search through the closet to find something to wear. Most everything in here feels like silk and provides very little coverage. The merpeople don't have the same modesty values humans do, which is something I'll have to get used to.

I settle on a blue shirt that's a cross between a crop top and a bralette, along with a similar color skirt with built-in pants. The sides of the skirt flare open, allowing me to freely move my legs. There's a lot of skin on display, and normally I would feel self-conscious, not of my body shape—I quite love the way I look—but rather the bruises that usually adorn my skin.

None are there today. None will ever be there again.

I walk out of the bathroom with a smile on my face

and straight into Allarick. The man still hasn't put on a shirt—I doubt he owns one—but he wears a pair of black pants that hug his thighs sinfully.

"Do I look okay?" I ask, suddenly feeling self-conscious. Is this appropriate attire for the future queen? Should I wear something more elegant?

My fears and insecurities are put to rest with the look Allarick gives me. It's molten-hot, burning me from the inside out. Wetness pools between my legs from that look alone. This man calls to my body in a way I no longer thought possible.

"You look ethereal. The incarnate of beauty."

Well, shit. Who says things like that? Incarnate of beauty? Men like Allarick only exist in old romance novels found on grandmothers' bookshelves.

"You're good for my ego. I might keep you around," I tease, trying to hide my obvious lust and discomfort at being complimented.

"I'm your humble servant." Images of him *serving* me fill my mind, and I have to press my legs tightly together. Allarick on his knees in front of me. Allarick pinning me to the bed. Allarick with his—

*Get a fucking grip, Erin. Stop acting like a horny teenager. Have some decorum,* I chide myself.

"I think we should check out the one downstairs." Allarick's words break through my lust-filled fog.

"Hmm?"

"The music room. The one downstairs is bigger. Do you mind checking that one out?"

Oh. Music. Right.

"Can you play music underwater?"

My question is greeted with a smile, and Allarick nods. "You can. Works similar to above, I imagine."

Intrigued and more than a little excited to have my kraken back, I follow Allarick out of the room and down the hallway. We pass the music room, and my fingers itch to caress an instrument—any instrument. It's been so long since I've been able to play, and I've missed it. James hated the noise and would become irate when I played. So, I stopped.

Allarick gets in the water first, and a small whirlpool surrounds him. A few seconds later, the water clears, and his legs are replaced with tentacles. I'm not sure I'll ever get over the awe of the magic here, but I hope I never lose the sense of wonder.

"Come," he says, and I take a tentative step down. The water is warm and soothes my cold feet, and as soon as I'm deep enough in, Allarick envelops me in his embrace. He's so gentle with me, like if he squeezes too hard, I'll shatter. He's probably not wrong.

"This way." He grins, and we take off back through the first story of the castle. I'm content with being pulled along, at least until my swimming skills get better.

The castle is alive this morning with staff, all wearing the same black button-down shirt. There are also a few in what looks like armor with spears at their sides. All bow as Allarick and I swim by. Even though everyone is working, there is an abundance of smiles and laughter. There's a sense of community within these walls, and that's a testament to what kind of king Allarick is.

We pass the meeting room from yesterday and head to an open room across the hall. The doors must have been closed yesterday, because there is no other way I would have missed this room. Like most rooms in the castle, all but the interior walls are glass. A few murals hang on the exterior walls, showcasing various ocean scenes and important-looking figures.

But what catches my attention is the number of musical instruments throughout the room. Most I recognize, but some I don't. A piano sits in the center of the room, surrounded by couches. A violin and harp perch in the rounded corner of the room. Something that looks like a tuba and another stringed instrument I've never seen before sit on the opposite side.

My eyes gravitate toward the piano and harp, two instruments that sound beautiful alone or accompanied by others. They both produce a tranquil sound that always helped calm my body after a stressful day of school.

I don't realize I'm swimming toward the piano until Allarick asks, "Do you play?"

"Yes...well, I used to. My mother signed me up for piano lessons when I was a young girl. At first I hated it because I just wanted to play with my dolls and the other children outside, but over time I grew to appreciate it more and more. I picked up harp in high school, just on a whim, and fell in love with that too.

"For my sixteenth birthday, my parents bought me my own harp. Some teenagers want cars, but I wanted musical instruments." I laugh, feeling the familiar ache I always get when I talk about my parents. It's bittersweet, but I love talking about them. It makes me feel like they are still alive in some way.

"Your parents sound like they were amazing people. They had to be to raise such a strong, intelligent, and talented woman," Allarick says. "If you don't mind, I would love to hear you play."

My cheeks hurt from smiling. "Really?" No one has asked me to play for them in years. "I might be a bit rusty."

Allarick shrugs like he doesn't actually think that's a possibility. "I don't mind."

"Right, okay. Let me..." I pull out the piano bench, wondering how I'm going to sit and play while keeping myself afloat. But I'm surprised to find my body sinking gracefully onto the bench, with my feet planted firmly on the ground.

"Gravity works a bit differently in some places here," Allarick says by way of explanation.

"Magic, I presume?"

"Ah, you're learning." He grins, making himself comfortable on the couch. His tentacles fan out around him while he sinks into the furniture.

I play a note, and the sound reverberates around the room. The piano is tuned perfectly, though Allarick probably has someone assigned to that job. I play a few more notes, my fingers remembering the keys even though it's been years.

"Is there anything you want to hear?" I ask after a moment.

Allarick ponders the question briefly before saying, "Play me a song that reminds you of happiness."

I think of my parents and the very first song we learned together. The song I played at all their birthdays, even though they both had heard me play it a million times. They always claimed it was their favorite, and it quickly became mine too.

Closing my eyes, I take a deep breath as the notes and melody come back to me. Then I open my eyes and play the first note to "Let it Be" by the Beatles.

# CHAPTER 19

# ALLARICK

I've never been one to pay much attention to music. It's not that we don't have music; we have plenty of extremely talented musicians who frequently perform at social events. It's not even that I don't enjoy music. I do. But it's a luxury I don't often find myself indulging in.

Until now.

Erin's lithe fingers run over the keys in a mesmerizing dance. I'm unfamiliar with the song, but that hardly matters. I'm captivated all the same. Erin's eyes flutter between open and closed—something I'm not sure she knows she's doing. Her body sways with each key she plays, hypnotizing me with every note and movement.

A sense of tranquility washes over me, quieting all other thoughts. I can't remember a time when my thoughts have been this silent. Erin's playing draws me to her. I fear nothing, other than being apart from her.

All too soon, the song comes to an end. I'm left

feeling empty, until clapping from behind me pulls my attention away from Erin. Floating by the door is Delmare and a few other staff members. Delmare has the decency to look sheepish, but the mermaids with him do not. Boldly, they swim into the room, ignoring me as they approach Erin.

Ignoring a king is a punishable offense, but punishment is the last thing on my mind at the look of wonder the mermaids give my future queen. Pride swells my chests at how my people look at Erin.

"Apologies, my king, but we heard playing from down the hall and—" Delmare starts but is quickly interrupted by a young mermaid, new to staff and castle politics.

"My lady, that song was beautiful," she gushes.

I'm tempted to correct her and have the mermaid refer to their queen properly. But she's not technically their queen. At least not yet. That title will only come through marriage.

"I was in the middle of polishing dinnerware when I heard the most beautiful sound. I felt pulled to the source, almost like a siren song. Except this pull was so much stronger," the young mermaid squeals excitedly. "You play beautifully, my lady."

"You do. Quite beautifully. If magic had a sound, it would be your playing, my lady," Iris, an older mermaid and Delmare's wife, says. She's usually a stickler for the rules and never barges into a room occupied by me without requesting access. I trust her the most out of all my staff, which is why I assigned her to attend to Erin. This intrusion is out of character for the seasoned maid.

Not even Delmare is able to ignore the music. The kraken prides himself on abiding by protocol and is always professional. But he's drifting toward Erin as if being pulled by an invisible string. This whole interaction is…interesting. Unexpected, but not unappreciated.

"Can we hear one more, my queen?" Delmare asks.

"Oh, well…" Erin shifts uncomfortably in her seat. She's smiling, and I sense her desire to play more for her new audience, but her self-doubt creeps in. She seeks me out amongst the group, and we lock eyes. I see the question she's not asking.

Erin doesn't need my permission to play. She can do as she pleases, but she does want my reassurance. I'm happy to give her just that for as long as she needs it. I nod, and her entire face brightens.

"Okay, I'll play one of my favorites," she says as the small group around her all find somewhere to watch her play. Iris swims over to Delmare, who wraps his tentacle around her waist, pulling her close. The two have been mated and married for years now, and still their love burns brightly. I've always envied him for that.

Erin starts to play again, and the feeling of peace consumes me once more. The feeling is almost tangible, like silky seaweed wrapping around my body. This song is slower than the one before but just as beautiful. It ends as quickly as her first song, but, at the request from the young mermaid, Erin starts another.

She plays and plays and plays without tiring. More people have wandered in, and soon the large room is nearly filled with my castle staff, all in varying states of amazement. Guards station themselves outside the doors, but they also peer in to listen to Erin. She doesn't even realize how many people she's attracted to her music until the end of her seventh song, when she picks her gaze up from the piano to look around the room.

Her posture changes, tensing and curling in on herself almost as if she wants to make herself appear smaller. Her eyes widen as she takes in every person in the room. Someone behind me starts to clap, and many more join in until the entire room is thunderous with applause, all praising her songs. Erin's cheeks redden, but she timidly thanks those closest to her. I quickly foresee a problem when more and more people surround my future queen. She's a guppy in a sea of sharks, eyes darting around for a swift exit.

I rise from my seat, swimming above the others. "My betrothed must rest. If she wishes, she'll play for you another time. Leave us, please," my voice booms around the room, and all chatter ceases.

Disappointed gazes meet my own, but no one tries to defy me. Each person bows in my direction, and, to my surprise, Erin's direction as well, before they leave.

"Delmare," I call for my guard before he makes it out the door.

Delmare whispers something to Iris that has her smiling before swimming away. "Yes, my king?"

"See to it we aren't disturbed."

"Yes, my king. I'll stand guard." Delmare turns and swims out, shutting the door behind him.

With him stationed outside, I don't worry we will be interrupted again. Finally, I'm alone with Erin.

Erin still looks like a cornered guppy, and I fear the

crowd may have been too much for her. I swim closer, hoping to provide comfort. "Erin, I'm sorry. That was—"

"Amazing," she finishes. Now that we're alone, she stands taller, her body vibrating with excitement. "Allarick, that was amazing. Those people came to listen. To *me*! Can you believe that? I haven't played in front of an audience in so long, I forgot the rush that it brings you. I can't believe I just did that."

Erin flings herself into me and wraps her arms around my neck. My body stiffens, but only for a fraction of a second before my arms come around her waist and pull her tightly against my chest. I haven't held Erin like this before, her curves flush against my body. Holding her like this, I know I risk causing her distress, but I still can't bring myself to let her go.

She smells of honey. Of salt and the sea. My head drops, nuzzling close to her neck. A soft whimper leaves her mouth as my lips brush her skin. I don't dare kiss her, though everything in me wants to do exactly that.

How easy would it be to give in to my carnal needs? To elicit more of those pleasurable sounds and have them turn into sultry moans? I want to see Erin writhing for me, begging me to touch her. Perhaps these are thoughts from a kraken who hasn't lain with a woman in some time, but I don't believe that to be true.

I don't want any other woman.

I want Erin.

The pull has been there since the moment I saw her broken and bruised in Ender's arms. Even then, I knew she was special. The time I've spent with her only confirms what I already knew to be true. Erin believes herself to be weak, but she's wrong. I see her strength. It's quiet and sometimes fragile, but strength doesn't have to be loud or unbreakable to be valid.

Sometimes the mightiest are the smallest.

"Erin…" My voice comes out raspier than I intend. My sweet girl stiffens in my arms, and I'm doused with reality. Erin's mind and body appear in battle with each other. Perhaps she wants me just as much as I want her, but she's shackled by her past. James stole her innocence and twisted her until he broke every piece of her body and soul.

You don't simply walk away from something like that so easily, no matter how strong you are. It takes time and energy. I believe Erin has the capability to heal from her past, but I'm also not so naive to think the short time with me has changed her. I'm not that arrogant of a man.

With great reluctance, I release my hold from around her, drawing back. Erin doesn't pull away at first. Instead, we stand chest to chest, her arms still around my neck as she looks up at me.

"Thank you," she says.

I watch her pouty lips, wanting to reach out and rub my thumb across them. Through the grace of our goddess, I somehow find the strength to refrain. "For what, sweet girl?"

"For letting me play. For being patient with me. For accepting me as your future wife when you probably expected someone a lot braver and less broken than me." Her cheeks redden at the last point.

Does she truly believe she's not brave? *Still?*

"Erin, don't speak of my future wife like that.

Because, as far as I'm concerned, you are the bravest person I know. You've looked true evil and darkness in the eyes and didn't let it destroy you, even if that would have been the easier option. You saved yourself time and time again, all the while agreeing to take on a husband and a kingdom you knew nothing about. If that isn't bravery, then I don't know what is. I have seen men crack under the same stress you've had to live with most of your life."

Erin's lips part in silent surprise, like she can't quite believe my words. I watch as she opens and closes her mouth multiple times, words eluding her. Then, she leans up and presses her lips to my cheek. It's soft and perfect. Not enough, but everything at the same time.

Her lips linger, only for a minute before she pulls away, this time out of my grasp. A cheeky smile crosses her lips before she swims away. "Do you want a private show, King Allarick?" she asks as she swims over to the harp this time.

I definitely want a private show. One that involves less clothing, but this will do for now. "I'd be honored, my queen."

And for the next hour, I watch and listen to Erin as she gets lost in the music.

# CHAPTER 20

# ERIN

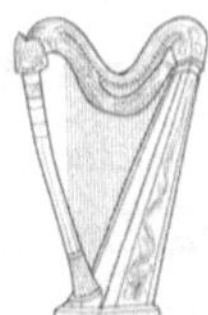

My new home is nothing short of magical. Tetria is a vision of beauty and grace. Creatures I once believed only live in dreams and fairytales come to life. Beautiful merpeople and hauntingly alluring sirens. The krakens hold their own majestic charm that I've come to appreciate over my week in Tetria.

Most of my time has been spent with Allarick. He's a busy man but makes time for me. He gives me the choice to go to any meetings with him, and I've taken him up on a few, but I've mostly been escaping into the music rooms. They've been my favorite places in the palace.

"My lady, King Allarick has requested your presence for lunch. Would you like to join him?" my new maid, Iris, asks. I learned recently she's married to Delmare, Allarick's favorite guard, who now watches over me when Allarick isn't around. She's also one of the few maids who can switch between having legs and having a tail.

I like Iris. She's kind and a motherly figure. Her job title is maid, but she spends most of her day with me, and I try to keep her from fussing over me—"try" being the key word. Iris swears she enjoys the job, so I need to get used to having someone do things for me.

Admittedly, maids and guards have been the hardest thing to wrap my mind around during this transition. I'm not used to people waiting on me hand and foot and making sure I'm safe. I would almost feel guilty about it if it weren't for Allarick's constant reassurance that my safety and comfort are a priority.

Still not sure I fully believe him, but I go along with it, regardless.

"Join him now?" I try to keep my voice as neutral as possible, but judging from Iris's smirk, I failed spectacularly.

Ever since four days ago when I willingly went into his arms and let him hold me, I haven't been able to get the feel of his body off my mind. Or the way I kissed his cheek but desperately wanted to feel his lips against mine. I can't remember the last time I've wanted to be kissed or the last time I even had butterflies for someone.

"Yes, my lady. He awaits you. And he wanted me to assure you he isn't the one cooking," Iris says.

I laugh, thinking back to the meals Allarick cooked me back at his sister's cabin. They were edible...but that's about the only compliment I can give them. I appreciated his efforts, but I don't think I can stomach more of his food.

"Good to know. I'm ready to go now." I push off the

piano bench, having had another successful day of playing. Like always, I drew another crowd of merpeople, but Iris took care of them a bit ago. A vain part of me loves the way people gravitate to me while I play. The look of pure tranquility that overtakes them is something truly special. Like I can make them forget about their problems for just a little while.

Goodness knows we all need that.

"I'll escort you, my lady." Delmare swims next to his wife. Her body instantly molds against his, and Delmare's shoulders relax. Their love is quiet, yet so evident. Something that feels a lot like jealousy stirs in my chest. I want that. Not with Delmare, of course, but with...somebody.

A certain kraken king, perhaps.

I push all thoughts of my betrothed aside and follow Delmare down the hall. We resurface on the second floor. The moment my clothes hit the air, they instantly dry. Even my hair dries, thanks to a serum I comb through my hair every morning. Tetria has really done everything they can to accommodate humans. I wonder what it was like when more of us walked the castle halls and swam these oceans.

Delmare surfaces behind me, shirtless and only wearing brown pants. Thankfully, I didn't have to awkwardly look away and pretend I didn't notice his dangly bits. I'm really starting to like Delmare and Iris, and the last thing I want is to have to pretend I've never seen her husband's penis. So far, so good.

"This way, my lady." Delmare takes the lead, even

though, for the past week, Allarick and I have taken most of our meals in this dining room, so I know how to get there on my own. I'm content with letting him lead, though, because it gives me time to take in the beauty of the palace and the vast ocean that surrounds us. I'm not certain I'll ever get used to it.

Allarick is already seated by the time we arrive. He's frowning, tapping his fingers against the table. But the moment he sees me, his whole demeanor changes. He stands, stunning me with his beautiful smile. "Erin. It's good to see you."

"You saw me this morning." I giggle, trying to hide my blush and racing heart.

"And yet, I still managed to miss you."

Allarick reaches for my hand with a tentacle, bringing it up to his lips and placing a soft kiss to my knuckles. His gaze never strays from mine, and the act appears more intimate than it should. His touch doesn't scare me. My body no longer tenses up in anticipation like it did when I was around James. My kraken is gentle. I find myself feeling less anxious underwater. I don't feel the need to constantly look over my shoulder in case danger is following me.

"Thank you, Delmare. You can leave us." Allarick dismisses the other kraken. Delmare isn't offended by his abrupt dismissal. He simply bows and takes his leave with Iris at his side. She winks at me before the door closes. I'm both excited and slightly nervous to be alone with my future husband.

A lot has changed between us since the day I ended up here in his care. It's amazing how much a person can heal from past trauma when put in a safe place and surrounded by people who want them to thrive and succeed. Allarick hasn't magically cured the last few years of my life, but he's giving me the strength to move ahead and not look back. Maybe I've had it in me all along, but I needed help finding it.

"How was your meeting?" I ask as one of the kitchen staff members brings out our food. I have to do a double take because I expected fish. Just like we eat every meal, which is fine. But the chicken on my plate makes my mouth water.

"I thought we could use something different." Allarick winks.

"How did you manage to get chicken down here?"

Allarick just laughs at my question. Not cruelly, though. "We do trade with the people of the land. I figured you'd appreciate a change."

"I do. Very much. Not that the fish hasn't been good, but chicken is my favorite," I say and take a bite. It's juicy and cooked to perfection, bursting with taste. I let out a small moan, eagerly cutting a second piece off.

"I'll make sure to bring you chicken more often, then," he muses. I feel his gaze boring into me. My whole body flushes just like it does every time his eyes linger too long.

"My meeting was actually to meet the new recruits," Allarick says after a moment. "Since the threat of the Leviathan and Nephilim, I've opened up the guard ranks for recruitment."

"Are they really that big of a threat?" I hate that I'm ignorant when it comes to the enemies we face. The enemies I'm supposed to help Allarick and the people of Tetria defeat. I've heard Allarick speak of them back at the cabin when we first met and at the meeting he invited me to sit in on, but I can't wrap my head around the danger they pose.

"The Nephilim are the biggest threats to our world. The Leviathan are the biggest threat to the ocean people. We cannot help our allies on land until we take care of the problem in the sea. If the Leviathan escape and seize control of the ocean, the Nephilim will have full access to ports, making sneaking into territories easier."

When Allarick finishes talking, a tense quiet envelops the room. Panic threatens to sour my mood because who am I to help Allarick win a war against an enemy I know nothing about? I'm not strong or a leader like him. I'm just a broken girl from Grym Hollow who couldn't defend myself from a man with a god complex.

A hand covers my own, bringing me back to the present. Back to Allarick. His presence is calming, chasing away the darkness that always seems to linger just out of reach. "Whatever happens, we will face it together," he says. "There's no one else I want at my side than you."

His words are sincere and almost convince me I'm capable of everything he expects of me. I want to be that woman, and maybe she's inside me somewhere. Deep down, begging to be let free after years of being locked away in a box.

After a moment of deliberation, I nod slowly. I'm agreeing to...trying? Not being afraid? Being with him?

"What do you need of me?" I ask.

Allarick squeezes my hand. "Come with me to the surface tomorrow to check in with my sister. She has sent word she has information for us. I want you to be with me when I hear it."

That much I can do. So, I agree but secretly wonder just how long I can mask as his brave queen.

# CHAPTER 21

# ALLARICK

I'm not keen on leaving Tetria so soon. A week home isn't enough, but my sister would never meet me in my kingdom. I can't blame her, especially when she does so much for me. I may not fully understand her fears of being in the ocean, but I can at least respect them.

Erin and I surfaced ten minutes ago to a note left on Atina's door.

*Meet me at Sonny's.*

Sonny's is a tavern that sits on multiple territories. It's considered neutral ground. As much as I would rather have met Atina at her house, I'll oblige her. Erin disappears into my sister's cabin to get dressed and fix her hair. She's been quiet since we've surfaced, but so have I. There's a lot on my mind in regards to the Leviathan and safety of my people. The pressure of the disappearing Tetria citizens weighs on me.

As a king, I've never had to face an enemy I know little to nothing about. Disputes between kingdoms are rare, though they do happen. But I have advisors who are experts on each kingdom in Mescos. I have nothing but old books and vague prophecies to help me figure out the Leviathan. I had prepared for the Nephilim—to the best of my ability—but the Leviathan are a surprise in more ways than one.

A gentle hand touches my back. I didn't hear her approach, a testament to my spiraling thoughts. I turn and am greeted by a sweet but shy smile. I return it before my eyes drop down to what she's wearing. Erin wears a dress that must have been left in the cabin. I love this woman in a dress. This one is yellow and complements her brown skin perfectly. The bodice is a corset, cut low. Her breasts are pushed up, teasing me with their fullness. The skirt of the dress flares out around the hips, stopping just below the knee.

She reminds me of the sun, warm and glowing in her radiance.

"Beautiful." I make sure she knows just how stunning she is.

Erin doesn't shy away from me or try to hide her face. It's a small improvement, but an improvement nonetheless. She reaches for my arm, which I willingly give.

She squeezes my arm before asking, "Ready?"

THE TAVERN IS quiet when we arrive. A lone wolf sits at the bar, lost in the bottom of his glass. A pixie flutters by the fire, speaking to a fae male. They share a few laughs. A few other patrons nurse their drinks and look up when the bell above the door rings. Some simply glance at me and then away, back to their drinks. But others do a double take and straighten up in their seats.

These people may have never met me, but they know a king when they see one.

But it's not me who holds their attention. It's Erin. The only human in the tavern. My body hardens, and I pull her closer, glaring at any fool who dares to stare at her for too long.

"Allarick," she whispers, tugging her arm away from me. Disapproval colors her features, but in the next second, it's gone, and she looks away.

"Yes, sweet girl?" I prompt because I don't want her to have to hold her tongue around me.

She looks reluctant at first but then says, "You don't need to growl at everyone who looks at me. It makes me feel like I'm your property."

Did I growl? I don't remember growling. I just remember seeing men stare at Erin like they were waiting to eat her up, and something inside of me flipped. I wanted to defend her. Show them that she...

Belongs to me.

Oh.

Damn.

Property belongs to people. People don't belong to people. I can't control the way people stare and look at Erin, but I can control my asshole nature. I can't take her disappointment in me. It cuts worse than any blade.

"Forgive me, sweet girl. That was unacceptable. The last thing I ever want you to feel like is property."

Erin blinks in surprise, like she hadn't ever heard an apology for one's behavior before. Maybe she hadn't. Gingerly, she places her hand back on the crook of my arm. "Forgiven. Thank you for keeping me safe. I know you didn't have any ill intentions; it's just that James…"

She trails off. I didn't need to hear what that bastard did to know it wasn't good. He'd be a dead man walking if he were in Mescos. I wouldn't be able to stop myself from inflicting the greatest amount of pain until he left this world screaming. Erin might be upset, but I would rather get on my knees and beg her forgiveness than have that monster walking around.

"I understand. No more growling." I smile, trying to lighten the mood.

"Well, I wouldn't be opposed to some growling." She smirks. Her voice takes on a new cadence, one that sounds like flirting.

Heat blooms low in my stomach, traveling south. My cock stiffens in my pants. It's the last thing I need right before meeting my sister.

Oblivious to my growing need, Erin scouts the room before pointing to a table by the window. "Oh, there she is." She smiles, pulling me along. Seeing my sister hunched over her drink is a douse of cold water over me.

Something is wrong.

My worries are further confirmed when we get closer, and I see the dark circles under her eyes. Her hair is a mess, and her shirt has some questionable stains on it. Atina's eyes are glossy when she looks at us, and it takes her a moment to realize who we are.

"Ah, Brother." Her words are slurred. "Come join me

in drinking." My sister has never been a heavy drinker, much preferring to keep her wit. To see her like this is unnerving.

Erin's smile drops when she takes in Atina's state. I approach her like one would approach a hungry shark: delicately and alert. I pull out Erin's chair and wait for her to take a seat before I take mine.

"You two look cozy." Atina smirks, but her eyes remain dull.

"What happened?" There's no other reason why my sister would take to drinking other than something terrible happening.

"No pleasantries, Brother? No declarations of brotherly love for a sister who works her ass off for her kingly brother?"

"Atina," I growl. "This isn't a time for jokes. Tell me what has you finding the bottom of your bottle."

Atina, my impossibly larger-than-life sister, slumps forward. For a moment, the meek little girl I grew up with peeks through. I'm reminded, for all my sister's bravado, she's not as fearless as she claims to be. She cares too much, and caring begets fear. It's the price we pay for loved ones.

"Is there anything we can do to make you more comfortable?" Erin asks, wearing her beautiful heart on her sleeve. "Clearly this is really hard on you. You don't have to carry that burden alone."

A ghost of a smile pulls at my sister's lips, and something passes between the women I'll never fully understand. Both are strong warriors in their own right. Not by choice, but by the hands they were dealt.

Atina traces her finger around the rim of her glass before pulling out a map she's tucked within her pocket. "We've located the Leviathan." She rolls out the map of Mescos, pointing to a coordinate forty-five leagues southwest of the Lycan Forest shore. She's marked the spot with a small red X.

"Not an easy sea to navigate. Rough waters and high winds. But those bastards are here, locked away in an underwater cave," Atina says.

"Are you certain this is the location?" I pull the map closer.

My sister is silent for a beat too long before she nods. "Aye. Lost three men. I don't lose men, Allarick. Not to the sea, at least. Never to the sea." She whispers the last part to herself, looking off into the distance.

Next to me, Erin lets out a deep breath. "I'm so sorry for your losses, Atina."

"Families have been told. Never want to see that kind of pain again. I learned one was expecting his first child." Atina laughs bitterly. "It's going to get worse before it gets better."

I don't want to dredge up painful memories, but there's no other way around it. "I need you to walk me through exactly what happened."

"Allarick, we should give her a moment. She's clearly hurting."

"It's okay, lass. Their sacrifice won't be in vain. We'll get retribution." Atina glowers at me, expecting me to make sure that happens. If at all possible, I will.

"It started out mostly the same as last time. We heard the sound off and on. It was low singing. Weak because we were still too far from it. I had the crew plug their ears and stay vigilant still. Just in case. Not even five minutes later, the singing became louder and harder to ignore. Even my seasoned crewmembers were struggling. Hell, I was struggling. It was the three new lads I picked up who didn't make it."

"They weren't our people?" I ask.

"That's the thing, Allarick. They were. But they jumped into the sea and never resurfaced. We heard them scream and then nothing. Everything, even the singing, went silent. I stayed for as long as I could, but the song was still affecting my other crew members. I had to get out. I had to. I would have lost more crew members if I didn't."

"Of course you had to," Erin assures. "You had to keep your crew safe. That couldn't have been an easy decision, but you saved the lives of the rest of your crew."

Atina takes a long swig of her ale until nothing remains but a few drops. "Aye, but no one should have died."

"You can't blame yourself for that." Even as I say the words, I know how hypocritical I sound. Every death that happens during my reign is a death that weighs heavily on my conscience. My people look to me to keep them safe, just as Atina's crew looks to her. Every death is felt heavily.

Atina flags down a barmaid for another ale, but both Erin and I decline when asked if we want anything to drink.

"What do we do now?" Erin asks after the barmaid

places Atina's mug in front of her. "It sounds like the Leviathan's song is getting stronger."

Atina nods at Erin's assessment. "It is. More powerful than a siren. The pull is strong and only going to get stronger."

"How do they get more powerful?" Erin reaches out to place her hand on my thigh. I'm not sure she even realizes she's doing it, but I cover her hand with mine, and she doesn't pull away.

"According to lore, which is all we have to go by, they steal the energy from other living beings."

"Like their souls?" Erin asks, horrified.

"Precisely," Atina sighs. "They steal their souls from their bodies, leaving their victims withered and hollowed. If we allow them to become too powerful, Tetria and the rest of Mescos will fall to them and the Nephilim. My crew and I have noticed ocean creatures acting strange, too, because of the singing. We plan on investigating that. After..." Atina gestures to the drink in front of her.

The harrowing thought sobers the table. Atina's mouth is set in a grim line, while Erin tries to convey her sympathy. Not for the first time, I question my choice to bring Erin here. To force her into a war she otherwise would have no part in. If anything ever happens to her...

No, I can't think like that. And I can't say I forced her when Erin signed a contract. She knew what she was getting into. Without her here, my people would surely suffer.

"May I make a suggestion for your next move?" Atina asks after a while.

I value my sister's opinions and advice. I may not always heed it, but she's never steered me wrong before.

"Of course. You know you always can," I say.

Atina leans forward until both of her elbows are on the table. She looks between Erin and me before meeting my eyes. Her jaw clenches, like she doesn't want to tell me what she knows. I stay silent, giving her time.

Atina sucks in a deep breath. "I've gathered information on these creatures and studied the history books Delmare found. In one of them, they show how the prison keeps the Leviathan in."

"Well, that's good news, isn't it?" Erin looks between us. "If we know how to close it, then we need to do it."

But nothing is ever that simple. If it were, Atina wouldn't look as defeated as she does. "In good news, we sometimes find bad," Atina says. "The prison gates are holding for now, but will weaken as the Leviathan get stronger. The gate to their prison can be sealed off, but only if it is closed by members of the royal family. In every text I've read, there's always been more than one person and always blood relatives."

I'm the last of my family. The only other person who shares my blood is sitting in front of me, but would her blood status as bastard-born be enough? And even if it were, getting her into the ocean would be near impossible.

"But I think I know what you can do in order to have the strength to close the gate yourself, Brother." Atina catches my eye, and I know what she's going to say before she says it. "If you really want to strengthen your kingdom and give your people the best fighting chance, then you two must marry. And soon."

# CHAPTER 22

# ERIN

We don't head back to Tetria that night. Atina offered up her cabin, and Allarick didn't want to be too far from his sister tonight in case she needed him. He tried to get her to come back to the cabin with us, but Atina was firm in her refusal, saying she had answers she needed about safely approaching the Leviathan and would contact us when she could.

No one spoke about her suggestion of marriage.

Not even as we were leaving.

Not even as we walk back to Atina's cabin.

It's dark by the time we finally leave the tavern, and my sight is nearly nonexistent, so I hold Allarick's arm. The only light comes from the moon and the warm glow from the tavern. Even though Allarick is quiet and distracted, I still feel better next to him.

I had hoped Allarick would say something—anything—before we reached the cabin, but he doesn't. He opens the door for me, and I walk in, expecting to have a conversation. Instead, he goes into the kitchen and starts making tea.

This is how I find myself sitting alone on the couch, replaying Atina's words.

*"If you really want to strengthen your kingdom and give your people the best fighting chance, then you two must marry. And soon."*

In my desperation to leave Grym Hollow, I signed a contract with the town's Guardian. I read over every inch of the contract, and even knowing I would marry a king to help his kingdom overcome a dangerous foe, I signed on the dotted line. Despite the fact that I didn't know this enemy or even the man I was to marry. It all sounded better than staying home with a man who would have surely killed me one day.

Now knowing what Allarick and I are up against, I still can't find it in me to regret my choice. I'm out of my league with mentions of Leviathan and Nephilim, but I see how much Allarick loves Tetria and his people. I want to save *that*. Want to save the people he loves and serves daily. Because I'm starting to fall in love with Tetria too.

Soft footfalls turn my attention toward the kitchen just as Allarick rounds the corner with two steaming cups of tea. Our eyes meet, and he stops walking. My breath hitches, and we just stare at each other. Questions dance on the tip of my tongue. His own stiff body language tells me he's thinking the same thing, but he's unsure where to start.

Soon, we both break the silence at once.

"I think we should talk," we say in unison.

Allarick gives me a shy, sheepish smile as he moves

into the living room and takes a seat close to me on the couch. He offers me one of the mugs, and I can already smell the soothing chamomile.

"Thank you," I murmur and bring the mug to my lips, tasting the hot tea. It burns my throat deliciously, and I hum in approval. "Much better than your cooking."

Allarick laughs deeply, and heat rushes through my body. This man is going to make me spontaneously combust one of these days.

All too soon, Allarick sobers up. His hand drops to my thigh, and I tense. He takes my reaction as negative and tries to pull away, but I cover his hand with my own, keeping him in place. One day, I'll stop being so jumpy at his touch. I like it, but you wouldn't know that by my reactions.

"Erin, we need to talk about what Atina said earlier," he starts.

"About the wedding," I interrupt.

"Yes, that. I know you are here to become my wife, but I don't want anyone to marry against their will. I cannot get you out of the contract, but I can buy you more time if you aren't ready. I'm not sure how much time with everything happening, and—"

"Allarick," I say gently and put down my cup of tea. He stops talking and stares at me like a lost puppy. I reach out and place my hand on his cheek, feeling the stubble of his facial hair against my palm. His body is warm, and he leans into my touch.

"I appreciate everything you've done for me and everything you are still doing for me. Very few other men would see a broken girl and notice the strength hiding beneath. I'm not sure I see it yet, but I'm trying. I still have a lot of healing to do, but you've helped me reach a place where I've experienced genuine happiness and what it means to be treated properly.

"So, I'm not afraid to marry you. I would be honored to be your wife. And maybe somewhere down the road, you and I will find more than friendship in our bond." I'm already more than halfway there, but it's still so new and raw. And maybe the fear of rejection has kept me from admitting my true feelings.

The softness in Allarick's eyes once would have made me question his sincerity. But not anymore. He is a man —no, kraken—of his word. If he stares at me like I'm the object of his desires and the star of all his dreams, then who am I to call him a liar?

"I do have one condition though..." I try to pull together the strength Allarick believes me to have. If there is ever a time to be brave, it's now.

"Anything, sweet girl. Name it, and it shall be yours."

Now or never. I can do this.

I take a deep breath. "I'm not sure how weddings operate in Tetria," I start, getting distracted by his lips. They are so close. All I need is to reach out and...*focus!* "Uh, but in Grym Hollow, the newlywed couple shares a kiss when their vows are complete, and they are pronounced husband and wife."

"We share a similar tradition," Allarick says, and I swear his body shifts. He's closer to me. His breath is hot against my skin.

"So, we are going to have to kiss." My voice comes out more breathless than I mean.

Allarick gives me an odd look, raising his brow. "Is that not what you want, Erin?" There's a sadness in his tone that he tries to hide, but it bleeds through.

"What if I say it's exactly what I want?" Be brave. Be bold. Be a woman who knows what she wants. A woman who isn't constantly plagued by James and the monster he was.

The man before me is the furthest thing from James. Probably because he is no man at all. My kraken is kind and gentle. Patient and attentive. He puts others before himself, and he makes sure people are taken care of. He made sure *I* was taken care of.

This time when he moves closer, I don't imagine it, and I don't pull away, even though he gives me the opportunity to.

Be bold.

Be brave.

His rough yet gentle hand comes to rest on my cheek. I lean into his touch, starved for some sort of true affection that I've been denied for far too long.

"Do you want me to kiss you, sweet girl?" His voice is warm honey, sending jolts of electricity straight down my spine. He stares at me like he can see into my soul and knows exactly what I want and need at this moment.

I need for my lips to touch another's, someone who isn't James. I need a kiss that will leave me completely breathless and desired. I can't remember the last time I had a kiss that didn't reek of alcohol. The memories of alcohol on James's lips are burned into my brain. I need something to replace it. I need to tell Allarick exactly what I want.

Be bold.

Be brave.

"Yes. I want you to kiss me. Now." Okay, maybe that was a little too forceful, but I didn't want to lose my nerve.

The corner of Allarick's mouth cocks up. Before I know it, he's pulling me closer until I'm sitting on his lap. My breath hitches as every hard curve and angle of his body presses into mine. He keeps one hand on my cheek while the other falls to my hip, keeping me in place. But not too tightly, leaving just enough room for me to pull away in case I change my mind.

This kraken is too perfect for the likes of me.

"You don't know how badly I've wanted to hear those words," Allarick whispers. And I'm completely stunned. He wants to kiss me? For how long?

Before I can verbalize any of those questions, Allarick moves forward, and his lips are on mine. My brain short-circuits, not accustomed to being kissed. His lips are so soft and taste vaguely of salt and the ocean. Butterflies burst in my belly, and I feel like a young girl getting kissed for the first time.

*Now kiss back.*

Right. I haven't moved since his lips touched mine. My body finally reacts, and I press closer to him, kissing him back. A low growl leaves his throat, vibrating my lips. This growl, I like. His hand on my hip tightens, but I don't feel suffocated by him. I want more.

He kisses me in earnest, and I give in to him, content

with letting him control this moment. His tongue runs along the seam of my lips until my mouth parts for him on instinct. Then Allarick, my gentle kraken, claims my mouth.

He drinks me in, tasting me like he's never had anything sweeter. A soft, needy whimper leaves my lips, but I don't have time to be embarrassed about it. Allarick's tongue mingles with mine, and he kisses me like he can't get enough of me. Like just one second away from my lips is too long.

My body grows hot. Wetness pools between my thighs. I've never gotten turned on by a kiss, but then again, I've never been kissed quite like this. Something hard presses into my thigh, and when I curiously grind down, Allarick groans.

Oh fuck, this man is getting hard. For *me*.

He doesn't push me to do anything other than kiss him. He's too much of a gentleman to ask for more. Logically, I know that's for the best because I'm not ready for more than kissing my kraken, but still, a part of me yearns for what could come from this.

Allarick kisses me until my jaw hurts and my lips are swollen. He kisses me until he steals all the breath in my lungs, and even after that, he kisses me more. When he finally pulls back, I let out a disappointed whine, but it only makes him chuckle as he reaches up to push a few fallen strands of hair behind my ears.

"We'll have many more years of kisses, sweet girl. This first one is just for us."

I smile at the thought. I don't know how I would have reacted if the first time I kissed Allarick was in front of his kingdom. I would be too nervous to enjoy the moment. It would be a kiss more out of expectation and not genuine want and need. The first time deserved to be just ours, away from outside eyes.

"Many years, you say?" I smile, leaning my head against his chest. His hand runs soothingly up and down my back.

"Many, many years," he promises. "You're in Mescos now. Humans live longer here."

"I'm going to hold you to that." I like the idea that I get more time with my kraken. My eyelids get heavy and start to droop. Feeling at complete peace makes me tired. Maybe because I don't have to fear what will come for me in the dark. Not when the deadliest thing is Allarick, and I'm certain he would die first before hurting me.

In no time at all, I lose the battle to sleep, drifting away in Allarick's embrace. The last thing I remember before sleep claiming me is Allarick's lips on my forehead and his soft hums of a lullaby.

# CHAPTER 23
# ERIN

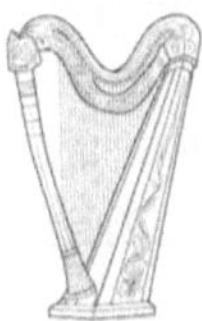

Today I'm getting married to my kraken.

I never thought I would say those words. Most little girls dream of marrying their prince or princess. I doubt many girls dream of marrying a sea monster. To be fair, Allarick is the furthest thing away from a monster. He's my gentle giant. My king.

And about to be my husband.

My lips still tingle from the earth-shattering kiss we shared last night. It was just a kiss—well, a lot of kisses —and yet I can't stop thinking about it. The way he made me feel. Both safe and desired. How I wanted more but didn't know how to ask.

We left early this morning for Tetria. I'm not sure how Allarick did it, but when we arrive back home, Iris and Delmare await us. We decided—after much back and forth—we want to marry immediately, which explains why the castle is already buzzing with activity; merpeople, krakens, and sirens all rushing around. Some hold decorations in their hands, and others bark orders. The one thing they have in common is they all stare at me, smiling widely like they have a secret I'm not privy to.

"We received your message, my king. The wedding preparations are going on full force," Iris says. "We should be ready by this evening."

"Good. See to it that Erin is comfortable," Allarick says, and my stomach drops.

"You aren't staying with me?" Of course, I should have known he wouldn't be getting ready with me during our wedding day, but I had the childish hope he would. I kiss him once, and suddenly I'm attached.

Allarick's features soften as he turns to me. He rests his hands on my hips and leans down to press a kiss to my lips. My cheeks burn bright red because both Iris and Delmare are there to witness this. Not that they haven't done the same thing a million times, some in front of me, because they are married.

"Iris will help you get ready for the wedding, sweet girl. I have a few things I need to do to get ready as well. Make sure things are in order for the ceremony. Delmare will assure your safety while I'm away."

"No harm will befall you, my queen," Delmare vows. And I don't doubt his ability to keep me safe. He's just not Allarick, who brings me peace and helps to keep me calm.

I don't want the nerves and the small voice that tells me I don't deserve someone like Allarick to ruin our day. I smile and nod, not able to trust my voice right now.

Allarick squeezes my hips before Iris takes my hand and leads me away. I swim besides Iris, allowing her to lead while Delmare follows from behind.

I expect Iris to take me up to my room, but we stay on the main floor, and she takes me into an interior room. "I can take it from here, my love. The queen will need to dress," Iris says to her husband. Delmare nods in understanding.

"Let me secure the room first." He swims inside, inspecting every inch of the room. When he's sure there isn't a killer shark in the corner or an angry siren fixed on ending me, he swims back out.

"Safe." He stations himself right outside the room.

"Thank you." Iris shuts the door behind him. There are no windows in this room, which I'm thankful for. I'm still not fully comfortable with undressing in front of Iris; the last thing I need is for the entire ocean to be able to see me. Even if Allarick stresses they can't see in. I'm not willing to take that gamble.

The room is set up with three large mirrors adorned with colorful seaweed. A slightly raised dais stands in the middle. There's a large walk-in closet and many trunks around the room. "This is our royal dressing room. It's where I've been getting most of your clothes," Iris explains, leading me to the dais. "Start stripping, my queen."

Iris disappears into a closet. I hear her rummaging through trunks and grunting as she heaves something heavy. When she reappears, she's winded. "Found it. Pesky thing was trying to hide from me." She smiles as she carries what appears to be a box. "We haven't had a royal wedding in some time, and I've always wanted to see the dress in person."

Iris undoes the locks on the box and lifts up the lid. She pulls out a shimmering opal bodice and inspects it before holding it up. The bodice is made up of hundreds of scales with small pearls sewed in throughout. It looks heavy and breakable. "That's gorgeous, but are you sure I should be wearing that?"

Iris stares at me like I've sprouted a second head. "This dress is made for a queen. You will be queen. Therefore, this was made for you, dear."

I finish taking off my clothes, balling them up and tossing them into an empty, open trunk as Iris wraps the bodice around me. She begins to tie it in the back, sucking me into the damn thing. Breathing and moving are clearly not needed today.

The panties she gives me to put on are hardly panties at all. More like three strips of...whatever fabric they're made up of. Hides absolutely nothing. Still, I pull them up over my legs and shimmy into them. "And the skirts, my queen."

In Iris's hand is a full white skirt made up of organza material. The light hits it just right, making it sparkle like a million rainbows. It's beautiful and the nicest thing I'll ever wear on my body. I help Iris get the skirts on me. They dance in the ocean, fanning out around me. There's no hiding in this outfit.

Next comes my hair, which Iris twists into several medium-sized braids before doing an elaborate pin-up. She uses pins with tiny seashells at the end to keep my hair in place. Makeup really isn't a thing here—at least from my brief encounter with Tetria—so she rubs various oils on my body until I smell like a fresh bakery.

"Just a few final touches." Iris starts on the jewelry. A pearl necklace with matching earrings. Bracelets of various shades of blue to add a pop of color. And then, finally, a tiara made from coral and shells. She places it on my head and swims back.

The woman in the mirrors staring back at me is not the same woman who showed up to Mescos broken and scared. She's not full of bruises with sadness in her eyes. No, this woman has faced hardships but survived. A newfound determination shines in her eyes. The need to live that did not previously exist burns in her. For the first time in my life, I feel powerful.

I feel like a queen.

"You look beautiful, my queen," Iris says from behind me. I see her smile in the mirror, looking over my dress. "It's time. Let's go marry your king."

I HEAR the crowd before I can see them. A cacophony of voices vibrates down the hall. My pounding heart thrums in my chest, louder than all the voices. The too-tight bodice squeezes me uncomfortably, making it hard to breathe. Iris holds my hand, leading me down the hallway lined with guards. Delmare swims behind us a respectable distance. Iris whispers sweet encouragements to me, but I can barely hear her.

All I hear is my pounding heart. Fear threatens to overwhelm me, and the walls feel as if they are caving in on me. My body stops.

I tend to avoid crowded places because loud noise and unfamiliar people watching or touching me trigger something inside me. Years and years of insecurities and verbal lashings come back to me at once, assaulting my senses.

*I'm not good enough. No one wants me. I'll be a shitty queen. I don't deserve love.*

Over and over, the mantra plays in my head, creating my own personal hell. My body shakes, unable to hold in the panic coursing through my body.

Not now.

Not here.

"My queen!" I hear someone shout—probably Iris. Everyone is too close. Too loud. Voices ring in my ear, and I try to block them out, slapping my hands over my ears.

"Stop. I need...I need..." My voice trails off as my body begins to betray me. My chest heaves as I desperately try to catch my breath. I need quiet. I need everyone to stop touching me. I need to find my damn voice. I need...I need...I need...

"Get Allarick. Tell him it's urgent, and the queen needs him," a gruff, masculine voice barks. The small hands on my back pull away, and bubbles follow her as she departs.

Delmare reaches out to me, but I scream, jerking away. I don't mean to do it, but I can't have him touch me. My hands fly to my head, blocking my face. I'll feel bad about it later, but I don't want his hands on me. They're too big. Too rough. Just like James. James who used me as his personal punching bag as he told me everything he hated about me. All my shortcomings. All my failures.

A flurry of commotion sounds from ahead, and someone barks, "Leave us!"

I hear people scramble, swishing their tails to get away. Then I feel something slither around my arms. Something else wraps around my waist, and I'm being pulled into a hard, naked chest.

"Sweet girl," Allarick purrs gently. He's here. My Allarick. My safety. He's here.

More tentacles wrap around me until they cover my body completely, cocooning me in their embrace. Protecting me from others, but also myself. "Listen to my heart. Count the beats. Match your breathing with my own. In. Out. In. Out. Try it, sweet girl."

His voice is a security blanket, keeping the monsters at bay. I count his heartbeats. *One...two...three...* And try to match my breathing to his. *In and out. In and out.* My breathing starts to even out, and the crippling panic that immobilized me starts to fade. My body unclenches as it relaxes in Allarick's embrace.

"There you go. Come back to me, Erin. I need you."

*I need you.*

"Allarick," I croak. "I...I don't know what came over me." It's a lie. I know my triggers, and usually I can prepare for them, but my mind was so focused on the wedding that I didn't even think about the audience and stares our wedding would bring.

"Perhaps you missed me." He grins, almost boyishly.

I laugh but gently smack his chest, which is colored with blue markings. He quickly covers my hand with his before I can pull away. Then the teasing expression is gone, replaced by something more serious. More determined. "If you aren't ready, we do not have to do this today."

I think of all the people waiting outside. All the rushed planning and setting up it took to get the wedding prepared on such short notice. Not to mention our marriage can make him more powerful for when he needs to seal off the Leviathan's prison. It isn't as easy as saying no, I'm not ready. Because that would diminish all the hard work everyone put into this. People would leave disappointed, and rumors would fly as to why the human queen did not marry the king.

No. Postponing the wedding isn't an option. Besides, I don't *want* to postpone it. Maybe that's crazy since my relationship with Allarick is so fresh and new, but I've never been a conventional girl.

"I want to marry you, Allarick." My voice, thankfully, stays strong. "I just didn't anticipate what all the commotion would do to me. I think I just needed to feel you wrapped around me." I tilt my head back to smile.

Allarick's stare bores into me with its intensity. It's so raw and full of something akin to admiration. Maybe more. "I will always be there when you need me, Erin. You have carved your name into my heart, and I'm afraid it can't be undone."

Definitely more.

Despite being surrounded by water, my throat goes

dry. By his words alone, this man has unwound me. He saw something that not even I could see and believed in me.

"Allarick?" I whisper.

"Yes, Erin?"

"Marry me."

# ALLARICK

Erin is a vision in her dress. She stands out like the goddess she is. I've only ever heard stories of the ceremonial dress, once worn by my mother and many queens before her. To think that Erin is now part of that history fills me with fierce pride.

The white skirts swish around her, giving the dress a more ethereal look. She wears a crown similar to mine, looking like the queen she was always meant to be. The carnal desire to see her in nothing but that crown as she writhes in pleasure underneath me hardens my body. Ever since our kiss from last night, I can't get the thought of her body against mine out of my mind.

This woman has wrapped herself around my heart and consumes all my waking thoughts.

The kiss wasn't enough. I want more. Need more. But I also don't want to push her until she's ready. I will wait for Erin for centuries if I have to.

Erin looks around, scanning the faces of our people. After she recovered from her panic attack, I brought her out to the balcony. A crowd has formed, which I expected, but my guards create a barricade. I can tell that Erin is still uncomfortable with so many eyes on her, so I squeeze her hand to try and provide some comfort.

"Tetria! We are gathered here today to celebrate the union between our faithful king, King Allarick, and his human bride, Queen Erin!" the spiritual advisor booms, getting the attention of the crowd.

Erin fidgets with a piece of her hair, eyes darting everywhere but to me. Her body is stiff, and she looks like she wants to bolt. She probably would if I wasn't holding her hand. Not exactly how I pictured my wife would react to me on our wedding day, but I know Erin's reaction isn't because of me. It's being the center of attention. In time, she will learn to love it.

"Hey, sweet girl," I whisper just low enough for her to hear. The spiritual advisor drones on about commitment and expectation. It is all part of the ceremony and easy enough to tune out.

Erin turns her attention to me, biting her lip. Her chest rises and falls faster than normal, and I need to calm her.

"It's just me and you," I say. "Look at me. It's just us."

"Just us?" she whispers softly.

"Just us. Allarick and Erin. Husband and wife."

At the mention of "husband," a red tint colors her cheeks. My sweet girl likes that title, and it feels like an accomplishment. Three words play at the tip of my tongue, but Erin doesn't need to hear those words yet. She needs to see them in my actions. She needs to know that, no matter what, it's her and I, and I'm not giving up on us.

"...the sacred oath. The goddess-bound promise that connects you in this life and the next," the spiritual advisor continues. This is an extremely condensed version of the ceremony, but I don't want Erin to stand here any longer than she has to. No matter how beautiful she looks in her wedding dress.

*She'll look even more beautiful with it off.*

The thought crosses my mind and travels straight to my cock. I'm thankful I'm in kraken form so Erin and the others won't notice my raging hard-on. I pride myself on being a gentleman, but Erin is my ultimate test.

The spiritual advisor produces a golden rope and begins to wind it around our clasped hands. This part of the ceremony is symbolic as much as it's necessary. "The rope, blessed by the sea goddess herself and used since the start of our people, connects kraken and human. Let the blessing of our goddess tie these souls together."

It is said that the golden rope forms a bond of the souls. Many married mates have attested to feeling a connection snap into place, but I have always been skeptical. It was simply the words of two lovers who have experienced heightened emotions.

The spiritual advisor waves his hands over our bound hands, muttering words in ancient Tetrian. My chest grows tight as a jolt sparks through my body. Erin lets out a low gasp, eyes growing wide.

She felt it too.

Invisible threads form between us, knotting so nothing can sever the new connection. Emotions not my own assault my brain. I feel and sense Erin better than I have ever felt anyone before. The feeling is all-consuming and fills me completely.

"To bind you in eternity in this life and the next, we will end this ceremony with a kiss," the spiritual advisor booms. I gauge Erin carefully, using our newly formed connection for signs of uncertainty or discomfort.

I find neither.

Instead, with her free hand, she tucks a strand of her hair behind her ear almost shyly. "Well, you heard the man. You gotta kiss—"

I don't let her finish. In an instant, I wrap my tentacles around her and pull her forward until our bodies collide. My lips find hers in a moment of pure need and passion. This isn't like the sweet kiss we shared the other night, alone at Atina's house. No, this is a kiss of true need.

Erin moans softly, arching her body against me. I feel every soft curve and dip of her body. My hands are desperate to touch her, but I keep them firmly on her hips. There'll be time for that later—hopefully.

Loud cheers from the crowd remind me that I'm not alone with my new wife, and I reluctantly pull away from her. Erin lets out a cute whine as she tries to pull me back. A weaker man would have given in to her demand, and I wanted nothing else than to be a weak man at that moment. But I fear if I start kissing her again, I won't be able to stop.

Instead, I place a gentle, lingering kiss on her forehead. "My queen."

At last.

"People of Tetria, I present King Allarick and his wife, Queen Erin!" The spiritual advisor's words are met by a chorus of cheers. Erin giggles, and my heart swells to see the happiness on her face.

"We will spend the day celebrating our king and queen. Let the festivities begin!" he says and unbinds our hands. He places the golden rope back into his robes.

"Festivities? What festivities?" Erin asks as the crowd of people starts to disperse, eager to celebrate.

"Drinking, mostly," I joke. "It's a day of celebrations. A feast, games, and dancing." And a lot of drunken sex, but I wisely keep that part of the tradition to myself.

"Oh. That sounds...like a lot." Erin's giggle gives way to her nerves. "When was the last royal wedding?"

"My parents. That was long ago, but I was told it was beautiful. My mom wore that very same dress."

Erin smooths down the skirt of her dress. "I bet she was a stunning bride."

"You, sweet girl, are a stunning bride." And she's mine. Ender brought us together because he knows something we don't. The Guardian is mysterious in many ways, but I can't bring myself to distrust him completely. Not when he brought me Erin.

"You don't look too bad yourself, Husband." Erin purrs the word "husband." It goes straight to my cock, and I'm once again tempted to sweep her away to find privacy. The carnal need to fuck out every last memory of James is strong. I want her to come with my name on her lips, loved as a woman like her should be loved and cherished.

Erin brings her hand to my chest, tracing the bioluminescent markings covering half of my body. "What are these?"

"Ceremonial markings. They tell a story of our past and the hope for our future. It also signifies that I've reached the highest honors of soul-binding to my mate. That my purpose is to serve my wife."

"Serve your wife, you say? Hmm, I think I can get used to that." Erin smiles, her hand lingering on my chest. Electricity sparks between us, sending jolts through my body.

"I will serve you well, Erin. Whenever you want. In every way you want."

Erin bites her lip, and I desperately wish I could catch a glimpse of her thoughts. I feel her lust and need, but what is she thinking?

A moment passes between us, and then Erin clears her throat, pulling her hand away. I try not to convey my disappointment. "Should we celebrate with our people? Maybe get something to drink, and then we could dance?" she suggests.

"Yes, but first I want to show you something." I take her hand. "I think you're going to like this."

"Well," she laughs. "Color me curious."

# CHAPTER 25
## ALLARICK

The music room is empty, as I thought it would be. Most people are in the grand ballroom or simply celebrating our union in the streets. I lead Erin into the room but pause right outside. "No one comes in. See to it that we aren't disturbed," I command the guards on duty outside the room.

"Yes, my king," they say in unison, taking up their positions.

I nod and follow Erin in, letting the double doors close behind us. "You brought me to the music room?" She smiles, immediately gravitating toward the piano. She plays it almost daily and always draws a crowd. I hope the party raging outside is enough of a deterrent to keep people away.

"I did, but for good reasons. It's custom to exchange presents on our wedding day," I say.

Erin's face instantly pales. "I...I didn't know that. I'm so sorry, Allarick, but I don't have anything for you." She sounds truly apologetic, and I don't want her to spiral into self-doubt again. She doesn't need to give me anything more than simply her trust.

"I didn't tell you that to make you feel bad, sweet girl. You have already given me a gift that will strengthen our people. I'll never be able to repay you, but that doesn't mean I won't try."

Before she can ask a follow-up question, I swim away toward a closed door. "I may have lied about one of my previous meetings."

"Oh?" Curiosity colors her voice. "Then where were you, and why was it so secretive you couldn't share it with your wife?"

*Wife.*

Never a sweeter word.

"Forgive me, my queen, but I didn't want to ruin the surprise." I search the dark room until my eyes land on the instrument. It was not easy getting it here and hiding it from Erin, but Delmare and Iris did a good job at keeping her distracted.

I grab the pearl-white instrument and am once again surprised by how heavy it is. The siren who made this assured me it was the top of the line and the only one of its kind. I know very little about musical instruments apart from liking the way they sound, so I'm hoping the man is right. More importantly, I'm hoping Erin will find it satisfactory.

An audible gasp sounds from behind me, and when I place the instrument down in the center of the room, I turn to see Erin. My wife's hands cover her mouth, eyes wide as she takes in the harp. The light hits the instrument to create an opal-rainbow effect around the room.

"I've seen you favoring the harp recently. Iris said you made a comment about the old one being out of tune."

"So you bought me an entirely new one?" She giggles. "Tuning would have sufficed, but…" Erin swims over to her present, gently running her hand down the sound-box. She hums appreciatively, moving to glide her fingers against the strings.

The music is sweet, and although I have no ear for correct tuning, even I can tell it sounds beautiful. "Allarick…" Erin's voice catches, her voice dripping with emotion.

Her gaze meets mine and holds. There's something different in the way she's looking at me, almost as if she's seeing me for the very first time. Really seeing me. Not just the man she had to marry to escape James. But rather her husband she's…falling in love with? Love is a strong word and perhaps not the case, no matter how much I want it to be.

Erin's love needs to be earned. She'll find I'll do anything for it.

"I can't thank you enough for this," she says after finding her voice. We gravitate toward one another, and I capture her in my arms. Erin, without hesitation, leans into my touch and places a soft kiss to my lips. "You are not what I expected," she whispers against our kiss.

"And what did you expect, sweet girl?"

"A man," she says. "But I'm learning I'm much more of a kraken sort of girl." She smirks, and I lose all semblance of composure.

My lips come crashing down upon hers, and Erin moans. It goes straight to my cock, painfully pushing against my pouch, wanting to be free. She opens for me, and our tongues collide. I drink her in, loving her soft whimpers each time my tongue strokes hers.

My tentacles wrap around her arm and waist, feeling her lush curves. What would it be like to explore her body with nothing between us? To see her writhing in pleasure as my hands and tentacles roam her body, bringing orgasm after orgasm. As she said, I am no man, and I don't fuck like one either. My queen will be treated as such, her body worshiped in bed.

Erin breaks away, chest heaving in her bodice. Her lips are swollen from my kiss, and the way she's biting her bottom lip nearly brings me to my knees. The heat and desire in her gaze make me want to pull her back and tangle myself with her until we don't know where one of us ends and the other begins.

"I don't have a wedding gift for you," Erin says again, placing her hands on my chest.

"It's fine, Erin." I didn't expect anything from her. She doesn't know all of our traditions, and I was being honest when I said she's already given my people and me a gift we can't ever repay.

"But I have a song I've been working on. For you. It's not completely ready, but...can I play it for you?" she asks nervously.

I've had stories written about me and dances made in my honor. But never has anyone written a song for me. My heart swells. As badly as I wanted her a moment ago, that can wait. I need to hear what my wife made for me.

"Please. I would love to hear it." I untangle my limbs from her lithe body and float back until I'm draped over the couch. Erin retrieves the seat from the old harp and brings it to the new one.

"It's rough," she warns.

"Luckily for you, your husband knows nothing about music other than it sounds pretty. So I'm sure I'll love it." My words are meant to encourage her, and I think they do. She doesn't shy away from me but sits up straight and brings her hands to pluck gently at the strings.

"I can't put my feelings into words. I've never been very articulate, so I hope this helps me explain how I feel about you," she says.

And she starts to play.

The song sounds melancholy when it starts, as if she's weeping. The melody reminds me of lost love. Erin's eyes close as she gets lost in her own music. The tune changes gradually to something sweet and soft, reminding me of the days we spent in Atina's house together. Then the sound morphs into something else entirely.

The notes are faster. Stronger. Her hands flutter across the strings, plucking each with an intensity only a seasoned musician can achieve. The sound is that of a siren, beautiful and new. Full of sorrow and hope. I've never been one to be brought to tears during a song, but this isn't just any song.

It's about us.

Our short history together.

Her fears. Strength. Love.

It blends together, creating a story. The story of us.

My eyes lock with Erin, and I see I'm not the only one

drowning in emotion. Her eyes are rimmed in red, conveying everything her melody is and her words can't.

*Please don't hurt me.*

*Cherish me.*

*Be my home.*

Just like that, the music fades to one last note. One that reminds me our future is yet to be written, just like the rest of this song. I've never been more excited to hear the ending. What lies in store for the pair of us.

I don't get to ponder long because, in the next moment, Erin launches herself at me.

# CHAPTER 26

# ERIN

I'm a goner.

I come apart at the seams by a sweet gesture that means more to me than any other gift I've ever received. A beautiful harp picked specifically for me. It's not the harp I care for, though it is a beautiful instrument. It's the man who went out of his way to learn my fears and desires. To look at all the broken parts of me and not be scared away. To learn what I like and truly listen when I speak.

Allarick has taken an interest in me from the beginning. He's been nothing but sweet and patient with me while I try to figure out these conflicting feelings. Slowly, I'm unwinding myself from James's web and falling hard for my sweet kraken.

There's no mistaking this feeling. All-consuming and powerful. Love is patient, and our love is quiet. Perhaps it's not even acknowledged, but it's there for the taking if I want it. It blooms more and more with each passing day.

I may not know what our future holds, but I do know one thing. I want my husband. No...I *need* my husband. Need to feel the last bit of James scrubbed away from me for good. I don't want him to be the last man I've had sex with. The faked orgasms I acted out just to get the drunken man off me. I want to know what it means to be truly appreciated by someone.

When the song finishes, I still have more to stay. My body acts of its own accord, and I close the space between us, launching myself into his arms. But only my actions can speak for me now. I waste no time in finding his lips. Those beautiful, full lips I want to feel all over my body. Would he draw out my orgasm until I'm begging him to let me come? Or would he get me to completion as fast and as many times as possible?

I'm not sure which one is more appealing.

Part of me knows there's no turning back. I'm certain I don't want to. My only doubts are if Allarick wants me in the way I need him. But those are smothered as soon as Allarick wraps himself around me, his tentacles pulling me flush against his body. He kisses me like a starving man, and I'm his last meal. He kisses me like I hold the secrets to the universe, and he's determined to discover every single one of them.

Allarick bites my lower lip and sucks it into his mouth. I let out a needy moan I might be embarrassed about later. He pulls back with a pop, but I don't let him get too far away from me. I fear I'll lose my nerve if we stop now.

"Is this your way of thanking me, sweet girl? Because if it is, expect many presents." He chuckles, trying to lighten the intensity brewing between us. He's not as unaffected as he seems though. His body is rigid, and his gaze is heated. Tentacles tighten around me, one stroking up and down my hip.

"Allarick..." Nerves threaten to overtake me, but then visions of rough hands and drunken thrusts plague my mind. Of nights of pain and drunken sex. Of saying no and wanting to stop.

That's not good enough for me anymore.

It never was.

I deserve better.

Newfound confidence fuels me, and I lock him in with my stare. "Allarick, Husband, I want you."

He doesn't appear shocked or disgusted by my bold proclamation. "Is this what you truly want, Wife? Because, if I have you once, I'll want you again. My resolve around you is crumbling, but I won't take from you something you aren't prepared to give."

I appreciate him checking in with me and letting me make my own decision. But my mind is made up. I want this. I want *him*. He is what I choose.

"A husband should make sure his wife is satisfied on their wedding night," I say.

Allarick drops his gaze to my lips before his darkened stare meets mine again. My heart pounds rapidly against my chest, threatening to burst free if he doesn't touch me and soon. I'm surprised he can't hear it. "We can't have that, sweet girl, can we? Let's go back to our room, and I'll change—"

"No," I say with too much ferocity. "I don't want you as a man, Allarick."

Realization dawns, and his lips twitch up into a predatory smile. Warmth rushes to my core just as it does every time he looks at me like that.

"Not a man," he repeats. "My wife wants her kraken husband, then? To feel my hands and tentacles all over this pretty body?"

"Yes. Allarick, please."

His tentacles caress my side. It's too slow. All too slow. I want him to unleash on me.

My wishes are granted in the next second.

Allarick brings me to his chest, his lips leaving a trail of kisses from my lips down to my neck. I tilt my head to the side, giving him full access to my neck. His teeth brush against my skin before he gently bites down. Goosebumps form on my arms, and my nipples harden to painful points.

His finger glides down my back to the ties of my corset. The instant exhale when he loosens it has my whole body relaxing. "Damn, Iris really knows how to tie these things." My boobs, which were pushed up nearly to my chin, settle back to their natural position.

"She's efficient," he says as more of the ties loosen until I can finally breathe properly. Allarick wastes no time unclasping the front. When he's got half of them unclasped, he runs his big hand up my stomach. He spreads his fingers wide, nearly encompassing my entire stomach before moving up. His touch burns me, sending molten heat straight to my core.

"Are you—"

"If you ask me if I'm sure one more time, Allarick, I won't ever show you my boobs." It's a threat I'm not prepared to see through, but at this moment, I will do anything to make my kraken drop his gentleman persona and his need to treat me like I'm a porcelain doll. "If I want to stop, I'll tell you."

I need him to see me as his wife.

A woman he desires.

Faster than my eyes can track, the last few clasps of my corset open, and my breasts spill out. The corset floats to the floor, and I think about picking up the beautiful garment so it doesn't get damaged.

But then Allarick's mouth is on mine again.

And his hands cup my heavy breasts, kneading them.

Everything else is forgotten.

I moan, arching my back. It's not close enough though. I want nothing between us. I want to feel his body flush against mine. I want to find his cock, because, admittedly, I have no idea where a kraken cock is located or what it even looks like. I've seen plenty of krakens, and I think I would have noticed if they were swimming around with their cocks out.

Probably.

Allarick snakes one of his eight tentacles around my hips and pulls. I spin in his arms. My back hits his chest, and I feel his hot breath against my neck before his lips sear my skin. He leaves a trail of kisses in his wake. I press my legs together, desperate for some friction. Desperate for Allarick. Need like I've never felt courses through my body, begging for more.

"Where do you want to be touched, sweet girl?" he asks. "Here?" He brings his tentacle up to my chest, teasing my nipple by swirling his tip around it. And, *oh god,* it feels good. Like really fucking good.

I've never considered myself particularly kinky. Or more accurately, I never got to explore that sexual side of myself. James was a missionary guy, which was...fine, but the moment he passed out, I would take the vibrator I kept hidden in the bedside table and finish the job. Sex was never enjoyable, but orgasming was. James was a no toy kind of man, so the fact I even hid a vibrator from him was amazing.

I've seen tentacle dildos before on the rare occasion I would wander into Richard's, the only sex shop in Grym Hollow. I had always been too scared to make any purchases, but it didn't stop me from window shopping. I always gravitated toward the...nonhuman penises. I knew my interests were different the time I overheard two women making judgy comments about the nonhuman dildos. So, it only remained a fantasy.

Until now.

"Or maybe you want to be touched here?" Allarick moves between my legs, my skirts bunching up and creating a barrier between his tentacle and my pussy. My clit begs to be touched; it's almost painful. Almost too much.

"You're teasing me," I manage to pant.

Allarick laughs deep in his throat, sending shivers through my body. "I am. I plan on taking my time with you, Wife."

"Well, *Husband,*" I say, though it comes out as a sneer, which I don't intend, "your wife needs more. Now." This woman who demands things is not one I'm familiar with, but I can't help but like this part of me that voices what she wants. I've missed her.

Allarick must like it too, because I feel a quick tug on my skirts before he pulls them away from my body. I only wear the barely-there panties Iris made me put on. Allarick hums in pleasure, fingering—tentacle-ing?—the tops of my panties.

Allarick makes quick work of removing the garments, and for the first time, I'm naked in front of him. I wait for the embarrassment or shyness to settle in, but it never does. Not with Allarick, at least. His hand travels down the curve of my breast all the way down to my hip bone. "You are exquisite, Wife."

If he keeps saying things like that, I'm going to fall in love with him. I'm already more than halfway there. This could also be the horniness talking.

"I'm going to make you feel good, Erin," Allarick purrs in my ear. "But you say stop, and this will end. It's as simple as that. Say you understand."

"I understand," I say immediately.

"Good." The hand on my hip slides lower until he cups my mound. I groan softly while his capable finger traces my seam. "Are you wet for me?"

I could be a brat and say I'm wet because I'm in the damn water, but I'm incapable of lying. "Yes."

"Good girl," he says, and I fucking melt. I always wondered if I had a praise kink, and now I have my answer. I most definitely do.

Allarick uses two fingers and makes a V, spreading my lips. I expect him to press his finger inside of me. But he doesn't. Instead, one red tentacle snakes between my legs, tip nudging at my entrance. We both groan as he nudges himself slowly inside of me. The tip of his tentacle isn't wide, but I still feel a little stretch. But the more he gently presses in, the more my pussy stretches around his girth. He works me slowly, taking his time so I can adjust to his size.

His tentacle is so damn big and—*oh!* Something slides over my clit and suctions over it. I writhe in Allarick's arms, moaning. What the hell is that? Whatever it is, it feels so fucking good.

"My tentacles have suckers. How does it feel?" he answers my unasked question. His voice is smug because he knows exactly how it feels.

I don't answer him quickly enough, and another large tentacle wraps across my chest, his suckers making my already sensitive nipples almost painful. It's too much. But it's also perfect. Everything about this kraken is perfect.

The need to orgasm for him is strong. Like a greedy, wanton thing, I grind down on his tentacle. He's ruined me for any other man.

"Baby, please," I groan, the pet name leaving my lips unknowingly.

Allarick growls, leaning down and kissing my neck. "Do you want to come, sweet girl?"

"Yes. Please. I need it."

Part of me wonders if he's going to tease me, prolonging my orgasm for as long as he wants. I'd be unable to do anything other than let it happen. I'm his willing captive, desperate for release.

Thankfully, Allarick takes pity on me and fucks me

faster with his tentacle. Moving in and out at just the right speed. Not too fast, but not a teasing pace either. The suction of his suckers on my clit feels like his mouth is on me, pleasuring me with his tongue. The sensation coupled with the added pleasure from my nipples sends deep pulses through me and has me crashing hard.

I scream—honest-to-god scream—as my orgasm takes over me. I've never come that hard and that quickly before. Honestly, I didn't know another person could make me feel like that. Allarick has proven he knows his way around my body better than my boyfriend of multiple years. Except Allarick cares about my pleasure. Cares that I feel good and satisfied.

I'm utterly and completely ruined.

# CHAPTER 27
# ALLARICK

She comes so prettily on my tentacle, and my cock is jealous.

What an obscene, yet beautiful picture we must create right now. With my tentacles wrapped around her body and one deep inside her tight pussy. I have been with many different lovers in my time, of all genders, but none of them have affected me quite as much as Erin.

My perfect, beautiful human. Made for me, just as I am made for her.

I'm not keen on letting her go, and from the looks of it, Erin is more than content to catch her breath, wrapped up in my tight embrace. It's perfect...minus my raging cock. It pushes painfully against my pouch, begging to be let out. My tentacles feel good inside her, extra sensitive. And I can usually get off with tentacle play, but me and my cock are greedy for our wife. I need more.

Erin slowly turns in my hold. Pointy brown nipples

scrape against my chest, and a moan threatens to leave my lips. I remove my tentacle from inside her, and she pouts, but only for a second.

She's so damn perfect.

"It's your turn," she purrs like a seductive land cat playing with her mouse. I'm no mouse, and I won't pretend to be one. But if my wife wishes to please me, who am I to deny her?

Her gaze moves up and down my body, stopping at my hips. I know what she's looking for, and it pleases me she's as eager for my cock as I am to give it to her.

"Can't say I've ever had to ask this, but, erm, where is your…" Erin's face flushes a light pink color. It's almost as if she's forgotten I had my tentacle inside her not too long ago. But asking me where my cock is? She's shy. It's adorable. And a valid question.

I reach out to intertwine my fingers with hers. She lets me guide her to my hips and then down. Down until I reach my pouch, the hidden enclosure my cock stays behind. Just like human men hide their cocks behind pants, this serves the same purpose. I let her feel the slit before sliding her hand inside. Erin makes a face of surprise and confusion, but it quickly changes when her hand bumps against something hard.

I remove my hand, letting Erin take control. She's not looking at me, but rather down to where her hand disappears inside my pouch. She moves her knuckles down my length and groans at what she finds. I can't help but smirk.

"Is your cock…*ribbed*?" She whispers the last part,

apparently forgetting we are alone, and there's no need for secrets. Not between us.

"See for yourself, sweet girl."

My words are the consent she needs to wrap her hand around my cock. I groan, my body tensing. This woman doesn't know the effect she has on me, and I feel like a guppy who is having sex for the first time. It takes all my concentration not to thrust into her hand and chase my own orgasm, but I don't want it to end that quickly.

Erin slowly—torturously—pulls my cock from my pouch, exposing every inch of me. My wife sucks in a deep breath as she takes me in. "Are you sure that's not another tentacle?"

Despite the growing need for her, I can't help but laugh. Even for a kraken, I'm big. My cock is a darker red than my tentacles, ending in a mushroom tip. As Erin pointed out, my cock is ribbed, ready to give my partners the most intense pleasure. Despite the size and color, though, it clearly doesn't resemble another tentacle.

"Very sure." To prove it, I fist my cock, giving myself a rough stroke. The pleasure is intense, but not what I want. My new wife bites her lip as she takes me in. She's always been beautiful, but at this moment, she's never looked better. I want to devour her.

Erin moves closer, swatting my hand away and replacing it with her own again. "Let me take care of you." I make no arguments.

Erin lowers herself. It's awkward at first, since she's fighting against the water and still learning how to move in the ocean. She's gotten better at moving with the water since she's been here, and, in a matter of seconds, she's on her knees, looking up at me. I remain still, each muscle of my body tightening. It's pure, sweet torture, but one I'll endure for her.

"How are you real?" she asks in reverence, as if I'm the one who should be worshiped. I am but a humble servant to my beautiful wife. But I don't have the chance to respond, because Erin takes my cock into her warm mouth. And my brain stops. All it knows is pleasure.

Erin hums around my length, her mouth open obscenely wide as she takes more of me down her throat. She wraps her hand around the base of my cock and starts to move. With each bob of her head and stroke of her hand, I'm pushed further and further into madness.

I hadn't expected this. Hadn't planned for my bride to be on her knees taking my cock on our wedding day. Not that I hadn't thought about it. I did. More often than I care to admit, but Erin's been through hell with a man who didn't appreciate her. It left her having to pick up the pieces he chipped away at for years. She's just now beginning to put herself back together, stronger than before.

So I never wanted to push her.

Erin's sharp nails dig into my cock. I hiss, bucking my hips forward. She groans and relaxes her mouth. That sinful mouth pulls moans from my lips.

"Fuck, sweet girl. Keep this up, and I'm not going to last much longer." My words only serve to drive her harder, sparking something within her. She sucks my cock like it's her job. Like every second I'm not orgasming is a disgrace.

I come undone. Hard. My mouth opens and closes, and then, only a strangled groan leaves my lips as I come for her. I expect Erin to pull away. Hell, I even start to pull away, but my wife is incessant. She pulls me back, sucking and licking me throughout my orgasm. It's messy. It's hot. I fear I'm addicted.

When she takes everything from me, Erin pulls back with a pop, a cocky smile on her face, one I have never seen before. It looks damn good on her. She licks her lips, clearing the last traces of my arousal away. "I see why men could never get me off now," she hums.

"Oh? And why is that?"

Then Erin says something that cements my feelings for her.

"Because I was always meant to be a kraken's wife."

I don't let her get far. I grab her and pull her up to me. My lips meet hers with a hungry need, despite already having her once. It's not enough. Never will be enough.

Together, we fall back on the couch, and this is where we stay for the rest of our wedding celebration.

# ERIN

I don't remember getting back to our room last night, but here we are. Sometime between getting railed by real-life tentacles and now, I must have been carried up to our bedroom. Allarick is angled toward me, still fast asleep, with his arm over my chest.

My bare chest.

Allarick, now back in human form, is naked as well. The thin white sheet covers the best parts of him, but his strong thigh is on perfect view. I can't help but wonder what his human cock would look like. Would he be just as long and thick? Would he taste different?

Never in my life did I think this is something I'd need to consider. Life can change in a blink of an eye, and mine has changed dramatically. The Erin who entered Mescos? She's gone. I'm not the same Erin who is constantly looking over her shoulder, scared for her life. This new version of me is something I didn't think possible.

I've taken the broken pieces of me that have been

chipped away for years and slowly reconstructed them into something I never thought I could be. Brave. Strong. Opinionated. Resourceful.

Allarick had a big hand in helping me heal, and a big piece of me was healed yesterday after our wedding. I gave myself to the man I'm falling for. Allarick is the last person who has seen my body, and the person I gave myself to willingly. Perhaps it was too soon, and maybe others won't understand my choices. But it doesn't matter because I don't regret the decision. I would make it again and again if it leaves me feeling like this.

Like I'm finally a person worthy of love and respect.

Allarick stirs next to me, his grip on me tightening as he pulls me closer. His locs tickle my chest, but I lean against him regardless.

"Good morning, Wife." Allarick's morning voice is… pure sex. A delicious caress to the senses. He has me pressing my legs together; my wayward thoughts go straight to what he did yesterday with his tentacles and wondering when it could happen again.

"Good morning. Did you carry me to bed?" I reach out to finger his hair. I'm itching to retwist his locs the next time he needs it. I learned at a young age, having practiced on my doll. I learned the best ways to style my own hair to keep it looking healthy.

"I did. You fell asleep on me after a while. I'll pretend my pride isn't wounded," he teases.

I laugh. "It shouldn't be. I fell asleep because I haven't orgasmed that hard in a long time. Or ever. I slept really well last night though, so that's good."

"Very good indeed." Allarick pulls me to his chest and

leans down to capture my lips in a slow but passionate morning kiss. His tongue lazily strokes mine, drinking me in like I'm his morning coffee. He's certainly mine.

And I need more.

I don't know where the boldness comes from. This sex-crazed woman isn't me, at least it wasn't before Allarick. My hands go to his chest, and I push him away. His stunned expression is almost comical, but I pay it little mind as I move to straddle him. Allarick's eyes darken, a low chuckle coming from his throat. "Does my wife need attention?"

"Yes," I say, not shying away from him.

This moment feels important, just like yesterday when we had sex. This is another thing I'm reclaiming, and having sex while my husband looks human is important to me. Man or monster, he needs to be the one who claims me entirely. Just like I'm about to claim him.

I reach down between us, my hand finding the tip of his cock. I grip him, and Allarick groans, eyes fluttering. He looks so sexy. Part of me still can't believe he's my husband. I don't know what I did to deserve such a gentle and loving partner, but I know without a doubt that I don't want to lose him.

"Touch me, sweet girl," he purrs from underneath me. Heat blossoms in my core, scorching me from the inside out.

His cock is no less impressive in this form than it is in kraken form. He's still long and thick with the same mushroom tip. The only difference is that his cock isn't red or ribbed. I'm only a little sad about the last part, but it doesn't last long. I stroke him, and the room fills with his groans. It's so hot and goes straight to my clit.

"I want you inside of me," I pant, drunk with lust.

"Then do it, sweet girl. Take your husband."

*My husband.*

My body is prepped and primed to take him. There is still a delicious ache between my thighs, but it doesn't deter me as I line him up against my slick folds and guide him inside me. We moan in unison. My head falls back as I slowly take in every damn inch of him. If all the merpeople are hung like Allarick, there has to be many happy—albeit sore—partners swimming around.

When he's fully seated inside me, I'm stretched obscenely wide for him. Allarick glances down at where we connect and licks his lips. His hands then come around to grip my ass, which he squeezes. This already feels different than what I had before. Better. I'm not a toy to Allarick. Something he could use to take his pleasure while ignoring mine.

I haven't done this before, so I'm slow to roll my hips, hoping I don't shatter the lust-induced spell we're under. Allarick moans, and it's the hottest thing I've ever heard. It fills me with confidence I desperately needed to roll my hips again.

"So perfect. So damn beautiful," he grunts, squeezing my ass. I soon feel the absence of his hand, but then his thumb finds my clit, and everything else fades away.

"Allarick," I moan his name, body tingling all over. Every inch of me is sensitive and needy for touch. *His* touch.

I move my hips faster, riding him in earnest. I chase

my pleasure as he continues to rub circles around my clit. Pleasure builds, and underneath me, I feel Allarick tense, breath hitching. "Erin," he says my name like a warning. Or perhaps it's permission. He's close, just as I am.

The muscles in my thighs strain, and my breaths come out in pants. I try to form words, try to warn him, but all that leaves my lips are moans and whimpers. Allarick understands though. I know he does. He moves his thumb faster, and I'm almost frenzied with my own movements, chasing my pleasure.

And then I burst. "Allarick!" His name stays on my tongue as I orgasm, and he follows suit. He moans. Or I moan. I don't know anymore.

He comes with a roar as he fills me. It's dirty. Unplanned. But perfect. I've never been more thankful for my IUD than I am at this moment.

My arms give out, and I'm falling onto his chest. Allarick wraps me up in his arms, peppering my face in soft kisses, murmuring sweet praises in my ear. If this is a glimpse into what the rest of my life looks like, I can't wait.

I'm not sure how long we stay like that. Wrapped up in each other and learning every inch of the other's mouth. It's forever and a minute rolled up in one.

I'm tempted to stay here the whole day, and, judging from the hardness forming between his legs, Allarick wants the same thing. But this morning, I get the first dose of what it means to be a queen because we get interrupted by a knock on the door.

"My king, I do not mean to interrupt, but I must speak with you." Delmare's voice travels through the door, an edge to it I haven't heard before. He's not one to demand to speak with Allarick first thing in the morning. Unease settles within my stomach.

Allarick sits up and covers me with the blanket, which I'm thankful for. I may be comfortable with my husband seeing my body, but I'm not eager for others to see it. When he goes to retrieve pants, I get a brief glimpse of his sculpted ass before it's covered up.

Pity.

I don't get long to mourn the loss of my husband's ass because, in the next second, Allarick gives his permission to enter. Delmare walks in, nude from the waist up. His pants are similar to Allarick's, hugging his muscular thighs almost indecently. I don't know what these krakens eat, but people would sell their firstborn for a bottle of whatever turns these guys into Herculean men.

Delmare bows. "My king," he says and then looks at me. His gaze doesn't stay on me for long because it's evident I'm naked under this thin cover. "My queen."

"Good morning, Delmare," I greet awkwardly and sit up, still keeping myself covered. Allarick steps in front of me, providing another layer of protection. My husband is a good man, but I don't think he'd take kindly to anyone seeing me naked. Even his best guard whom he admires and respects.

"Good morning, my queen. I apologize for interrupting, but this couldn't wait."

"Out with it then, Delmare. What is the urgency?" Allarick asks, not unkindly.

"Reports have come in from civilians and new

recruits about suspicious activities surrounding our borders."

"What kind of activity?" Allarick asks.

"Unusual sounds. People are disappearing. Two more families have come forward and said they are missing several members of their families," Delmare explains.

Allarick curses under his breath. "Is anyone within our borders claiming to hear a sound?"

Delmare frowns. "No, but the healers have reported a suspicious rise in headaches and fatigue cases. It could be nothing, but—"

"I'm not willing to chance it," Allarick interrupts. "I need to see and hear this sound for myself. Get a group together. We will be leaving shortly to look into these claims."

"Yes, sir. I'll gather a few trusted guards," Delmare agrees.

"I want to go too," I say, and both men turn to look at me.

"My queen...I'm not certain that's a good idea," Delmare says gently. His words take me by surprise. Delmare has never been one to speak out against me. Hell, he hardly ever speaks when he's following me and Iris around.

"Why not? I should know what's going on in Tetria, shouldn't I?" I pin him with my stare. Delmare has the decency to appear appropriately chastised.

"Will you leave us, Delmare? My wife and I need to speak," Allarick says.

I bristle, slightly hurt that Allarick didn't immediately agree with me. I understand why though. I'm not exactly a strong swimmer, nor do I know these waters well. I'd be a liability and a distraction.

"Of course. In the meantime, I will get a group together for the mission." Delmare bows and leaves hurriedly.

The moment he shuts the door, I address my husband, "I want to go."

Allarick sighs and drops back down on the bed next to me. "I know you do," he says in a way that does little to ease my nerves. He reaches for my hand, and I let him take it in his. "But I'm not sure that is the best idea."

Even though I expected it, it still feels like a blow to the gut. "But why? Am I not your queen? Your equal? Tetria is my kingdom too. I want to help, Allarick."

I pull my hand away from his, and Allarick doesn't fight me. I'm not sure if that fills me with relief or not.

"You are correct, and I'm not denying that. Which is why I need you to stay here. Both of us leaving the castle during this time is dangerous. What if something happened while we were out investigating? Who would rule the kingdom in our absence? Our people have to focus on defeating the Leviathan and Nephilim. They can't be focused on battling for the throne."

My lips purse, and I hate how much sense he's making. It wouldn't make sense for both of us to leave the castle. We're married now, and our Leviathan problem is only getting worse. We are up against enemies we know little about. I know even less than Allarick, who has been here his entire life. I'm still learning this world and the people in it. If anyone should go, it only makes sense that it's Allarick.

Doesn't mean I have to like it.

"How long will you be gone?" I sigh, giving in.

Allarick relaxes, reaching for my hand again. I let him. "A few days at most, but if we are lucky, then only a day."

"And you'll tell me what you discover?"

"I'll tell you everything until you command me to shut up and please you instead." He smirks, and I can't help but smile.

"Fine. Please be safe. We just got married. It would be terribly inconvenient if something happened to you. I don't want to have to find a new husband." If I don't make a joke, I'll cry. And I've cried too many times in my life.

It's pathetic that I feel lost and on the verge of tears because Allarick is leaving. He's my safety. Taking him away means battling through darkness alone.

"I will. I have someone I need to make it home to." Allarick smiles, pulling me close. I lose hold of the sheet covering me as he pulls me into his arms, but I don't care. "Because I will be coming home to you, Erin. If you ever miss me while I'm gone, play your harp. Let your music comfort you."

Our lips meet in a hungry kiss, and I pray to whomever will listen that we will have many more. For now, I let Allarick soothe me the best way he knows how: with his lips.

# CHAPTER 29
# ALLARICK

Leaving Erin behind at the castle isn't an easy decision. Leaving my wife after only one night together isn't how I want to start off my marriage, yet here we are. In truth, I didn't expect our wedding day to end with my tentacles in her sweet pussy and her sinful lips around my cock. It was the best present she could have given me. Her trust, body, and, if not love, something close to it.

Erin ruined me yesterday, and I loved every second of it.

I would feel better if Delmare stayed with his queen because I trust him the most, but the reality is that he is needed alongside me. I still made sure to leave Erin in good hands with Danika, a woman who has proven herself loyal and capable. She's been a guard for a long time and knows how the kingdom runs. She can be an asset to Erin if my wife likes her.

My wife. I don't think I'll ever get used to that.

"My king, are we ready to leave?" Delmare asks.

I gather with five other guards at the front of the castle. To not cause any more alarm, I instructed my men to carry their normal weapons of choice and nothing more. Fear is a disease and, once bred, will ignite the entire town into chaos. I want to avoid spreading more, if at all possible.

"Almost. Everyone needs to put noise cancelers on. We cannot risk prolonged exposure to this unfamiliar sound. We must take precaution," I say.

Delmare nods, disappearing back inside before coming out with a glass bowl full of silicone putty. Each guard breaks some up, rolling the putty between their fingers to create balls. It's not the most effective noise canceler, but it will do the job for today.

A few of the guards mount their hippocamps, big steeds that will be essential to our mission. These creatures are similar to horses but are made for the water. Their hearing is better than ours, and they will alert us when we get close. I choose to swim; being able to move swiftly and freely through the water without the hindrance of a hippocamp is more appealing. With Delmare and me leading the way, we set off.

We journey through the rural part of the kingdom, not wanting to stir up any unnecessary concern from the civilians. Each mile away from the castle, I'm more acutely aware of Erin's absence. Is she okay? Is she scared? How is she handling being thrown into a leadership role with no training?

A better man would have prepared his queen for the duties and responsibilities of the throne before thrusting her into it. Granted, we haven't had much time in our kingdom and even less since our wedding, but a plan should have been put into place before Erin was even brought to Mescos. I thought I planned for everything, but where it counts, I failed.

Despite this, I still trust Erin with my life to lead the kingdom while I'm away. She has all the qualities of a leader. Fair. Brave. Compassionate. She just needs to trust herself and her decisions.

Doing my best to push all thoughts of Erin behind, I focus my attention on what's ahead. I don't get to enjoy the beauty of my kingdom, the playful sea creatures, or the temperature of the water. I strain my ears to hear. Nothing out of the ordinary, but we haven't reached the outskirts of the kingdom yet.

We swim for two hours, stopping periodically to assess the sound situation and make sure the hippocamps aren't acting strangely. We reach the edge of our border, where the ocean is darker and quieter. None of the infrastructure, like the coral houses, shops, or bubble homes, reside in this part of the water. There are caves occupied by merpeople who want a quieter life outside the kingdom.

The water is eerily calm today. None of the usual dwellers swim by. In fact, the ocean feels desolate. It's true there's never too much activity, but it feels like we are the only merpeople left in the ocean.

I'm not one to shy away from danger. As the king, my whole life has been filled with danger around every corner. It seems odd to say you get used to the feeling of knowing your enemies are one lucky shot from taking you out, but if I start each day fearing for my life, I doubt

I would get out of bed. That said, I still swim into the dark ocean with caution.

We travel in silence for the next hour. It's only broken up when the hippocamp to my left huffs. I don't think anything of it until another hippocamp does the same thing. Then, as one, the hippocamps stop and shriek. They jerk back, nearly knocking their riders off. The riders desperately try to calm them, but to no avail. They jerk and twist in obvious distress.

"Take them back!" I roar over their cries. Delmare barks my order, getting the two on hippocamps to go back. Watching the guards try to tame their distressed water horses almost makes me miss the way the guard next to me tenses.

It happens in a blink of an eye. I turn in time to see the guard's eyes gloss over. Phyns's emerald eyes change to a milky white. The hand poised on the hilt of his sword drops, and he swims forward as if being led by an invisible hand.

"Phyns!" I call, hoping it will break through whatever spell he's under, but Phyns doesn't stop. He doesn't even falter or acknowledge he's heard me. Before the guard can get much further, I lunge for him. My tentacle wraps around his arm, but Phyns doesn't seem to notice.

"Noise cancelers. Everyone! Now!" I yell, taking my own putty and cramming it into Phyns's ears. Only then does the guard blink, eyes slowly going back to normal.

"My king?" his voice shakes, looking back at the other guards staring at him with various degrees of grim expressions.

That's when I hear it.

It's faint. Easy to miss. A light cascade of sound. It's not just one voice but many coming together to create a song of ruin and destruction. My body tenses as the voices overwhelm me. "Phyns, give me your noise cancelers," I speak loudly, not only for the guard to hear me but also to block out the song.

Phyns fumbles with something in his vest before handing over the putty. I'm quick to place it in my ears and feel the instant relief that comes over my body. I still hear it, but it's dulled and easy to ignore. True fear seeps in, and it would be so easy to give in to the fear. Fear for my kingdom. Fear of the Leviathan and Nephilim. Fear for Mescos. But as king, I don't have that luxury.

"Head back!" I command. Delmare frowns, looking like he wants to have a conversation right here, but I need to be away from this noise. I need all the guards to be away with a clear mind. Luckily, Delmare doesn't push it as we swim back toward the kingdom.

It's probably overkill, but I have us swim for an entire hour before giving the okay to take out the putty. "It's getting stronger, my king," Delmare says as soon as everyone can hear again.

"I'm aware." I try to keep my irritation at bay. After all, I'm not upset with Delmare. I'm upset because I'm woefully unprepared.

"The sound is strong. Stronger than any siren I've ever heard. And we were still miles away from where your sister pinpointed their location. If this makes it to the kingdom..." Phyns trails off, but he doesn't need to say what we are all feeling.

If this gets to the kingdom, we won't survive.

It's time to make a plan to silence the Leviathan once and for all. I just need more time. Until then, things in the kingdom will have to change in order to keep everyone safe.

"We must instill mandatory curfews to make sure all are accounted for. No one out past tide change. We'll issue noise cancelers to civilians and post more guards along the border. No one comes in or out without my knowledge. We'll have the siren mages erect a sound wall over the kingdom," I say.

Heads nod, and I know this team will see to it. A sense of dread blooms in the water around us.

Our siren mages are powerful, but never have they created such a magical barrier expanding over the kingdom. This will test their abilities and spread them thin. It's unfortunate, but something we need done.

War has come to Tetria. It's time to see if she'll stand proud against her enemies. I hope Erin is the key to our victory like Atina and Ender claim.

But sealing the prison gates again doesn't come without risks. I'm one person with the strength of my human wife. Is that enough?

# CHAPTER 30

# ERIN

Allarick came home two days ago, though he might as well still be far away. I've seen very little of my husband since his return from the deep sea. He's pulled to our kingdom's borders, making sure the guards we placed there to protect our people know what to look and listen for. He's met with groups of sirens—those he calls mages—to help make some sort of sound barrier to surround our castle.

He's offered to bring me along, but I wouldn't be much help. I know little about defending our borders and knowing what to listen for. I would simply be a hindrance rather than a help, so I opted to stay at the castle and aid where needed.

It hasn't been bad though, minus missing Allarick. Iris has been glued to my side since the day Allarick left, and Delmare joined us as soon as he returned. I've grown fond of both of them, but especially Iris. She's become more than my maid, though I hesitate to say friend. I've never been good at making and keeping friends, and this new, fragile relationship is not something I'm willing to let slip through my fingers so easily.

Over the past two days, the castle has experienced more activity than normal. People complaining of headaches. Some claimed blackouts in their vision, losing entire hours. Many more took to the castle out of fear. With the uptick in guard presence and the fear of missing family members, the kingdom feels unsettled.

The role of queen is thrust upon me, whether I'm ready or not. For the first time in my life, people flock to me for support. I understood the fear breeding in the castle like a plague, the constant anxiety of not knowing what would come next. The general consensus is that Allarick will protect his people. But even supporters have their doubts. Everyone's trying to remain as positive as they can.

Today I've decided to open up the first floor of the castle to the public. I didn't run it by Allarick, but he said I had free rein to run things as I see fit. He trusts my judgment, which is refreshing. My fondness for him grows, especially during his absence.

The first floor of the castle is a large enough space to accommodate at least two hundred guests. Not that I think we'll have that many merpeople coming in for sanctuary, but I want to be prepared if we do. Iris helps me greet the merpeople and directs them to the kitchen for food. Delmare stays by my side throughout it all, and I'm glad for his presence because the merpeople look at me like a diamond in the rough. I'm a marvel they haven't seen in years, and everyone wants to question me. Delmare's job is to mostly steer them away, and he takes it very seriously.

Interestingly enough, their stares don't bother me like they once would have back in Grym Hollow. They aren't staring at my poorly concealed bruises or looking at me with pity. They don't see the sweet girl who fell in love with the wrong man. No, the merpeople stare at me out of curiosity and some with reverence. It's...nice.

"More than yesterday came. It seems like people aren't eager to spend their time outside," Iris says as another family and their pet sea turtle swim in.

"Can you blame them?" I ask softly, not wanting anyone to overhear us. "People are nervous. They aren't sure what's safe and aren't willing to risk their families."

The songs of the Leviathan have reached the outskirts of our borders. It happened so quickly after Allarick returned. The voices are getting stronger. Most merpeople can't hear the calls yet, which is a small relief. But a few civilians with exceptional hearing have made reports of a low buzzing call, hard to resist.

I fear for the day all of Tetria hears it and wonder if I'm doing enough.

"We need to lighten the mood, my queen. It's not good for morale." Iris frowns, hands clasped in front of her. She hasn't stopped swishing her tail since we arrived. I know she's on edge too. Just like most of the people in this room.

I rack my brain to think of something that might help soothe the crowd. At the very least, something that will provide a distraction. Visions of a pearly white instrument come to mind, and a thought occurs to me. I grin and quickly whirl on Delmare.

"Delmare, can you retrieve the harp from the music room and bring it out to the foyer? I think I would like to play." My fingers itch to strum the strings and hear the beautiful melody it makes. I haven't since our wedding night. Even then, it didn't last long because Allarick and I got distracted.

*Really* distracted.

Delmare nods, though he doesn't look eager to leave my side. "I'll wait right here with Iris until you return. Danika is right down the hall too. We'll be fine," I say to ease his worry.

"Of course. I'll be right back." Delmare bows and swims away to the music room, looking back to make sure I don't move. I can't help but notice Iris's eyes on him as he leaves. The way she stares longingly at him fills me with guilt because I've been occupying most of their time. As mates, I'm certain they would appreciate alone time.

Just like I would kill to have some alone time with my husband. Sacrifices must be made all around though.

A few moments later, Delmare swims out with the harp Allarick purchased for me on our wedding day and a stool for me to rest on while I play. He sets it up, and I thank him before taking a seat. "Music has a way of healing the soul. Do you think they'll mind if I play?"

Iris and Delmare share a glance, as if thinking it over. Iris smiles, though it doesn't reach her eyes. These last few days have done a number on her, and I know she's tired. "I don't think they'll mind at all, my queen. You often get an audience when you play. I think it'll be lovely and maybe even calm some of the restless guppies."

I survey the room, seeing stressed parents trying to corral their children, merpeople holding their heads as if fighting back a headache, and others chatting, but their body language is too stiff. True fear hasn't settled upon Tetria, rather a guarded caution. If I can make everyone's mood just a little brighter, then I've accomplished what I wanted to do.

Like always, my eyes close when I pluck the first string. It's a soft vibrato I let linger before picking back up the note. Music takes hold of me, and my fingers glide effortlessly. James really put a new meaning into starving artist after taking away my music. It felt like a piece of me was missing. A hole in my heart I couldn't fill no matter how hard I tried.

The commotion around me fades away as each note rings loudly in my ear. I play a song of happiness and hope. I don't stop at one though; my fingers eagerly pluck away at three more songs, all upbeat and full of hope because that is what we need right now.

When the last note hits, I exhale a deep sigh and sit back in my chair. My hands fall to my sides, and my eyes flicker open. The floor in front of me is suddenly occupied by a handful of children—guppies, as they call them. Merpeople who were once on the opposite side of the room have huddled close, a look of serenity on their faces.

Delmare isn't next to me anymore, and Iris is hunched over an older kraken who had been sitting alone in the corner, holding his head. He had one of the stronger headaches of the bunch and was slouched over in his chair all morning.

But now the same man stands tall, speaking excitedly to Iris. She nods and says something to the man I can't hear, then she hugs him. She visits two other merpeople who have all complained of headaches before swimming back to me.

"Are they okay? Do we need to call the healers?" I don't think I need to, judging by their smiles, but I offer anyway.

"No, my queen. Those three merpeople I spoke with all came in with horrible headaches. You remember? Slouched over in corners. Well, they said as soon as you started playing, their pain went away. Just like that," Iris says.

"Well, music is said to be healing." I smile, but Iris doesn't return it. She's too busy spewing about others who have made comments of relief.

"And a mother who couldn't get her newborn to sleep in days finally got the guppy to sleep. The woman was in tears, she was so happy."

My cheeks flush. Iris's tone teeters on excitement. I just don't understand why. She's happy, but also...suspicious? "Music is a good lullaby." I shrug, trying to brush off her words.

"There's more," a voice booms behind me, and I jump as Delmare reappears. "The siren by the window reported hearing a strange call earlier. The moment the music started, he stopped hearing it."

"Okay, well, that happens when you play music. You

tend to hear the sound closest to you." I laugh, trying to lighten the mood, but, in reality, my body is on alert. What are they getting at, and why do I feel like I'm in trouble? "Not to sound rude, but I'm not sure what you are insinuating."

Delmare and Iris do that thing where they look at each other and seemingly have an entire conversation with just their eyes. Part of me envies them for having such a strong love over the years, they can tell what the other is thinking without asking. Right now though, it's annoying.

Neither speak up at first, and the tension growing between us only heightens until Iris speaks. "We could be wrong, but we think your music might be healing."

Now it's my turn to stare. And stare. "You mean like... metaphorically?" Because she couldn't possibly mean anything else by it. Right?

Except the way she bites her lip and the way her tail fidgets from side to side speak a different story. "I'm not explaining this well," she says quickly. "Let's just wait for King Allarick to arrive so we can tell him what we observed."

I want to urge her to explain herself, but that's when I feel something slither around my midsection, pulling me back into a hard chest. Then a voice that stars in all of my dreams asks, "What have I missed?"

# CHAPTER 31

# ALLARICK

"Queen Erin's music has healing abilities," Iris blurts out the moment I have Erin wrapped in my embrace. Her body eases, only for a fraction of a second, before growing tense again at Iris's words.

They are interesting words indeed.

"She doesn't mean literally—" Erin starts to say but is swiftly interrupted by Iris again.

"No, I mean literally."

I feel the discomfort wafting off my wife and squeeze her tighter, hoping the pressure can provide a little comfort. She presses back against my chest, and I can't help myself. I lean down and kiss her neck. The soft whimper of surprise has my body on full alert.

I want to ask more about what Iris means, but Erin is obviously uncomfortable. This is a conversation better suited for just the two of us.

"Iris, Delmare, I see my wife has opened the castle for merpeople. Please attend to the guests. I need to steal my wife away. Please don't let anyone disturb us unless it's critical," I say, hoping we are allowed one night of rest.

"Of course," Delmare says.

Iris offers Erin an encouraging smile before I take my wife's hand and lead her away from civilians. I don't stop until I reach our private chambers on the second floor. Water drips down my body, pooling on the stone floor until I'm completely dry. Erin's eyes bore into me, and I let her drink her fill. It fills me with wicked satisfaction to have my wife lusting after me.

Being pulled out to secure our borders, I've seen very little of Erin. I waste no time getting her into our room and pulling her into bed, even though she hasn't completely dried off yet.

"Allarick!" She laughs, trying—and failing—to fight me off, but I pull her closer to my chest. "We've made a mess of our sheets," she complains.

"Not yet, we haven't." It's adorable to watch red flush her cheeks. She bites her lip but playfully swats at my chest. As much as I want to devour my wife, Iris's words ring through my mind.

"We should discuss what Iris said," I say after a moment.

Erin rolls her eyes. "It's really nothing. People like music and enjoy listening. It's not deeper than that."

"Perhaps," I say gently, not wanting to rile her up. "But your music is different from what I've heard played here before. It calls to you like that of a siren song."

Erin tilts her head up to look at me. "What do you mean?"

"The music played by our skilled musicians is beautiful and can be moving. But the way you play music, it's...different. It seeps into your skin, warming you from the inside out. Everything else fades away, and there's only your beautiful sound. It feels cleansing." There's no other way to describe it other than a full body and mind cleanse after a day of being pampered.

Erin seems to consider this, thrumming her fingers against my chest. After a pregnant pause, she asks, "So, you think my music holds magic? Real magic?"

"I don't think we should discount it. Ender saw magic in you. Knew you were destined to take up the throne alongside me. If this is your gift, you may very well help combat the song of the Leviathans."

"They're getting stronger," she says.

It's not a question, but I answer anyway. "They are. Which is why I think your music is so important to our people right now. It's not only beautiful, but healing."

"That only works if they can hear it." Erin props herself up with her elbow to look at me. "And I've been thinking... It could be dumb, so you don't have to agree to anything."

It's been a while since I've picked up on her insecurities about her ability to lead. Anger heats my body. Not at her, but at myself for not being around to give her the validation she rightfully deserves.

I cup Erin's cheeks, and she sucks in a deep breath, eyes downcast. "I will only say this once, sweet girl, but your opinion and guidance mean more to me than anything. Speak, and I'll hear you. I'll always hear you."

Erin's frown slowly spreads into a grin. "Careful, Allarick. You sound like you love me."

"You make it easy to love you." The words come out so effortlessly. It's not a loud declaration of love, or even a fancy one. It's soft. New. Fragile.

Erin's lips part as she opens and closes her mouth, looking like the fish swimming through Tetria. She doesn't have the words, and that's okay. She doesn't have to return the sentiment. I'm a competitive man, and when my sights are set on something, I'll do anything I can to achieve it. Earning Erin's love will be the most rewarding prize yet.

Erin clears her throat, quickly getting us back on topic. "If the song is getting stronger, I think we need to take protective measures now before it's too late. Not just mandatory curfews and border cutoffs."

"What do you propose?"

"Well, I don't really have all the logistics for it yet. I'm not entirely sure it's possible, but I think we should open the castle for families to move into temporarily, not just someplace they can spend the day at. This would help eliminate missing family members and keep people safe. From the sounds of it, some merpeople are already picking up the song. Pretty soon, it will do more damage than just a headache."

I consider her suggestion. The castle is grand, built to host and house many sea creatures. We wouldn't be able to supply everyone a private room, but we could provide meals, shelter, and security. It's not a bad idea, especially since the song is becoming more than just a nuisance. I want to attack the noise head-on, but the civilians need safety in the meantime.

Not every merperson will come. I have stubborn

subjects, but perhaps those who choose to remain outside the castle will help guard our borders against the Leviathan.

"It would only be temporary. Until we can seal the gates off," Erin adds, but I don't need any further convincing.

"We will prepare the castle tomorrow."

The smile Erin gives me melts my heart. It's pure joy and excitement. "Really?"

"Really. I think that's an excellent call to keep our people safe until we can rid our waters of the Leviathan. I've spoken to the siren mages, and they will continue to strengthen the sound barrier. That, coupled with your suggestion, is our best chance at keeping our people safe." I trail my hand down her back soothingly. "Your people are in debt to your brilliance."

"Just my people?" she asks coyly, trailing a hand down my chest.

The fire reignites within me, feeling every inch of her touch. "Your husband as well." I roll over, capturing Erin underneath me. Her legs spread for me so I can settle easily between them. "Do you wish for me to show you how thankful I am, my queen?"

Again, Erin bites her lip, but this time, I lean down and suck it into my mouth. We moan in unison, her body responding to mine as she arches into me. "I wouldn't be opposed," she says, almost breathlessly.

"You know, the first time I had my tentacle inside your pussy, I was jealous." I kiss down her chest, stopping to kiss both nipples through her shirt. Even covered, I feel the hard nubs.

"J-jealous? Of what?" she asks.

I continue my descent to her form-fitting pants that save little for the imagination. Every dip and curve of her body is on full display, though the mound of her pussy is hidden behind the black material. "Jealous of the fact that it wasn't my tongue fucking his queen. Not knowing what you taste like."

"Allarick..." she moans, reaching for me. I catch her wrist in my hand, gently stroking her palm with my thumb.

"I'm going to feast on this pussy, Wife. If you want me to stop, tell me now." I wait for her to push me away. Wait for her to tell me no.

She doesn't.

I smirk.

"Good girl. Now, put your arms above your head. Hold on to the headboard. Can you do that for me?"

Erin obeys my command. I let her hand go, and she shivers. Her arms go above her head, and she grips the bedpost, chest heaving in what I hope is anticipation. For a moment, I allow myself to wonder what it would be like to have her tied to the bed. Would she let me? Trust me enough?

It's something I want to explore later on.

My thumb hooks in the waistband of her pants. "Consider this an apology also. For working late hours and spending little time with my new wife." In one swift motion, I have her pants pulled down, exposing her entirely. Her pussy gleams with her eagerness.

"This is the only way I'll accept apologies," she says breathlessly.

I chuckle low in the back of my throat, parting her legs. "Noted." The scent of her pleasure hits me, and I groan. I'm a starving man with no patience. I grab her thighs, keeping her spread for me, but I flick my tongue out and lick up her seam.

The strangled moan that leaves Erin's lips spurs me on. I lap at her wetness, her tangy taste coating my tongue. I'm a man undone. The need to hear her moan and make her come on my face is strong. "You taste so good, sweet girl."

"I do?"

"Delicious. Has no one ever told you that before?" I remove one hand from her thigh to part her folds.

Erin blushes. "Uhm, no. No one has... James didn't like..."

I stop what I'm doing and gaze up at her. "Knowing that no one has feasted on this pussy is criminal. But I can't deny that I love being the only one who has tasted you."

Before she can respond, I suck her clit into my mouth. Her hips jerk up, and she grinds her sweet pussy against me. I tease her with my tongue, eating her out in earnest. Erin moans, and her hand comes back down to rest on the back of my head.

I stop immediately. "Hands on the headboard frame, beautiful," I remind.

"I want to touch you, Allarick," she whines, and I'm tempted to give in. But my need and desire for her complete obedience overwhelm me.

"And you will. But not now. Headboard, sweet girl. Now," I say gently yet firmly.

Erin pouts but ultimately listens to me. "You're a bossy apologizer."

"I like to think I'm a *thorough* apologizer," I punctuate my words with another lick to her seam. Erin moans and tries to close her legs, but I keep her spread wide.

My cock is hard, needing to feel her stretched around me. I remind my dick that this isn't about me. This is about my wife. She can come on my cock later.

Erin's moans only get louder. I roll my tongue over her clit and press two fingers inside her. She's so wet, they slide in easily, and she clenches around them. "That's right, sweet girl. Take your pleasure."

"Fuck...Allarick." She grinds down on my fingers, riding them as if it were my cock. Or tentacle. My wife is fond of those.

I help coax her to her first orgasm, switching between licking and sucking and fucking her with my fingers. It's too much, and soon Erin moans my name and tightens around my fingers. I lap at her sweet cunt, licking the evidence of her orgasm away.

When I pull back, I'm sure my mouth is shiny with her release, but Erin doesn't seem to care because she quickly lets go of the headboard and reaches for me. This time, I let her, and our lips meet in a clash for dominance. She submits to me, parting her lips as I thrust in my tongue, letting her taste herself. She does so eagerly.

"Best apology and show of gratitude ever," she pants once we break apart.

I have to say, I agree.

# CHAPTER 32

# ALLARICK

After Erin's suggestion last night, it was time to see my queen's plan take motion. When she fell asleep after I ate her out for the second time, because once wasn't enough, I slipped away to find Delmare. The poor bastard was eating a very late dinner with his wife. I nearly turned around to leave him to his night, but Iris noticed my presence.

We spoke in hushed, urgent whispers about the plan to open up the castle. Delmare is my most sensible guard, and even he saw the logic behind Erin's plans. Iris, though not part of my guards, is still a valuable employee of the crown and agreed to help Delmare carry out the plan.

We spent our night recruiting guards to help set up family spaces and prepare the castle for our citizens. The normal furniture was stripped from the bottom story and carried out to storage. Cots and storage were set up throughout the ballroom and greeting room. A healing center was set up in the dining room.

We worked well into the night.

When I finally got back to bed, I laid my head down, pulled Erin close, and fell asleep.

It didn't last long.

Movement in the room causes me to stir. My lids feel heavy, not ready to wake up. Absentmindedly, I reach out for Erin next to me, but the bed is empty. That's when my eyes snap open to see her side of the bed. Growing alarm wakes my body immediately.

I jolt out of bed. "Erin?"

"Allarick," a sweet voice cuts through my fear, and a soft hand touches my arm. Turning my head, I see Erin's kind face staring down at me. I'm again hit with just how beautiful this woman is. How could anyone have her and want to cause her harm? If I'm ever able to ask one more thing of Ender, it will be to bring James here so I can dole out my own justice.

"I didn't mean to wake you. You looked like you could use more sleep." Erin reaches out to caress my face. I'm tempted to wrap my arms around her waist and pull her back into bed.

Except we have too much to do today.

And she's right, I am exhausted. But I've worked on less sleep. "People will be coming in today." I kick off the blanket.

Erin nods, not looking surprised. "Iris has been here. She told me what you did last night." A small smile spreads across her lips. She leans in and kisses me gently. "Thank you for listening to me."

"Of course. You had a great idea to keep our people safe. It's only temporary until we hear back from Atina."

"Have you heard anything from her?" she asks.

I frown, shaking my head. "No. It concerns me. I figured we would hear from her by now." Sending guards out to track her down has crossed my mind more than once, but if I'm overreacting and she's fine, Atina will be pissed I sent people from the sea after her, considering her history with us.

"I'm sure we will soon," Erin assures, squeezing my shoulder. "You should rest up some more. Delmare is waiting outside to take me down to the first floor. I can meet you there later."

"I'll come," I say.

Erin looks like she wants to argue but nods after a moment.

Five minutes later, Erin and I meet Delmare and make our way to the first floor, hand in hand. I didn't know what to expect, not sure if my people would be willing to leave their homes and come here. The last thing I want is to cause mass hysteria, so part of me fears what I'm walking into.

Merpeople, sirens, krakens, and a few sea creature pets crowd the lower levels. My staff show families to cots and where to store their belongings. There's a whirlwind of activity, but none of it is disorderly or filled with a sense of dread. It's more a matter of logistics. Like knowing where to house each person and figuring out the needs of the civilian.

A family of three swim by, a mother with her two rambunctious mermaid daughters. She holds one, trying to soothe the crying guppy, while the other one drags behind her. The older daughter, only a year or so older than the small guppy in the mother's arms, whines in attempt to get the mother's attention. It's clear the mother is flustered, trying to corral her daughters during this hectic time.

I'm about to jump in, but Erin beats me to it. "Let me help," she says and swims over to scoop up the young mermaid. The girl looks up at her with large eyes. "What's your name, sweetheart?"

The girl turns to her mother, as if asking permission to tell Erin her name. The mother gives her an encouraging nod. "Gabriella," the child says softly.

"Gabriella. That's a beautiful name. How old are you?" my wife asks.

Gabriella holds up four fingers.

"Oh my, you are such a big girl. Do you mind if I help your mommy take you to your own cot? You know, I bet I could find some toys somewhere in this castle. Do you think you could help me?"

Gabriella's eyes light up. A big smile spreads across her lips. "I can help! I love toys." She starts to talk about the coral animals she has back at her home.

The mother's body visibly relaxes. Moments ago, she had looked on the verge of tears trying to juggle two small children alone. "Thank you, my queen. Thank you so much," the woman praises, barely restraining her emotions.

Erin's cheeks redden as she smiles shyly. "Of course. Is it okay if she comes with me to find toys? I'm sure some of the other children will want to play too."

"Yes, of course. Our cot is the last one in the ballroom. Right by the east doors."

"East doors. Got it." Erin nods. Then she looks down at the child in her arms and whispers something to her that causes Gabriella to laugh. My brain conjures up an image of Erin, with our child on her hip and one on the way. It's a beautiful future I desperately want.

One day.

We just need to survive the Leviathan and Nephilim.

That's the last I see of my wife throughout the rest of the day. I catch glimpses of her, and each time, she has another child following her. Iris helped her find my old toys from childhood, and they passed them out to the kids. They haven't stopped following after her since.

Other times, while helping our people to their cots or showing them where to go for food, I would hear soft but upbeat music playing. I caught a few of the guppies shaking their tails or swinging their tentacles around happily to the music. I knew Erin was playing because no one plays quite like her, and the sound created a sense of peace that swept through the crowds.

I finish up leading an older kraken to the healers for a headache when Delmare finds me. "My king, all cots are accounted for. If we have more people come in, we will need to figure out where to put them."

"My office. I already sent a few maids to get it ready. We turn no one away." I need to make myself clear for safety purposes. Not everyone has the abilities to defend themselves in their home. They deserve to seek sanctuary here and will not be punished simply because they didn't arrive earlier.

"Of course. Those who are staying behind, shall I

send a group of guards out to ask if they wish to volunteer for the watch?"

I nod. "Make sure everyone outside this castle has noise cancelers. Volunteer or not."

"Yes, my king."

"And, Delmare," I start. Delmare looks at me intensely. "Have you heard from my sister?"

Delmare's shoulders droop, and I have my answer before he speaks. "No. We've heard nothing from Atina. Shall I see if I can track her down?"

"Not yet. If we don't hear from her in a few days, I'll send you. Be ready."

Delmare bows. "Of course. I'm sure we will hear from Princess Atina soon."

I hope he's right.

# CHAPTER 33
# ERIN

I've never had so many children following me and begging me to play music. Honestly, I'm flattered. I've never had such a captive audience before. By the end of the third day, I swore my fingertips would fall off. It was all worth it, though. The music provided these kids and their parents some much-needed relief from the outside world.

Allarick has grown more worried over the last few days. A faint buzzing has made its way past our sound barrier, which I'm told is expected but keeps the noise at almost a silent volume. We have still not heard from Atina, which puts Allarick on edge, and none of us can afford to leave the castle to find her. I wish I could make him feel better, but nothing I can do will bring him peace of mind.

We also rarely have time alone. It's a small sacrifice to pay to keep Tetria safe, but I would be lying if I said I don't miss my husband.

This evening, we both find ourselves in the dining

room after I left Iris to attend to those in the ballroom. The staff has created a buffet line for meals. It's the most effective way to get meals out to everyone, as long as we keep the menu fairly simple. I've never had so much seaweed salad in my life. I would kill for a greasy burger and fries. I doubt that will fare well in the ocean though.

Allarick helps dish up plates by the time I bring the children in for the line. I make sure they are with their families before I swim over to my husband. He doesn't notice me at first, too focused on his task at hand. He smiles kindly to everyone he serves, giving assurances when someone speaks their fears about the impending Leviathan song.

I never thought much about what it means to be a king. Never had a reason to. Grym Hollow doesn't have kings and queens. It's full of regular people with mundane jobs—if you don't count The Guardian.

But when I look at Allarick, I see selflessness, humility, kindness, and love for his people and kingdom. All things I would say constitute a good king. I'm not sure when my feelings for him have changed, but this deep, floaty feeling can only be described in one word.

Love.

And I think I'm finally ready to admit that, but it doesn't seem like the right time while we are in this predicament. For now, my feelings for Allarick will be my own little wonderful secret.

I wait until the line dies down before approaching Allarick. I come up behind him and wrap my arms around him. His rigid posture instantly relaxes in my embrace. A tentacle wraps around my waist, keeping me close.

"Sweet girl." His voice is a purr, sending tingles down my body. "I've missed you."

"I've missed you too," I whisper. We saw each other last night and this morning when we woke up, but it still feels like a lifetime ago when we had time together. My mind wanders back to the cabin when it was only him and me. A part of me wishes to go back, but as long as Tetria is in danger, that won't be a possibility.

"Have you eaten?" Allarick asks.

My stomach rumbles, but looking at the same meal we've had the last few days, I can't muster up the will to eat. "Maybe later," I say instead.

I loosen my hold on Allarick, and he turns so we are chest to chest. Another tentacle wraps around my arm, and I feel so safe and secure. Who knew it would take a kraken with tentacles to make me feel this way?

Allarick runs his hands down my arms, down to my hands. His thumb brushes over the small abrasions on my fingers. He frowns, looking down at my injuries from playing harp as if they are a stab wound and not just a simple annoyance.

"The kids like to hear the music. It's helping everyone calm down and not think about the Leviathan," I explain.

Allarick brings each of my fingers to his lips and kisses them all one by one. This man fills me with butterflies. I've had his tentacles inside me, yet this somehow feels like the most intimate thing we've done.

"I'll rub a healing lotion into your hands tonight," he promises.

"Usually they don't get this bad. It's just been a long time since I've played like this." Back when I started learning the harp, I would make my fingers bleed and have to wait a few days before I could play again. Eventually, my fingers got used to the rough treatment, and it didn't bother me anymore.

"You've been incredible," Allarick's voice is soft, full of reverence, "through all of this. You've been thrown into a war that is not your own and cared for people you hardly know. A true queen is measured by her ability to care for others. Tetria couldn't have asked for a better queen."

Allarick stares at me like he's seeing me for the first time. My chest flutters, heart pounding so loudly, I'm sure he hears it. The tension between us sizzles, and I gravitate toward him. "Erin, I need to tell you something."

"Yes?" My voice is breathier than I intend, gaze dropping to his plump lips. All other thoughts fly out my mind, replaced with the need for him to kiss me.

"Erin, I—"

I never find out what Allarick is going to say because, the next moment, guards flood into the room. In the center of them is a disgruntled merman who looks vaguely familiar. The man pants like he's been swimming for a long time and is about to keel over.

"Nori? What is it? Did my sister send you?" Allarick's voice booms from next to me. It isn't until he speaks that I recognize this man. Nori is one of Atina's men. A man who can walk between the sea and water, like Allarick and some of the other merpeople can do.

The entire room goes silent when Nori speaks words that send a sinister chill down my spine. "I bring news from your sister. She wants you to know that attacks are coming. Get your people to safety. Her ships are on their way."

"What do you mean? What is coming?" Allarick demands, moving past me to get closer to Nori.

But Nori doesn't get the chance to tell us. Because, at that moment, a thunderous noise erupts, like something heavy just hit a cement wall, followed by bloodcurdling screams.

# CHAPTER 34

# ERIN

I scream. My voice is lost in the cacophony of sounds all around me. It was like a switch was flipped. One moment everyone was calmly eating their meals with their family or friends, and the next, people are swimming in every direction, screaming. Chaos erupts around us.

Someone pulls me away from Allarick, and I struggle against the hand. "My queen, it's just me! We need to get you to safety. Now!" Delmare's voice roars above the noise.

I turn my head, expecting to see Allarick where we left him, but my husband is gone.

"Allarick!" I scream.

"He's fine, my queen. He knows how to defend himself. We must get you to safety," Delmare repeats. He pulls me along, head darting from side to side. It takes me a moment to realize he's not just looking for safety, but his wife as well.

"Iris was in the ballroom." I reach out for the large

golden mermaid statue outside the dining room. Delmare pulls my arm, but my grip on the statue is unwavering. "Please, just tell me what's going on. I don't want to hide. Allarick needs me."

"You are a liability," he says, not unkindly. "I must get you to safety."

How can I hide when people I know are scared for their lives? What kind of queen turns her back on her people when she gets scared? It's not the queen I want to be, and it's not the queen Tetria needs. I've done enough hiding in my lifetime, I refuse to turn my back on people who need me.

Resignation washes over Delmare, and he runs a hand through his salt-and-pepper hair. "Sharks are attacking," he says at last. "They are trying to break the sound barrier."

I suck in a deep breath. Delmare doesn't need to tell me why this would be catastrophic for the kingdom. If the sound barrier keeping the Leviathan's song is destroyed, many will follow the song. These creatures keep getting stronger each time a person goes missing, and I fear they'll break out of the prison they're held inside if they take more of us.

Another loud crash shakes the foundation of the castle. I'm jerked away from the statue and into Delmare, who catches me. A white blur catches my attention from the corner of my eye, and I snap my head in attention. The light from the floor-to-ceiling window at the end of the hall darkens as a huge great white shark swims by.

Followed by three more.

Fear threatens to immobilize me. Until one of the

sharks rams itself forward. For a minute, I think the shark will break the window and come for Delmare and me. But it doesn't. It stops just outside the window, slamming against something. White, murky water ripples from the spot the shark just hit. "Is that the…"

"Sound barrier," Delmare says just as the shark rams against the barrier again. Only this time, a soft hum makes its way through.

People scream, scrambling to find their loved ones and cover their ears. Again and again, sharks ram the barrier, and more of the deadly hum pierces the castle. My body stiffens, and the sound grates on my nerves. I don't feel compelled to follow the sound, but I do feel compelled to block it.

I need to do something. Standing here like a fool isn't helpful. I can't fight, but I have other skills—none I can think of that would be helpful at this moment, but there has to be something. Something I can do to help my people.

Then something dawns on me. A moment of clarity.

Music.

My strength is music. It always has been.

I whirl on Delmare. "Remember when Iris said my music is healing?"

The question catches the kraken off guard, but he nods.

"Do you believe that too?"

This time there's no hesitation as he says, "Yes."

"Then take me to my harp. Or piano. Whichever is closer."

Delmare purses his lips in a firm line but nods. I

expected him to argue with me, but even he fears our current situation. I allow him to take my hand and pull me toward the dining room, the last place I used my harp right before I started helping the guppies get food.

We pass people crying, holding on to one another. We pass more trying to get out, but guards block the doors. Some already have a glazed look on their face, attempting to leave the castle any way they can. I don't see Allarick though.

He's okay. He has to be okay.

Delmare pushes past a few men stopped by a group of guards, begging to be let out. The guards don't budge, and I can't blame either party. Needing to run to safety is human—and apparently, merpeople—nature. But keeping everyone together within the last of our defenses is equally important.

Delmare makes his way through the throngs of merpeople until we reach my harp. Amongst the chaos, the instrument has not been touched. Simply forgotten and ignored.

I hesitate as soon as I see it. What if I'm wrong? What if my music can't overpower the sounds of the Leviathan? This could be a foolish mistake, but what other option do I have?

Strengthening my resolve, I take a seat on the stool next to my harp. Delmare stays rigid in place, his eyes scanning the room, looking for a certain blue-haired maid. "Go find her."

"Hmm?" Delmare asks distractedly.

"Your wife. Go find her."

At that, Delmare snaps to attention, turning into the

perfect soldier. "I won't leave you. Iris will be fine," he says, but his voice wavers, so I reach out for his hand.

"Go. I'll be right here playing. I won't move," I promise him.

For a moment, I don't think he'll listen to me. Stubborn kraken. He wars with himself until finally he lets out a sigh. "Gavin!" he barks at a nearby guard.

Gavin, a red-haired merman, stands at attention. He scurries over and salutes Delmare. "Yes, sir?"

"Watch your queen. If anything happens to her, what I do to you will be child's play compared to what the king will do," Delmare threatens.

Gavin pales, nodding like an obedient bobblehead. "Yes, sir. I won't let you down."

"See that you don't," Delmare huffs. Before he takes off, he spares me one last glance. "Play. Don't stop unless your life is in danger."

Sound advice.

I watch Delmare swim off. Gavin swims close to me, taking his job seriously. I try to ignore him as I close my eyes, centering myself. It's hard to block out the screaming and cries. The palpable fear is harder to block out, but I do my best.

My tired fingers pluck the first string, and the note reverberates around me. Just like every time, the music transports me to another place, where all I see and feel is the melody come to life. It's a soft, upbeat song with intricate finger work. These are my favorite pieces to play because of how challenging they are, with the constant movement of my hands to find the right note.

I play two songs in a row without opening my eyes. I

could say it's because the music swept me away, but the truth is I'm scared to see. I'm scared to look around and see failure. Or worse. Like, while I was playing, my people were slain. Logically, I know that's not the case, but my brain instantly goes to the worst-case scenario.

Despite my fears, I force my eyes open, fingers still dancing along the strings. Soft notes keep me calm as I look around the room. There is still plenty of fear. I have not taken that away. But the room has changed.

The group of irate and scared merpeople who were demanding to be let out no longer crowd the guards. Merpeople aren't swimming around, adding to the discord. People huddle in groups, gathering all around the room with their loved ones. Panicked and tear-stained eyes all stare at me.

In that time, Delmare returned, standing with Iris at his side. My maid offers a weak smile, clearly spooked as she holds on to her husband. "Keep playing," she whispers.

"Is it helping?" Despite the tense calm of the room, I don't know if my playing is actually effective. Even as I ask, I don't notice anyone nearby with glazed eyes trying to chase after the call. That has to mean something.

"Very. You're blocking out the song of the Leviathan," Delmare answers. "Please, my queen. Keep playing. It's the only thing keeping this room together."

I sweep the room once more, looking at all the faces depending on me. Men. Women. Children. It's intimidating, to say the least, but I don't want these people to hurt any more than they already do.

So, I play. And don't stop once.

# CHAPTER 35

# ALLARICK

I'm ripped away from Erin, pulled in the opposite direction. Delmare comes into view. He grabs Erin and pulls her out of the room, doing exactly what is expected of him. Protecting the queen.

The fear and confusion on Erin's face cut deep. I want nothing more than to go after her and promise her she's safe. Except my words won't be true. Only my actions can guarantee her safety, which is what spurs me on.

"We need to move, Allarick!" the voice from next to me booms. There's only one person here who wouldn't bother with royal titles.

My suspicions are confirmed when I turn to see Nori, Atina's crewmember, leading me out of the dining room. His usual calm demeanor is replaced with stoic urgency. I don't give a shit that he didn't use my title when speaking to me. But I care deeply that he clearly knows more than he's letting on.

"Tell me what is happening, Nori," I growl, ripping

out of his grasp. Chaos ensues all around us as merpeople attempt to gather their family and flee.

"The Leviathan's song has grown stronger, affecting sea life. We've seen changes in the animals and heard whisperings about attacks from various sea creatures. We didn't realize this until the problem was nearly at your front door. Atina asked me to swim ahead and let you know what is happening."

Just as Nori speaks the last word, a loud boom crashes around the hallway. I spot the reason for the sound immediately. Above us is a sixteen-foot predator, a shark with white, milky eyes and scars along his under-belly that look fresh. The shark swims around before zeroing in on our invisible sound barrier.

He rams it.

He rams it again and again until murky bits of the magic begin to crumble. Our only barrier between us and the Leviathan is on the verge of collapsing completely. Singing filters in through the cracks.

It's there and gone in the next second as the barrier struggles to knit itself back together, but not before the song gets under my skin. It was a pull. A *strong* pull. One that, if it went on longer, I don't think I would have been able to ignore it.

Seeing the stunned faces of guards and merpeople around me, I'm not alone.

Siren mages rush to the front line, singing their own magical songs to strengthen the barrier in hopes to buy us some more time.

Nori shoves something in my hand. "You'll want to wear these."

In my hand are two sound cancelers, different from the ones I issued. These are made with a different, firmer material and better shaped for ears.

"From above land. Should be stronger," Nori answers my unasked question. I shove them in my ears. They block out a lot of the noise, but not all of it.

Crying and screaming merpeople push their way to the doors, demanding their release. Sharks of all sizes and species ram against the invisible barrier. It's not meant to withstand attacks, meaning we are living on borrowed time. It will soon fail.

And everyone around us will be in danger.

"Nori, gather a few guards and issue noise cancelers to people who don't have them," I bark out, knowing Nori doesn't answer to me. He answers to Atina. Still, the man nods and rushes off to do as I say.

So much is happening at once. The screams from my people. The barks to "get back" and "calm down" from the guards. The guppies crying. The constant attacks by the sharks.

Through all of this, I hope Erin is okay. Delmare is a good man. I know he'll take care of her until his dying breath.

A new sound assaults my senses: a terrible ripping sound, like a limb being separated from the body. It's so loud, it makes everyone stop in their tracks.

I jerk my head up just in time to see the last of the barrier fail, no longer able to hold its magic from the shark attacks. It blinks once and then crumbles out of existence. Mage sirens slump to the floor, exhausting all their energy.

And then, for one glorious second, silence.

Until the song starts.

Even with the noise cancelers Nori gave me, I can still hear the low thrum of sound and the nagging pull to listen to their cries.

All around me, people scramble to block out the song. Guppies scream as if in pain. It's a harrowing sound. Death itself has paid a visit to us today. The real question is how many he'll take with him by the time this is all over.

Without further stalling, I rush to the nearest guard and take his sword from his sheath. He can find others in the armory, but I don't have time to make the trip myself.

Sharks swarm the castle, breaking through windows and crashing through doors. We live in peace with all creatures of the sea. A coexistence we have cultivated over millennia. But tonight, we are forced to be enemies. The Leviathan's song is growing impossibly strong if they can control these massive beasts.

I try to reach out to them, but my call is blocked. Again and again, I can't get through. Then a shark lunges for civilians. Its large, jagged teeth bite into a merman's arms. He screams, flailing, but it only makes things worse.

Later, I will beg the sea goddess for forgiveness.

Later, I will atone for the atrocities I will commit today.

But right now, I plunge my sword through the shark's rubbery skin. It's tough and not easy to cut through. I muster all my strength to push the sword in deeper until it comes out the other side.

Someone screams.

I think it's me.

The shark twists in my direction, causing my sword to slice through him. Blood colors the water around us until I can no longer see through the cloud of red.

The shark stops struggling and sinks to the floor.

Dead.

Because of me.

Because I killed it.

More sharks attack, and screams of pain nearly drown out the Leviathan's song. Nearly.

Guards take up arms against our cousins of the sea, slaying them in our own home. It's a massacre. Them versus us.

With each wound inflicted, my soul dies a little. The water bleeds red. A few guards try to spare their lives, but these creatures are relentless and not in control of their own bodies. They won't stop, despite the injuries given to them. Nothing but death—of the sharks or the Leviathan—will keep them away. My guards have no choice. It's kill or be killed.

Another shark comes from the red mist, right for me. I barely dodge its attack and swim out of the way. The shark hits another guard. A new recruit who started six months ago. The young kraken barely registers the hard impact of the shark.

The guard turns his head, and his eyes are the same color of murky white as the shark's. I check his ears but see he's not wearing any noise cancelers. He starts to swim toward the exit of the castle. None of the other sharks pay him any mind. They let him pass.

The young kraken isn't the only one. More people swim unprovoked through the castle. Not screaming or fighting. Eerily quiet as they all swim in the same direction. Each one of them with the glazed-over look on their face.

"HEY!" I scream, trying to get their attention. Anyone's attention. But none look back. It's as if I'm no longer here.

I feel powerless to help my people.

I can't let the feeling of defeat overtake me. I channel all of my fears into my attacks. It's not a good strategy. Fighting without a clear and sound mind is sloppy work at best and death at worst.

With each shark I cut down, three more take its spot. It's like we have the entire ocean at our front door. The water is almost too red to see through. Only dark shadows hint at where sharks could be. It's getting harder to make out who is friend and who is foe.

My body is already fatigued. I'm not sure how much longer I can keep the sharks at bay and from hurting any more of my people. A shark to my left swims straight toward me.

I lift the sword up.

The creature moves faster.

I'm ready.

But before the shark can make contact, and before I bring my sword down upon him...it stops.

The fog in the shark's eyes disappears as if never there. It looks disoriented, not sure where it is and why it's here. I no longer feel the blockage in its mind. The frightened shark glances at me before turning tail and swimming out of the castle.

I scan the room—what I can see of it, anyway—and more sharks follow in its wake. Guards and merpeople who had similar hazy expressions suddenly stop what they're doing. A mixture of horror and panic crosses their faces as they look around to see what happened.

What changed?

I hesitate but slowly pull out one of the noise cancelers. Music hits my senses, filling me with warmth and tranquility. It's not the song of the Leviathan; this is different. Happy. Welcoming. Beautiful. Safe.

Erin.

I know it's her. It has to be her.

My body moves on its own volition, carrying me to the music. To Erin. Getting there isn't easy. Broken glass and statues clutter the path. Dead sharks that need a proper funeral also litter the way toward Erin. They deserve better than that. I will atone for what I did later.

Right now, I need to get to Erin.

I maneuver my way through the throngs of merpeople, all gathered around my wife, blocking my view. I push myself to the front of the crowd and sag in relief when I see her. Safe and untouched. My sweet girl.

Erin sits on her bench, lost in the music she creates with her harp. Delmare and Iris stand behind her, keeping back anyone who gets too close. We spoke of Erin's ability to captivate an audience with her music and how it holds magic in the tune. I fully believed that, but I never thought about the music blocking out the Leviathan and bringing people out of their hold. Where I once thought her music brought only comfort, I know now she can counteract the singing.

Pride, love, and devotion for Erin swirl in my chest, making me choke on the affection I have for my wife.

But it's gone all too soon.

Because I know Erin can't do this forever. My people need a safe place, and Tetria isn't safe. Maybe one day it will be, but I can't risk the civilians. I can't risk Erin.

My sister's words from the tavern come back to me. Only a member of the royal family can close the gate to keep the Leviathan locked away. Erin has made me stronger. She has protected our people. My wife has done her job, and now it's time for me to do mine. I've waited long enough. There's no safest way to do this; it simply needs to be done.

I know what I must do now.

I have to break Erin's heart to save my wife and our people.

# CHAPTER 36

# ERIN

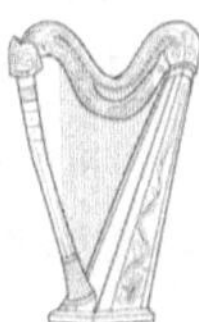

There's a hand on my back. No...not a hand. A tentacle. It caresses my shoulder and moves down to my hip. I shiver at his touch, knowing it intimately. My fingers hesitate over the strings of the harp. A lost note hangs between us.

Then I remember I can't get distracted. Not from fear or because my husband touches me.

But he's here. He's alright. He has to be.

I spare a glance over my shoulder, expecting to see my put-together husband, his warm smile and kind eyes.

The man behind me is Allarick, but not a version of him I've seen before.

Hollow eyes and a tight smile that looks painfully forced. A deep crimson stain colors his chest.

Blood.

His blood?

A sword swings at his side, clean except for dark flecks hanging off the blade. It strikes me that I've never seen Allarick with a weapon before. I should have known he would know how to fight, but seeing the evidence for myself makes my breath hitch. He looks frightening.

Sensing my poorly concealed alarm, Allarick leans down and presses a tender kiss to my lips. He lingers for a moment and reluctantly pulls back.

"Keep playing, sweet girl. Just a little longer." His voice is gruff, tired even. Maybe even melancholy. Dread settles over me, but I can't figure out why. Something just feels...off.

"My king?" Delmare questions, ready to take orders.

Allarick sighs. He brings both of his hands to my arms, rubbing me absentmindedly. I'm not sure he even realizes he's doing it, but I hope it brings him a semblance of comfort.

"We need to get our people out. Erin's music is the only defense we have against the Leviathan down here. She can't play forever," Allarick says.

I knew this would be a logical next step, but it still feels like a blow. Uprooting and displacing everyone will be no easy task and still won't solve our problem. True fear chills my body—something I haven't felt since leaving James.

"We need to test out Atina's theory. We must meet the Leviathan where they're at and shut the gate for good," Allarick says.

All color drains from Delmare's face. It's the first time I've seen the large, tough guard scared. It does little to quell the growing fear.

"So, what does that mean? What do we do?" The questions leave my mouth without second thought. If there's a plan set in place, my mind can focus on something else. It would give us a purpose. I continue with my music, making sure not to miss even a small note.

"We have an evacuation plan in place in case of disasters. I never thought we would actually have to use it, but..." Allarick trails off, a tortured expression on his face. He hates this as much as I do.

Allarick then looks down at me, squeezing my arms gently. "Do you remember the cove I took you to while we stayed at Atina's cabin?"

The cove he took me to while I was in the midst of a panic attack. He took me into the water and held me until I calmed down. I nod slowly.

"There are more coves similar to that along the coast and safe cabins located on the outskirts of the wolf and dragon territories. The ones surrounding my sister's cabin. Those who are able to stay on land will take the cabins. Those who need to stay in the water can stay on the rocks or in caves in the coves, close to land. I'm going to need your help though, sweet girl," Allarick says.

I don't have to think. I just nod. "Anything. Whatever you need."

"Keep playing."

It is the simplest of instructions, and yet it carries a heavy weight. I need to play to keep Tetria safe. No matter how badly my fingers hurt from the strings, or the way my back has started to ache from my horrible posture. Those are all small sacrifices in the grand scheme of things.

"What is it you need of me, my king?" Delmare asks, gripping Iris's hand. It is clear, whatever he does, his wife will be at his side.

If Allarick sees this, he clearly doesn't mind since he makes no comment. "We need to lead the people out of the castle to the current behind the city. It will lead everyone to the surface the quickest. Guards need to be stationed at the front and back of the groups. Have a few guards stay behind to accompany me to the Leviathan's prison. But warn them of the dangers and risks."

Delmare, ever the faithful servant, nods. He takes Iris, and the two of them head toward a group of guards to carry out Allarick's order.

Allarick looks at me. "I need to help them—"

"Go. I'll be okay," I say after seeing his hesitation. I want to hug him. To kiss him and make him see that I'm fine. But I'd have to stop playing, so I stay where I'm at, plucking the strings of my harp.

"I'm sorry, Erin." The distress in his voice hurts, but when I look up, Allarick is already gone. I can't tell him he has nothing to apologize for.

I'm not sure how long I stay here, playing any song that comes to my mind. It reminds me of my recital days, when I would play for an hour in front of a large crowd. None of those recitals ever held such high stakes before.

The tension in the room is palpable. Whatever comfort my music brings people is fragile, threatening to break at any time. Mothers grab their children. Lovers reach out for each other. Families crowd together. The guards attempt to keep the crowd calm as they direct them safely out of the castle.

Slowly, the packed room empties until I'm playing for an audience of one. The last guard remaining has something stuffed in his ears. He should be safe from the siren's call, but I don't want to risk it until Allarick comes back.

It takes another ten minutes before my husband returns with Delmare at his heels. Iris is no longer with him, so I can only assume my maid left with the others. Good. She needed to be where she's safe. She's also a calming presence, so I hope she can bring comfort to a family in need.

"You can stop playing, Erin. The song has stopped," Allarick says. Not *sweet girl. Erin.*

It concerns me that the Leviathan's song stopped, but I allow my hands to fall like dead weights down to my side. The reprieve I feel is instant, giving my sore fingertips a break.

Only a few merpeople stay behind. In total, there are six men, all older and more experienced guards, plus Delmare and Allarick. This is the team he's selected to go with him to the Leviathan prison.

I straighten up, giving my back a much-needed stretch after hours of playing. "Where are we going now?" I ask, though I really just want a nap. But time is of the essence, so my nap will have to wait.

None of the guards around Allarick meet my gaze after I ask my question. I try to catch Delmare but regret it. He's looking at me the way someone looks at a child who has just been left out of a friend group: with pity and sadness.

Finally, my eyes land on Allarick. He's staring right at me, as if trying to commit every part of me to memory.

Like he might not ever see me again.

Heat rushes to my face as a rising panic I'm desperately trying to keep in check forms. "Allarick?" I speak his name, though it's soft and almost frightened.

Allarick swims over to me. When he's right in front of me, his tentacles reach out and wrap around my body before pulling me flush against his chest. There's pain in his expression, but pain for what? For whom? And why?

He silences my overactive brain with a kiss. It starts off innocently enough. Soft touch of our lips. But it quickly turns into something more. Hungry, maybe even desperate. He kisses me like a dying man on his last breath. He pries my mouth apart, and I open for him. His tongue claims my mouth in a rough but passionate way. I can't help the small moan that leaves my lips.

I vaguely remember that we have an audience, but I don't have it in me to feel embarrassed as Allarick kisses me until I'm breathless before him. He pulls away from me, and I whimper, not ready for him to stop.

Because something in me knows his next words will shatter me.

"I love you, Erin Goodwin. You made falling in love with you easy. Ender brought you to me because he knew I needed you. Needed your warmth, love, and tenacity." Allarick's voice wavers at the end.

He loves me.

Allarick loves me.

He said it once before, but it feels different now. Like it's the most important thing in the world. To me, it is.

So why does this feel like a goodbye?

"Allarick, I—"

He silences me with another kiss that steals my

words. I kiss him with the words I cannot say but feel so deeply. He needs to know. He *has* to know.

Once again, Allarick breaks off his kiss. I see the regret but acceptance in his eyes. "Our people need a ruler if things go bad. They need you, Erin."

"No, they need us. Allarick, they need *us*," I cry, but he doesn't listen. "I need to go with you. I need to help you. Allarick, please!"

He can't be doing this. He can't possibly think of pushing me away now. Not when he made me love him. Not after he helped pick up all the broken shards of my heart and reconstruct the pieces even stronger than before.

But Allarick lets me go. He pushes me into Delmare's arms. Before I can reach for Allarick again, Delmare catches me and pulls me away. "Take care of her, Delmare."

"With my life, sir," he swears.

I scream. No one hears me, but I scream "Allarick!" over and over again, thrashing against Delmare. But my guard is much bigger and stronger than I am. He pulls me away from Allarick. Away from the man I love with my whole heart. Away from the future I pictured with my husband.

No amount of screaming or kicking loosens Delmare's hold on me. He pulls me farther and farther away until I can't see Allarick anymore. I scream until my voice is hoarse and my throat is raw. I scream until black dots cloud my vision.

I scream until it all goes dark and my body goes limp.

# CHAPTER 37

# ERIN

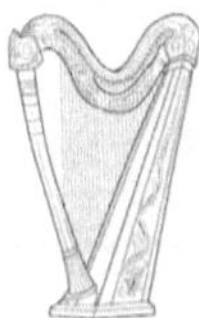

I'm no stranger to pain. It's a feeling and emotion I'm quite familiar with. The pain of having loving parents and losing them to time's cruel clutches. The pain of a sharp sting on my body from the hands of a man who was supposed to love me. Who claimed he loved me so much, it could only be expressed through black eyes and broken bones.

Despite living—and surviving—through that pain, nothing could have prepared me for the utter devastation that consumes me now. It's a pain that numbs the body one second and puts it through the shredder the next. It hurts like my heart has been ripped out of my chest.

My body is exhausted, and I have no fight left in me. I've succumbed to the darkness. I'm not sure how long I've been asleep, but when I wake up, my head pounds with a tension headache. I always got them after a stressful fight with James, and it has been a while since I felt one this strong and debilitating.

I awake on my back in a dark room. Rough fabric that feels like an old, worn blanket caresses my skin. There's a thin pillow underneath my head. It's like someone hastily put together a cot. It's a far cry from my bed in Tetria, and my body aches when I try to move it.

Something wet rolls down my cheek, and I brush it away. Tears, I think. I didn't think I had any left to shed, but a few stubborn ones remain. I force myself into a sitting position to get a better look at where I am and how I got here.

The last thing I remember is Delmare carrying me after my husband forced me away. That damn bastard. It was supposed to be us together. Not this. And now he's gone. Maybe forever. I don't feel much of anything.

Just...numb.

I glance around the room until my eyes adjust to the poor lighting. Only the cracks through the wood making up the four walls around me provide a modicum of sunlight. The room is small, only big enough for the cot and a small round table, looking like it could only hold a book, and a wooden chair that leans to the left.

The air smells of fish and saltwater. The room also sways, and the sound of seagulls filter in from outside. Am I on a boat?

My question is answered immediately when I hear a familiar woman's voice outside, barking orders. A few seconds later, the door to my room opens, assaulting me with sunlight. I squeeze my eyes shut at the sudden intrusion, giving them a second to adjust to the brightness.

"When I said put her on the ship, I didn't mean here.

I'll fucking kill the grandpa for putting you in here," a voice growls.

"He couldn't find anything else, and she needed to lie down!" Another voice I know.

It takes me a moment to make out Atina. I'm surprised she's here. I thought Nori said her ships were farther away. Atina's wearing her usual high boots, black pants, and white billowy shirt. Her hair is tied back, reminding me so much of Allarick. Fresh pain slices through my heart, and I have to look away at the other familiar face.

Iris stares at me with a mixture of sadness and pity in her expression. I wish she wouldn't. I'm sure by now Delmare told her exactly what happened. Or maybe she already knew. Maybe they all knew, and I was the only one left out of the loop.

Atina comes to kneel at my side. I should look at her, but I know I'll see Allarick in her stare, and I can't bring myself to see that. Perhaps that makes me weak or a coward. I can't bring myself to care.

"How are you holding up, Erin?" Even her voice takes on a gentle quality like Allarick's. Not one that sounds patronizing and makes me feel like a child. One that makes me actually think she cares.

But the question is absurd. How am I doing? After having my heart ripped out by the man I love? Knowing he's in danger and there's a big possibility he's not coming back, which makes Leviathan, Nephilim, and the citizens of Tetria my problem.

There isn't a word to describe this feeling. I fear if I open my mouth, only sobs will come out. So I just shrug.

"How do you think she's doing, Atina? That poor girl," Iris answers for me and moves to crouch down next to me. The three of us don't fit in here well. Too close. But apparently personal space is not something they care about.

Iris takes my hand in hers. It's motherly, and that alone is nearly enough to break me. A strangled cry leaves my lips, but tears don't sting my eyes. I can't even muster the energy to cry anymore.

"You poor dear. Don't worry about the merpeople. Delmare, along with a few other guards and Atina's crew are getting everyone situated in their new temporary homes. They are safe now," Iris assures.

Selfishly, I hadn't been thinking about the merpeople and how self-sufficient Allarick's guardsmen are. I guess they are technically mine now. Although I'm happy everyone seems to be safe, I can't work up the energy to show I'm happy. I just nod instead.

"Erin," Atina says softly.

Even though it's hard to focus on anything other than the debilitating pain, I turn my face in her direction. We stare at each other for what feels like a lifetime. Her warm eyes are full of sorrow.

"Why?" I croak. It's the one thing I can't figure out. Why Allarick forced me away.

Atina sighs. "Because men are idiots?" she supplies, and I know it's meant to lighten the mood, but it falls flat. "I suppose he did it because he loves you. He wanted to keep you safe, and he knew you could protect his people if he failed."

Part of me understands it. My music can counteract

the Leviathan, and if our people need another layer of defense, they are going to need me here. But Allarick needs me too. War rages inside me, not knowing how to feel other than devastated.

"I'm sorry for what my brother did. He should have communicated with you better. Whatever you decide to do next, know you have my support," Atina says.

"And mine as well, my queen," Iris says. Having the support of both of these women means everything to me. I just wish I knew what my next moves should be.

"Before we make any decisions, let's get Erin to my cabin. I'll fix supper, and she can sleep in," Atina looks around the small space and scowls, "something that doesn't resemble a broom closet."

Atina stands up, dusting off her black pants. Iris tucks a strand of blue hair behind her ear and offers her hand to help me up. I nearly decline, but instead I lean into her touch and allow her to guide me. When I'm finally standing, Iris leads me out.

"I just want you to know, when Delmare brought you here, I made him go back down and get your harp for you. I thought you'd appreciate something that reminds you of..." Iris trails off, suddenly realizing her mistake.

Fresh tears form in my eyes, but I blink them away. Apparently, I still have more to shed. My maid is sweet, but that damn harp is the last thing I want to see right now. It's a symbol of Allarick and what I lost. So even though the gesture is sweet, it's not something I want or need right now.

Iris picks up on that and rubs my back soothingly.

"I'll keep it with me until you're ready for it. Let's just get you something to eat."

Conversations stall as she leads me out of the small room and off the boat. We follow Atina in silence, and I count down the minutes to when I can close my eyes and leave this pain behind me for a few hours.

# CHAPTER 38

# ALLARICK

I can still hear her screams echo through these empty halls. See and feel the hurt and betrayal in her expression as I pushed her into Delmare's arms so he could carry her out of the castle, away to safety. My girl fought to stay, which only solidified my decision to send her away. No matter how much it hurt me to do so.

Erin is strong. She's a fighter, and our people need that. They also need her to keep them safe from the Leviathan's song. If this goes south, I need to know Tetria is in good hands. Even if that means breaking the heart of the woman I love most in this world.

I plan to make it up to her. I plan to survive. But if I don't...

"King Allarick," Nori's voice booms behind me, grounding me back in the present.

When everyone left for safety, Nori stayed behind. He's our best bet on tracking down the Leviathan's prison and eliminating the threat once and for all.

"Are we set to leave?" I ask, anxious to start our

journey while the waters are quiet. It's only a matter of time before the Leviathan's song starts up again, putting us at a disadvantage. Like sirens, they can't sing for prolonged periods of time, so once they rest, their deadly song will reach us again. We'll have the noise cancelers Nori brought, but who can tell if they will be effective the closer we get?

"We are. It will be a few days' journey, give or take," he says and then hesitates. "Allarick, sealing the prison isn't going to be an easy task."

"I figured."

"There is a good chance you won't survive. You're alone without family to help you."

My jaw clenches. "I'm aware." It was the whole reason I sent Erin away. Only those born into the Eldridge line can close the gate. Which is why it was important to send her with our people.

"But what other choice do we have, Nori?" I ask when the man looks like he wants to argue. "We knew it would come to this. The gate needs my bloodline in order to be sealed shut. I'm the only person who can do that."

It's not entirely true. There's one other person who could assist, but my sister has not set fin in the ocean for decades. I'm uncertain if she could even take on her mermaid form anymore if she tried.

No, it has to be me.

And I'm ready.

"Prepare the hippocamps. Pack provisions. Each guard needs to have their noise cancelers," I instruct.

"All of that has been done. Your steed is awaiting

you. I'm here on behalf of your sister and to make sure you understand that we could all be walking toward our death," Nori says.

"And doing nothing is also a death sentence. Not for us but for the entirety of Mescos. If the Leviathan are free, the Nephilim will have free passage of the seas. We have to try." My only regret is that innocent men accompanying me might meet their end. I don't say that though because they know. It's written across their faces.

Nori sighs, resigned to his unknown fate. "Then we best be off. And pray the sea goddess is on our side."

I nod and follow Nori down the hall, leading to the front of the castle where our steeds await us. The other guards are already mounted, waiting for further instructions. The mood is pensive, though not completely hopeless. A sliver of hope pulses through our troop.

Good.

We need to hold on tight to that hope. The moment it flickers out of existence is the moment our cause is dead. The moment *we* are dead.

I approach the group and stare at the men still with me. This is the part where I should give them a speech of heroism and the importance of our victory. But everyone already knows what's at stake. They know what happens if we fail.

So, instead I say the only thing that might breed purpose and inspiration.

"Remember who we are fighting for." I leave my words vague for a reason. Everyone here is fighting for our people, but they have loved ones they want to keep safe. It could be their mates. Their children. Their parents.

Sweet hazel-colored eyes come to mind. The melodic laughter. The softness of her skin against mine. I feel Erin with me. I keep her locked deep in my heart to give me the strength I need to battle our enemies.

Nori comes up beside me and dips his head. He grabs the reins of his hippocamp and commands the beast to go. I'm on his heels with the others flanking us.

My last thought before I leave my castle behind for who knows how long is Erin.

*I'm coming back to you, sweet girl. Wait for me.*

# CHAPTER 39
# ERIN

As it turns out, pretending your heart isn't broken into a million pieces requires a lot of energy. The day after arriving at Atina's house, I wanted nothing more than to stay in bed all day. Unfortunately, Atina had different plans for me.

After a quick breakfast of eggs and ham—I ate only a few bites—Atina pulls me outside and into the sunlight. "You need to show your face to your people." She takes me from cabin to cabin.

I put on a smile because what else can I do? Fear hangs heavy in the air, and I don't want to add to it. Atina leads me back toward the ocean. We pass Delmare, Iris, and a few other royal guards who are helping pass out supplies and food to those who need it. Guilt gnaws at me. I should be out there helping them, not trailing Atina like a lost puppy. I can't muster up more than a weak smile and a simple hello.

It's draining.

I spend most of my day with Atina, moving mechanically and not speaking. Atina tries to elicit any emotion from me, but she comes up short each time. Eventually, she stops trying. I don't blame her. I would give up on me too.

I see Allarick in everything I'm doing. I see him in the people who come up to me, telling me how strong I am. I don't feel strong, though. Quite the opposite, really. I see Allarick each time Atina turns on me with her brows drawn together. She looks so much like her brother, it's hard to be around her for too long.

But it's just a ghost because my husband isn't here. And I don't know if he ever will be again.

I make no complaints when Atina finally grows weary of me and offers to take me back to her cabin. I go without protest. "Are you hungry? I can make dinner." She's already halfway to the kitchen, not interested in my answer.

I'm not hungry.

But I somehow doubt she'll care.

After twenty minutes of her tinkering around in the kitchen, Atina sets a plate of salmon and rice in front of me. She takes a seat at the table and wastes no time inhaling her food.

"So," she says between bites, "do you have a course of action yet?"

I play with the rice on my plate before taking a bite. I'm sure it's a fine meal, but I don't taste anything. "No."

Atina sighs heavily, lowering her head. I don't wait for her to tell me just how shitty of a queen I'm being, so I rise and grab my plate. "Thank you for dinner. I'm tired and think I'll head to bed."

Atina doesn't even look at me as she nods. I hesitate, wanting to apologize but torn between her feelings and my own. Ultimately, my selfishness wins, and I walk to the kitchen and discard my plate. I make my way to the bedroom and shut the door. Atina insisted I take her bed last night—the same bed I slept in when I first arrived to Mescos—and I'm assuming that offer extends to tonight as well.

I don't even change before I climb into bed and hold a pillow to my chest. My only reprieve from this heartache is to close my eyes and drift off to a dreamless, silent sleep.

I'm not sure how long I stay asleep that night, but when I wake up in the morning and finally force myself out of bed, Atina is gone. I don't blame her after yesterday, but loneliness creeps in anyway. I'm sure she got tired of my mopey shit.

Although Atina isn't in the main room when I walk in, my harp is. I stop dead in my tracks, frowning at the beautiful instrument. I told Iris I didn't want to see it, but clearly my maid had other ideas for me. Delmare must have helped her carry it in here, and both left before I woke up. Not even Delmare and Iris want to be around the negative energy I possess.

Sighing, I stalk close to the harp, dropping down on the couch. My fingers graze the smooth body of the instrument. I'm sure they brought it here to cheer me up or have me play to calm everyone else, but I don't particularly feel in the mood for music.

I'm about to get up to get myself a glass of water when the door opens. I expect Atina or Iris to walk through the door, encouraging me to get out. I'm already exhausted just thinking about making rounds again. Two people peek around the door of my cabin, but neither is Atina or Iris.

Despite myself, I jump back.

"Sorry! We didn't mean to scare you," a woman with red hair says.

"We were told you might still be asleep," the other black-haired woman says.

There's something vaguely familiar about both of these women. They aren't from Tetria; that much is obvious from their clothes. The red-haired woman is wearing an emerald-green dress that doesn't look like any fabric I've ever seen before. It's like it's made from lizard scales.

The other woman's outfit is much more mundane and familiar. Tight black pants and a long-sleeved red blouse. Her black hair is braided back, showing off a tattoo on her neck. At least it looks like a tattoo, but I can't make out what the design is.

Both women enter the cabin, and realization dawns. I've seen these women before, heard stories from Sister Tammy about them.

"You're from Grym Hollow." My mind is having a hard time seeing two women from my hometown in this magical land.

The red-haired woman laughs. "We are. I'm Rose, and this is Hettie. We made the same deal as you did with The Guardian. He's not the most forthcoming."

The other woman—Hettie—scoffs. "It's easier to talk to a brick wall."

My interactions with The Guardian were minimal. I don't think we said more than a few sentences to each other. Our last interaction was him carrying my broken body out of James's house.

"What are you doing here? *Why* are you here?" The last thing I expected today was to have two people from Grym Hollow show up at Atina's door.

"Atina—apparently that's your husband's sister?" Hettie asks. I nod and she continues, "Well, she paid my husband and me a visit and asked me to speak to you. Rose happened to be visiting, so I brought her along. She helped me out a few weeks back, so I figured she'd be helpful in this situation."

"I don't understand." Was this Atina's attempt at helping me make friends in case I become a grieving widow? Was she already tired of putting up with me? The women before me both look strong and capable, but unless they can help me get Allarick back, I don't think their help is necessary.

Rose steps forward, hand coming to rest on her flat stomach. "Do you mind if we sit down? These days I can barely go a few hours without feeling sick."

Because I'm not completely rude, I nod. "Of course, take a seat."

"Thank you," Rose says graciously and moves to sit on the couch. She groans, holding her back as she sits.

"Are you okay? Can I get you something?" The woman clearly looks uncomfortable. She rubs her back before straightening up.

"I'll be okay in seven more months," she mumbles.

My brain is slow to process the words, but luckily

Hettie explains Rose's discomfort. "Rose is expecting. She and Malix wasted no time getting down to business." She smirks.

"Didn't you just tell me you and Rip want to start a family?" Rose teases.

"I did...do, but I'm going to let you push out the dragon baby and then consider if I'm ready to push out a wolf baby. Tallie told me Rip weighed twelve pounds. Twelve fucking pounds. I'll never recover from that," Hettie says, falling back on the couch dramatically.

From outside the door, there's a low growl, and then a male voice shouts through the door, "You'll recover just fine."

"Ugh, fucking alpha males," Hettie murmurs, rolling her eyes. Even as she feigns annoyance, I don't miss the smile she tries to hide. "That's my husband, Rip. Ignore him; I'm trying to."

"At least your husband isn't flying above head, scaring anyone who tries to get too close to the cabin." Rose laughs but then sobers up quickly, like she remembered why she's here. "Anyway, we didn't come here to talk about my pregnancy or our husbands. We are here to talk about yours."

Both women look at me as my brow lifts in confusion. "I'm sorry, I don't understand." Perhaps it's my brain fog, or maybe it's my annoyance at being caught off guard that keeps me from understanding.

"Can you tell us what's happening?" Rose asks. "Atina told us a little, but we would like to hear it from you."

I sigh, deciding to humor Rose and Hettie. It's not

like I have anything better to do, plus both women are from Grym Hollow. If anyone can help me and understand what I'm going through, it's them. I tell them about Allarick and the home he brought me to. About the Leviathan, which they seemed really interested in, and then finally about the last day we were together. How Allarick pushed me away and how I ended up in this cabin.

Sad. Lonely. Pathetic.

"So, I'm here waiting to see if my husband comes back. If not..." I cut myself off. Stubborn tears roll down my cheeks, and I quickly wipe them away. The last thing I want to do is cry in front of these women. I'm the acting ruler of Tetria and the merpeople who inhabit it; I can't show weakness to these other Grym Hollow women. No, not just women. *Queens.* They both signed contracts with The Guardian to become wives to their respective kings.

"Must be a requirement for Mescos kings to be so damn stubborn," Hettie says. "It's like they forgot the whole reason they brought us here is to help them save their kingdom."

"Do you know where he's going, Erin?" Rose asks. I didn't tell her my name, so Atina must have filled them in about me. Or they heard my name around Grym Hollow...which I hope isn't the case.

I shake my head. "He's trying to seal the gate that's holding the Leviathan. But I don't know where it is." I only saw the place marked on a map I couldn't read. Even if I could, there's no way I can navigate the sea without Allarick. The only person who knows the sea better than Allarick is...

Atina.

Something akin to hope flickers to life.

But it instantly extinguishes because, even if Atina could get me there, there's nothing I could do to help him. The door must be sealed by his bloodline. I would only be a distraction.

"There's nothing I can do to help him," I say at last.

Hettie and Rose share a look, and I can't help but feel left out. There's a friendship between them—one I envy.

"There actually might be," Rose says at last. "Have you or Allarick noticed anything you do that seems... magical?"

I nearly scoff and tell her absolutely not, but that's not the truth. The evidence is sitting right in front of me in the form of a beautiful pearlescent harp.

"Yeah, actually," I say slowly. "I'm a musician. I'm used to moving people with my music, but the way my songs capture the merpeople is...different. I've had a few of them say it's cured their headaches, and it brings peace to many. It also blocks out the song of the Leviathan when nothing else will."

And Allarick is going straight to the source. Without his best chance at success.

The lingering sadness I've felt since being forced apart from Allarick is quickly replaced with anger.

How dare he.

How dare he leave himself defenseless, knowing I could help.

He was wrong. Tetria doesn't need me. Tetria needs *us*.

"I believe it," Rose says. "Which is why I don't think leaving you behind was a smart move."

"Ditto. I'm all for defying your husband and doing exactly what they say not to do." Hettie grins. From outside, someone growls again.

If I had looked past my sadness and stopped my own pity party, I would have come to the same conclusion Hettie and Rose are getting at. Or maybe I wouldn't have. Maybe I needed two women who have gone through the same ordeal that I'm currently going through to tell me that seeing Allarick is possible. That helping him is possible if I defy his orders.

"I need to get to my husband," I say at last, looking between Hettie and Rose. These two women know better than anyone what it means to stand against your husband and fight for your chance at love.

Hettie smirks. "I like you, Erin. Now, let's get you to your ship."

# CHAPTER 40

# ERIN

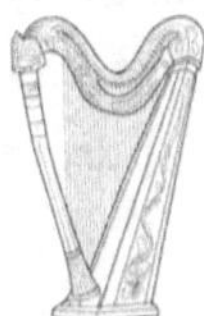

"These are your husbands?" My mouth falls open as I stare at the man and the damn dragon waiting outside Atina's cabin door. The man stands well over six feet and takes up the entire doorframe. He's shirtless, every chiseled muscle on full display. If I had never seen Allarick and every hard muscle on my husband's body, the man standing before me would overwhelm me with his hotness.

Hettie walks straight up to the man. Their size difference is almost laughable, but Hettie struts right up to the giant man and yanks his head down. She kisses him in a way that makes me blush and think I'm intruding on something I really shouldn't be seeing. Loneliness settles within me, making me think of Allarick and how I want to kiss him as soon as I can.

And then yell at him for leaving me behind.

Rose is more subtle in greeting her husband—the dragon. She goes over to the massive black reptile and touches his snout. The dragon huffs and nuzzles into her touch, reminding me of a dog greeting their owner after a long day. You know, if dogs were giant and deadly.

"Yes, unfortunately these are our husbands," Hettie says, still wrapped up in her man's arms. He huffs, but she just laughs and breaks away from him. "This is Rip, and that large lizard over there is Malix."

"They are...big," I whisper, but hear a snort from the dragon—Malix.

"Trust me, I know." Hettie smirks in a way that makes me think we aren't talking about the same thing. "If the women back in Grym Hollow knew who waited over here in Mescos, The Guardian would have a line ten miles long."

I laugh, nodding in agreement. The Guardian would certainly have his hands full.

Rip steps up, casting a shadow over me and Hettie. I'm unable to hide my nervousness around this intimidating man and step closer to Hettie. He seems to sense my discomfort and stops, dipping his head. "Queen Erin, it's a pleasure to meet you. Your husband is a good man."

"But a foolish one. Which seems to be a common trait amongst the males of the species here," Hettie says. That comment earns her a disapproving glare, which she returns tenfold. Neither one of them holds their ire for long, soon smiling like teenagers in love.

It's beautiful.

Also a little sickening.

My dumb heart flutters, thinking of Allarick.

"But Erin plans to join her husband." Rose steps away from her dragon, but Malix doesn't let her get too far, blocking her with his tail. "Don't you, Erin?"

"I do." My voice doesn't waver and thankfully doesn't convey my fear. I'm scared. Scared at what I might—or might not—find. But fear isn't going to stop me. Allarick needs me.

"What do you need from us?" Rip asks. "We know a threat to the sea will turn into a threat to our land. As long as the Nephilim roam, we must stay on alert."

"Isn't he hot when he gets all valiant?" Hettie giggles.

"Hettie," he groans, no true malice in his voice.

"Our fight is with the Leviathan, but from my understanding, they are cousins to the Nephilim and are just as dangerous to the sea," I say. Their pale expressions tell me just how uneasy they are with this situation. "I need to know my people are safe while I'm away."

"Done," Rip says immediately. "Wolves can patrol the area."

"Dragons too," Rose speaks for herself and her husband. "I would volunteer to stay myself but..." Malix's tail squeezes around Rose, pulling her close to his body. She laughs and rolls her eyes.

"But my husband barely lets me leave the castle these days," she finishes, placing her hand on her belly.

For just a moment, I picture my future with Allarick. We deserve a future filled with love and precious memories. I never thought about becoming a mother, but my heart does a weird flutter when I think of Allarick holding our half-kraken, half-human baby.

I want a chance at that future.

"What else do you need?" Hettie asks.

"I need someone to carry the harp onto the ship."

"Go, Muscles, that's all you." Hettie pushes Rip

toward the door. He disappears inside. A few seconds later, he comes out carrying the harp like it weighs nothing at all.

Even I swoon a little.

"We will take good care of your people, Erin. Worry about channeling your energy into your music. Everything else should work out the way it needs to," Rose says confidently.

I want to ask her how she's so sure about this, but something in the way Rose smiles at me lessens the knot forming in my stomach. She has faith in me. I need to have that same faith.

"You should get going," Hettie says gently.

She's right, but I'm not quite ready yet. I reach out for both of the women's hands. Something passes between us, an understanding only three women from Grym Hollow could have. They remind me that I'm not alone, that just because I'm human doesn't mean I don't have power.

"Thank you. Both of you. I wish we had more time." I think I could be friends with these women. Maybe even best friends.

"We will soon. Just go and save your husband's ass first," Hettie says.

We laugh, and I bring them in for a hug. "Thank you," I murmur one last time before letting them go.

And then I walk toward the ship with Rip at my heels carrying the harp. Crew members busy themselves inside and outside Atina's ship, working on whatever the hell goes into maintaining a ship and a crew.

We walk up the slipway, and Rip places the harp

down as soon as we board. "Good luck, Erin. I hope to see you again soon."

"Likewise. Thank you, Rip," I say as the large man exits the boat.

"My queen, what are you doing here? Are you okay?" A voice draws my attention away from Rip to see Iris strolling toward me. Delmare is right behind her, assessing me.

I don't blame Iris for being confused and concerned as to why I'm here. I haven't exactly made myself available. "I need to see Atina."

Iris shares a look with Delmare, who nods. "Of course, my queen. Right this way." Delmare leads me across the deck and up a few stairs. Iris trails behind us.

Atina and three others lean over a map and speak in hushed whispers. Delmare clears his throat when we draw near, and four heads pop up. Atina meets my gaze immediately and straightens up. "Erin," she says slowly. "What can I do for you?"

I push past Delmare and close the distance between us. "I need you to take me to Allarick. I need to help him."

Atina doesn't speak at first. She looks at me like she's trying to detect a lie, but I don't fold under her scrutiny. I expect Delmare to interject and say it's not safe. Or Iris to demand I reconsider. But they don't do either of those things. In fact, Delmare smiles at me like a proud father who was waiting for the moment I came to my senses.

Finally, just as nerves set in, Atina smirks. "I thought you'd never ask. Welcome aboard, my queen. Let's go kick some Leviathan ass."

# CHAPTER 41

# ALLARICK

We encountered no trouble on our journey to the Leviathan's prison. In fact, we hardly encountered anything. Only a few sea creatures crossed our path, but I felt the eyes of many upon us. The creatures were hiding. It's like the entire ocean is locked down and hiding in the sand and shadows.

The mood between us is somber. We stop once to rest, but rest doesn't come easy out here. All of my men have loved ones at home. It's not lost on any of us that we may never see them again. Thoughts of Erin fill my mind on our journey. Her beautiful music. The way her nose scrunches up when she laughs. Her body draped over mine when we wake up in the morning.

The thought of her occupies most of my time. I only come back to reality when Nori comes to a dead stop. He reaches up to his ear, taking out the noise canceler. After a moment, he gestures to me to do the same.

"We're here," he says as soon as I can hear again.

"Here?" I ask, assessing what lies in front of us.

This isn't a part of the ocean I've seen before, and I take pride in having explored many parts of our home. This place is in ruins compared to Tetria. Gray, lackluster sand coats the bottom of the seafloor. No corals and only the occasional seaweed grow here. Other than that, nothing living resides here. Sitting like an ominous beacon in front of us is a large cave made of limestone and sandstone. Sculpted at the opening of the cave are three archways with translucent gates barring the entrance.

Magic. Ancient magic.

In the hands of evil.

"My king, do you see that?" the guard next to me asks. He points at something close to the cavern gates, and my gaze follows.

At first glance, it looks like a random pile of rubble and rocks. But a low moaning sounds from that direction. I swim forward, trying to get a better look. That's when I see the "rubble" isn't rubble at all. It's skeletal remains, withered away until only a shell of their former self remains.

We've found where the lost family members have gone. Their souls were snatched by monsters of the deep. A moment of silence settles over us as the others piece together what happened. My stomach drops, knowing I wasn't able to protect my subjects. The time to mourn will have to wait until later though; we have a job to do.

Trying to ignore the withered remains, I look back at the gate to see it slightly open by a few inches—enough to unlock the power of their voices. It will only be a matter of time before they steal enough souls and power to break down the prison door for good.

"Atina says you need to close the gate," Nori says.

It shouldn't be too hard.

"But the Leviathan will sense you and do everything they can to stop you."

Never mind.

"What attacks should I expect?" I wish I had the forethought to ask Atina all of this the last time I saw her. Not that she was in any condition to tell me, though. She was on the verge of a drunken spell after losing three crew members.

Nori opens his mouth to answer, but a high-pitched hum erupts all around us. One voice turns into ten, turns into one hundred. My body tries to betray me, moving me closer to the sound. It's like a pull I can't resist. Before it wraps the noose tighter around me, I push the noise cancelers deep into my ears and shout out to everyone to do the same.

They know we're here.

It's too late for one of my men though. A guard glides forward effortlessly. Someone shouts as another guard grabs for him, but it's too late. The transfixed guard breaks free of the man's grasp and swims to the gates.

I don't realize I'm moving closer until Nori clamps his hand around my shoulder and doesn't let go. I'm helpless as black, shadowy hands, almost clawlike, reach for the man. He doesn't even try to fight them off; instead, he stands there and lets himself be wrapped in shadows.

When the shadows finally disperse, only the withered, skeletal shell of the man remains.

Gone. In a blink of an eye.

My resolve hardens. The gate needs to be closed once and for all.

"Noise cancelers! Now!" I shout.

Knowing the rest of the guards will follow, I take the lead and close the gap. The singing gets louder, stronger even, the closer we get. It's getting painful to ignore. The Leviathan know we are here, and they aren't holding back. More claw-shaped shadows slip through the small crack in the gate, attempting to reach out and grab us. I reach for the sword at my hip and bring it down upon as many claws as I can. There's something akin to a hiss before the shadows slither back inside the prison.

But two more claws escape and lunge for us.

Next to me, Nori takes up his sword and cuts down more of the claws. No matter how many get cut down, more take their place.

The gate needs to be shut, and it needs to be shut now.

I sheath my sword and throw my weight at the shimmering gate. I half expect to go through it like a veil to the other side, but it turns solid when my tentacles wrap around the bars. I pull, testing the strength of the gate. It doesn't budge, not even a little.

I should have known it wouldn't be so easy.

I pull harder, all the while trying to dodge the claws coming for me. The guards hit many away, but it's still too much. The song is too loud. My head hurts, and it makes thinking, let alone doing anything, extremely difficult.

More of my strength depletes at a rapid rate, drained by the Leviathan inside. They are strong. Stronger than I anticipated. The guards' movements around me start to slow until I no longer see the gleam of the blade swinging down. I risk turning my head, only to see glazed-over looks in the eyes of the men I brought. Some look like they are actually trying to fight the hold, but it's an uphill battle.

I scream, knowing they can't hear me, but hoping by some miracle they do. Next to me, Nori drops his sword and moves closer to the shadowy claws. "Nori! Fight it! Don't let them control you!" I scream. I scream until my throat goes raw.

Scream until my voice is scratchy and I can't scream anymore.

It's never been clearer that I'm alone in this.

We never stood a chance. In a matter of minutes, the Leviathan entranced and incapacitated every person I brought. If they die, their deaths will be on my hands. As well as every death that comes after.

If I'm to die, it won't be by sitting and doing nothing. It will be by defending my kingdom. There's honor in dying for those you rule over, knowing I did everything in my power to defend Tetria.

So, with what might be my last minutes with the living, I pull on the gates harder, fighting against creatures more powerful than me.

# CHAPTER 42
# ERIN

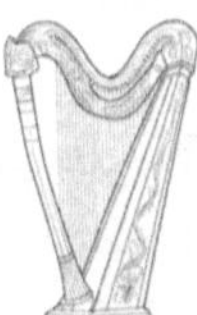

During the night, the calm of the sea slipped into a vicious storm. Loud thunder rattles the boat, making sleeping impossible. Not that sleep would have come easily anyway. Atina let me bunk with her, away from the rest of the crew. I'm thankful for that, considering how many people stuffed themselves below deck.

However, the makeshift cot is scratchy, and the blanket is threadbare. I don't want to seem ungrateful because Atina has already done so much for me, so I simply go along with it for the night. I manage to doze off for an hour or so, but the constant motion of the boat and the loud storm brewing outside make me ditch sleeping after several attempts.

Atina is no longer in the room when I finally get out of my cot. I tame my hair back as best I can and then give up, realizing I'm about to brave the elements. There's no use in trying to look presentable when, the moment I step out of this room, I'll be drenched.

When I reach to open the door, it blows back, nearly hitting me in the face. The wind whistles an ominous howl, flapping through the sails. Rain pours down in abundance. Lightning makes visibility possible, if only for a few seconds. Which is how I see Atina in the midst of all the chaos.

I feel my way along the deck. Multiple times, I bump into something hard or trip. Images of me falling overboard assault my mind. Being lost at sea terrifies me, even with my ability to breathe under water.

It takes an embarrassing amount of time to finally reach Atina. I'm soaked, feeling a chill deep in my bones. I shiver just as she reaches for me.

"What are you doing up? You should be sleeping," she yells over the storm.

"You expect me to sleep in this?" I counter.

"A seasoned seafarer could," she says, and I just stare at her. If my lack of —shipping? Boating? Pirate-ing?— wasn't obvious before, it is now.

"Right, forgot this is new to you. When I first started, I don't think I slept for weeks. It gets easier," she says.

I believe her, but I don't want to stay on the ship for that long. Ideally, I don't want to be on a ship after this for a long time. I'm starting to feel sea sickness on this rocking vessel.

"Where are we?" I ask in her general direction because, once again, it's pitch-black out here. A lightning strike shows Atina looking at a small gold compass.

"We are...here. I think," she says, and I suck in a breath.

"Here? Like here as in the prison holding the Leviathan?" I ask, as if we were looking for anything else.

Atina nods, but my confusion only grows. "Wouldn't we be able to hear them?"

"We did the last time we were close, but I think the thunderstorm is a blessing in disguise. It's blocking out the sounds," she says. "Their song is also not continuous. They have to break."

Well, yay for small miracles.

"And you are certain this is it? That we are above them?" I don't mean to sound condescending, but we are working on borrowed time. Every second counts.

"This should be it. It's the coordinates I've written down," Atina assures. "We need to get you ready."

I'm already wearing leggings and a form-fitting shirt, ready to be back in the ocean. "No, I'm ready. Are you going with me?"

Allarick told me Atina didn't go into the ocean because of the judgment of their people. However, none of the merpeople judged her while we made our rounds the other day, checking to see if everyone had what they needed.

I think her fear lies within the ocean itself and her ability to navigate an unfamiliar world. To feel like a stranger in one's own body. It's a feeling I know well and one that's hard to overcome.

But this is her brother's life.

Another flash of lightning illuminates the indecision on Atina's face. I know her answer before she speaks, but it still disappoints me to hear. "No, I'll find someone else."

"I will go with the queen," a new voice sounds from behind us, startling me. Next to me, Atina sighs.

"I suppose he works as good as anyone," Atina mumbles as Delmare approaches us. She feigns annoyance, but there's also an undercurrent of relief.

I want to tell Atina that she doesn't get to be picky about who accompanies me when she is refusing to come, but I hold my tongue. Besides, I hoped it would be my guard.

"Delmare, what are you doing up? Is Iris okay?" His wife seemed uncomfortable sleeping on a ship earlier this evening.

"Iris is fine. Asleep finally. But I couldn't. I thought I heard something above deck and came to check it out. I couldn't help but overhear your conversation. Most of it, anyway," he says.

"Shouldn't you at least tell Iris that you plan on accompanying me?" I think of my maid waking up in the morning only to find her husband is gone.

"She will understand, my queen." He doesn't elaborate, and I don't get a chance to ask.

"Can you get her to the prison site from here? It's straight down, but I'll give you the exact coordinates," Atina says.

"I can."

Having Delmare by my side makes the tension ease inside of me. He's strong and capable and knows these waters better than most. "Do you have something to block out the noise once we get down?"

"I do. Carry them with me everywhere these days." Ever the faithful guard.

"Good. Then I'm ready to go," I say.

"You'll need your harp. I'll carry it down," Delmare says.

I thank him because I hadn't even thought of how I'd get that down.

"This way then." Atina takes my hand.

I reach for Delmare to keep my balance, and we walk as a chain to what I presume is the side of the boat. I peer over, looking at the dark sea beneath. Fear threatens to overtake me, but losing Allarick is scarier.

"Allow me to go first," Delmare says.

"We're jumping?" I squeak. I should have guessed as much, but the scary water takes up residence in my brain and doesn't allow me to think of much else.

A light splash is the only answer I get. He already jumped.

"Your turn, queen," Atina says. "I'll toss your harp to you. I swear you chose a large instrument on purpose. Ever heard of a harmonica?"

"I think you're joking, but I'm too scared to think of something witty to say." My body shivers at what I must do. I know if I think about it too long, I'll talk myself out of it. I can't do that though. I need to jump. With shaky legs, I climb the side of the boat.

And then I jump.

I fall for what feels like an eternity. I expect the water to hurt when I fall, but it doesn't. Hands grab for me, pulling me up before I can sink and fall away from him. "Good job, my queen."

"Harp overboard!" Atina grunts from the ship above

us. Something splashes down next to me, and Delmare grabs for it.

The water is cold, but not unbearable. Still, I shiver, equal parts from the temperature and my own fear. Delmare gives my hand a reassuring squeeze. "Let's go. It won't be long now."

With me and the harp in his hands, Delmare starts his descent into the sea. I don't know how he knows how to navigate these waters, especially when it looks pitch-black to me. His tentacles work quickly, moving us effortlessly through the eerily calm waters.

It's so vastly different under the sea. No roaring storms, only peaceful quiet. It's almost scary how quiet it is out here. Not even a single fish swims by us. It's... haunting.

I don't know how long we swim, but every second that passes feels like an eternity. This far down, biolumi-nescent organisms light our path in a faint glow. For the first time in hours, I hear a soft humming noise. It grows louder the farther down Delmare goes. It's not a beau-tiful song per se, but it's one that holds deep emotion. Pain. Anger. Vengeance.

I know we're close.

Distracted by the song, I don't realize we've hit the bottom of the sea until my feet touch the floor. We land in the middle of a mostly barren area. Few seaweed and coral decorate the floor. Before us, off in the distance, is a massive rock structure leading into an underwater cave. The rock is sculpted in three large arches with moss adorning the surface, making it appear lost in time.

The sound is louder here. More urgent and pressing.

It's not pretty but otherwise doesn't bother me. Delmare visibly tenses next to me, so I know this is hard on him.

I squint, and that's when I see the middle arch is alight with a white glow. It looks like chains across the area. Something large bobs in front of the entrance. Several somethings, all reaching toward the slight opening in the white chains.

No...not something.

Merpeople.

And in the middle of them is Allarick, his back toward me. He's screaming at the unmoving men around him to focus, but none of them heed his orders. They reach past him, trying to make their way inside the arched gate.

To the Leviathan.

Dark shadows slither through the cracks of the gate. Black hand-like shapes reach through, attempting to grab the next victim.

"Delmare! He needs your help! Go!" I yell, but the guard doesn't hear me. Of course, he doesn't because of the noise cancelers.

I don't think. I just act. I swim for the harp, tugging it out of Delmare's hand. Finally, with his attention on me, I frantically gesture to Allarick and his men by the gates. Delmare looks like he wants to argue and stay with me. I don't have time to fight with him, though, so I push him as hard as I can toward Allarick—which, admittedly, doesn't move him much.

I turn my back on my guard and drag the harp closer. I fear I won't be loud enough, but I have to try. For Allarick. For Tetria. Hell, for Mescos.

Absolutely no pressure.

Before I can let the fear of the repercussions of losing this battle immobilize me, I stop dragging the harp and position it the best I can without a proper seat. I don't ease into a song, I just start playing, as loud as I can, a melody I hope will overpower the Leviathan's song.

And because I need to give Allarick the best fighting chance, I begin to sing.

# CHAPTER 43

# ALLARICK

I t starts out as a whisper.

A simple hum that rings in my ears. This isn't the same desperate, high-pitched melody of the Leviathan. No, this is a soft croon invading my senses. It's a warm hug that heats me from the inside out. The melody is strong and beautiful, one that reminds me of warm summer waters and lazy days in the kingdom.

Then a voice.

Ethereal. Fierce.

Erin.

That playing...that voice...I could place them anywhere. For a brief moment, I wonder if I died and this is my paradise. But the thought is fleeting because black claws grab my body. They dig into my tentacles and my chest, attempting to drag me away from the gate. They're so damn strong, and my hold loosens.

A flash of a blade next to me arches down and cuts right through the claws, sending them back. My head snaps to the side just in time to see Delmare bring his blade down again.

He's not the only one. Nori, who had once been under their influence, cuts through more of the Leviathan claws. The other guards quickly break out of the Leviathan's influence as well, brought back by Erin's music. A newfound determination blooms between us.

My eyes lock with Delmare's, and he nods. His unwavering faith in me doesn't shake, not even when things look grim. His presence reminds me that my wife is here, and the stakes are higher than ever.

My hold on the gate tightens. I pour every ounce of strength into closing the gap and locking the Leviathan away indefinitely. Delmare takes up position next to me, cutting down the shadowy claws.

I should be able to close it. If it were any other gate, that would be the case. But this isn't just any gate. It's a magical prison containing powerful creatures. Only those of royal blood can contain the creatures inside, which means me and me alone, with my wife playing in the background. It's the only thing keeping the Leviathans out of our heads and controlling us.

The gate gives a little, only a slight budge. I'm pulling with all the strength I possess, straining my body. The gate moves...but not enough. It remains open with no signs of giving in anytime soon. All around me, my men are locked in combat, straining their muscles as they fight enemies that never seem to go away and only multiply.

Doubt creeps in. My failure is inevitable. I feel it all

around me. The way my men struggle. How fatigue has set in. We were so close. So close and...

A soft hand reaches for my arm. I look down, seeing smooth brown skin. I flick my gaze up to where Delmare swims a few feet away. He's pale, eyes wide as if he's seen a ghost. Nori comes into view next to him, equally astonished. But his mouth quirks up in a smirk.

I turn my head and nearly lose my grip on the gate.

"Atina?"

My mind can barely comprehend what I'm seeing. My sister swims in front of me, red mermaid tail awkwardly swishing from side to side. Her face is drained of color, and she looks seconds from swimming away and back to land. None of that matters though, because she's here.

"Atina?" I say again, apparently only capable of my sister's name. The noise cancelers in her ears prevent her from hearing me.

My sister has not been in the sea for years, not since she was a teenager. Her heart is with the land and mapping out the world. Not below the sea. To her, it's a cage. An unknown abyss she hates.

Atina seems to remember where she's at, and her eyes narrow like I personally offended her. She doesn't speak—and even if she does, I wouldn't be able to hear her—as she swims next to me. Atina swats me with her tail, and I move over, giving her space to grab the bars. The moment her fingers wrap around them, the Leviathan's song turns into a screech, prompting my men to stop what they're doing and cover their ears.

I refuse the temptation, even though it's taking my

entire being to do so. I try to focus on Erin and the beautiful, calming cadence of her voice. It gives me the strength to pull at the gate, only this time I'm not doing it alone.

Atina throws her weight back against me, not used to her tail. Still, she's able to use her strength to pull, and together, the gate begins to move. It's painfully slow, but it's moving. The screeching only grows louder, laced with a newfound fear.

"Harder!" I yell, even though she can't hear me. The instruction is just as much for me as it is for her: a reminder that Tetria's safety is dependent upon closing the gate to the prison once and for all.

Little by little, the gate starts to close. The Leviathan grow louder in their frustration, almost deafening in the vast ocean. Atina jerks her body back as hard as she can. Her head collides with my chest, but she doesn't seem to notice. She's too focused on the task at hand.

The black claws retreat, followed by a chorus of screams. I only get a small glimpse inside the prison, but movement catches my eye. Dozens, if not hundreds, of black sea serpents thrash around in their enclosure. Yellow eyes meet mine, and for the first time, I've looked into the eyes of true evil. Malice and contempt stare back at me before the creature lunges.

I throw all my might into closing the door, and before the serpent can reach us, the last inch of the gate is closed. The gate molds into the rock, a white shimmer bonding it permanently together. The last scream rings out, and the white light of a magical lock explodes, temporarily blinding me.

Soon, more light follows. Small white orbs free themself from the cave and float to the surface. For a moment, I wonder if those are the souls stolen by the Leviathan. They escape, finally on their way to the sea goddess and their final resting place.

Then...

Nothing.

No sound. No claws. Nothing.

Just sweet silence.

For a moment, no one moves, too stunned to do more than stare in disbelief. I'm first to remove the ear cancelers, and the others quickly follow.

"It is done," Delmare voices our disbelief out loud.

Then everything happens at once. My men break out in triumphant whoops of joy, while Nori, Delmare, and I both ascend on Atina, attacking her with a forced hug. She hates it, but I can't bring myself to care.

"You fuckers! Get off me," she grunts and attempts to push us off her.

"Just fucking bear it." Nori grins and squeezes her tighter.

"You came." I'm still in a state of disbelief because my sister is here. In the ocean. Swimming right in front of me.

Finally, Atina pushes us all away and glares daggers at us. If looks could kill, we'd be sushi. "I couldn't trust you idiots to get the job done," she says, feigning nonchalance. I can tell how much this is affecting her though. I might not ever know her reasoning behind what she did, but I don't need to know in order to be eternally grateful.

"Thank you, Sister. We owe you everything."

"Start by acknowledging your wife. She's the reason I'm here." Atina lifts her head, motioning to something behind me. I turn just in time to see Erin swimming my way.

I don't think. I just act and swim to my girl. My tentacles wrap around her lithe frame and pull her flush against my chest. "Allarick—" Before she can say more, my lips are on hers. I have a lot of making up to do, and I will.

But right now, I need to feel my wife against me.

# CHAPTER 44

# ERIN

Allarick's lips feel like coming home after a long time away. The kiss is desperate—disbelief, worry, love, and success all packaged into one. To say it's overwhelming would be an understatement.

And yet I cling to Allarick, afraid we won't have a moment like this again. We were so close to failing. So close to losing everything we created together and the possibility of a future.

I break the kiss. "Don't ever push me away again. Anything we face, we face together. Don't leave me because you think it's the better option." I have more to say, more I want to yell and demand he never do. I also want to kiss him and tangle my body around his until I can't tell where I end and he begins.

But it isn't the time nor the place.

To his benefit, Allarick grimaces, shoulders slumping. "Not my finest moment, sweet girl. I thought I was protecting you."

"Sometimes I need to protect *you*, Allarick."

Allarick smiles, reaching to caress my cheek. I lean into his touch, needing to be reminded that he's here and safe. "Thank you, Erin. You came even after I pushed you away. I love you, and I'll forever be indebted to you."

Those three words hit me like a tidal wave. Allarick loves me. It's so damn good to hear out loud and gives me the confidence to say it to him. "I love you too, and I can think of a few ways you can pay me back." I wink, leaning up to kiss him gently.

His low chuckle follows me as I push away from him, looking at the woman who made this moment possible. She seems so far away, but her eyes lock with mine.

"Atina." I don't think I've ever seen the woman look so small and utterly uncomfortable. "You came. You helped close the gate. Thank you." My words don't accurately convey my gratitude for her. "It took a tremendous amount of courage to come here."

Atina laughs, though there is no humor behind it. "Do me a favor and never let there be a reason I'm down here again."

"We will do our best." Allarick smiles, coming up behind me. He places his arm around my shoulder, tucking me into his side. I'm not the only one who can't keep my hands off, out of fear he'll be ripped from me at any second.

Atina swims toward us with Nori glued to her side. Her movements are jerky and unnatural. When Nori reaches to steady her, Atina slaps his hands away. "I'm not an incompetent guppy," she hisses.

Nori doesn't try reaching for her again.

By the time Atina makes her way toward us, she's out

of breath. "Are you both okay?" she asks, inspecting our bodies for injuries.

"I should be the one asking. You are the two who did the brunt of the work. I didn't do much."

"You did plenty." I'm surprised by the intensity of her voice and the hard set of her jaw. "Without your music, neither Allarick nor I would have had the clarity of mind to shut the gate. We wouldn't be standing here right now because the Leviathan would have destroyed us and been let loose in the ocean."

"Which would have given a huge advantage to the Nephilim," Allarick says gently. "And all of our people would be dead. Your role in this was pivotal."

The intensity of their stares makes me shift uncomfortably, but I can't hide the smile on my face. I did something good. I helped protect my new home, and I get to keep the new family I've made here.

I throw my arms around both Allarick and Atina, squeezing them tightly. Allarick laughs and returns the hug, while Atina awkwardly pats my back, but accepts the group hug—at least for a total of ten seconds before she pushes us away.

"Well, this has been quite fun. But if someone doesn't get me to the shore soon, I'm going to become everyone's problem." She glares, and I can see just how ready she is to leave.

"We can take her to the surface, right? Our people are up there, and we can tell them the good news. That we'll be able to go home." I squeeze Allarick's arm, eager to see excitement and relief on the merpeople's faces.

"So, what I'm hearing is that it's time for a celebration? And no celebration is complete without copious amounts of alcohol." Nori grins.

"After today's events, I'm going to drink the bar dry," Atina murmurs.

Nori tries to reach for Atina again, and this time, she slaps his tail with her own. While they are distracted, Allarick pulls me to his chest, rubbing his tentacle up and down my back. "We shall have our own celebration as soon as our people are safely home."

"Oh yeah?" I grin. "Does this celebration involve clothes or no clothes?"

"Definitely no clothes."

"My favorite type of celebration," I hum.

I'm not sure if I'll ever get used to Allarick kissing me, or ever lose the butterflies that fill my stomach each time our lips meet. I hope I don't. To be truly loved is the sweetest thing in the world, something I would fight hundreds of Leviathan for. I've spent too long in the dark, thinking my happy ending would never come. But now that it's here, I plan on holding it tightly and never letting go.

"Let's go home, sweet girl," Allarick says when we finally break apart.

Home. Our home.

Pulling Atina between us, hooking her arm through mine, we begin our ascent to the surface. For the first time in a long time, I feel like I'm where I'm supposed to be.

And that's a damn good feeling.

# CHAPTER 45

# ERIN

ERIN

The glass feels cool against my body as Allarick presses me against the window. My nipples pebble at the cold sensation, and I let out a breathy moan. Not for the first time, I'm thankful for the fact that we can see out, but no one can see in.

Because they would be seeing *a lot*.

Allarick presses his body against me. His hard cock pushes against my ass, allowing me to feel every glorious inch of my husband. One of his tentacles is wrapped around my neck, applying just enough pressure to make me gasp in need. Another tentacle is deep inside of me, moving at an agonizingly slow pace. The sucker is positioned just right to tease my clit.

It's torture that has been going on for hours.

I can't feel my legs anymore, and my body is spent, but Allarick wants to coax out every last orgasm I can muster. Has anyone ever died from an orgasm overdose? Because I think I'm going to be the first one.

This has been my life every day since we closed the gate on the Leviathan's prison a week ago, thus saving Tetria. Allarick promised to show me his gratitude, and I naively thought that meant flowers and a nice dinner, but clearly he had other things in mind.

I'll admit, his idea is much better. He did manage to retrieve my harp, which I'm thankful for.

"Look at our kingdom, my queen," he purrs in a low, seductive voice. I have a hard time focusing on anything other than the giant kraken tentacle buried in my pussy.

"Look at the vibrancy. The abundance of joy and feeling of security you helped save," he continues and increases his speed. I moan, desperately trying to grasp for something, but my hands ball into fists on the glass.

"Allarick," I moan, my breaths coming in short, shallow gasps. I twist my naked body, trying to speed up my pleasure.

My husband just chuckles at my expense. "Needy girl, aren't you?"

"Yes." There's no need to deny it. My body is wound so tight, begging for one last orgasm before I shoo him away and hide my thoroughly used vagina from him.

"What is it you want?"

He knows damn well what I want. I can't see his face, but I imagine he's smirking. Pure male satisfaction. The sucker on my clit presses down harder, and I cry out.

"Baby, make me come all over your tentacle. I can't hold back anymore. I need it. I need *you*. Please!" My words are barely coherent and sound like a desperate woman. I certainly feel like one.

"That's my sweet girl," Allarick hums. Then, faster than my brain can process, his thrusts turn punishing. My body slams harder against the glass, nipples so sensitive from the constant rubbing against the window, it's almost painful with how good it feels. Allarick yanks my head back, and I moan.

He quickly swallows my sounds of pleasure when his mouth captures mine in a searing kiss. My body—and brain—short-circuit, and I can do nothing but give in to his will. He claims me, pressing his cock between my ass cheeks. I shiver at the intrusion, and even though he's not inside me there, I know it's only a matter of time.

"Allarick!" I scream as my orgasm overtakes me. I come for him, and he follows me shortly after. Something hot and sticky splashes my back, and I know he came for me.

"Fuck, Erin. You drive me crazy with need. The power you have over me," he groans, and I slump against him.

"I'm done," I pant, shaking my head. "I tap out. All my body holes are closed to you, you sex-crazed kraken."

Allarick just laughs as he pulls his tentacle out of me. I whimper at the sudden empty feeling, but my pussy also weeps in joy for finally getting a break.

"I just needed you to know how much I love you. I'm also not finished thanking you for your role in imprisoning the Leviathan or apologizing to you," he says.

"Well, you're done thanking me for today." I let my body float. I can't feel my limbs.

"I'm done because we have a meeting to get to."

I groan and almost start to cry. Almost. "Meeting? What meeting?" I sound like a whiny child, but I can't help it.

Allarick captures me before I can float too far away and gently rubs my back. "We're meeting with my sister and a few other kings to discuss Nephilim activity."

"Oh, right," I say, deadpan. Last week, Allarick sent word to his sister, asking for her help in arranging a meeting to discuss Nephilim above the sea. I just forgot about it. If I would have known, I wouldn't have ever let my husband fuck me for the entire morning.

Probably.

"I promise to give you a massage when we get home. I'm sure your muscles are sore." He sounds smug, and I shoot him a look, which he returns with a boyish smile.

"Fine," I groan. "Help me get dressed, will you?"

THE MEETING IS BEING HELD in wolf territory. Allarick tells me that is where Rip and Hettie live. I'm excited to see them again, even under these circumstances.

When we arrive, a tall, handsome man by the name of Thorne greets us. "They are in here, right this way." He leads Allarick and me through the giant house Allarick calls the "packhouse."

Thorne opens the door, and heads swivel in our direction. Hettie stands up, smiling wide as she comes and greets me. "It's so good to see you again. And congratulations for kicking ass down under." She winks, then takes my hand and leads me around the table.

"Let me introduce everyone. You know my husband, Rip. Next to him is his cousin and my best friend, Tallie. Thorne's her husband. And Rose and her husband." She points to Rose and the intimidating man next to her. That must be Malix. Last time I saw him, he was in dragon form. He doesn't look any less intimidating as a human.

"Next to them is Rose's friend and Malix's council member, Vivia. And you know Atina."

She smiles, and I take a seat next to Atina. "It's good to see you," I say to her.

"Especially above water." True to her word, Atina has not returned to below the water again. She was pivotal in closing the gate, and we will forever be thankful for what she did, which is why neither Allarick nor I have pressured her to come for a visit. We'll happily make the trek to see her above water.

"We may as well get started," Rip says. "The oceans are once again safe, meaning the Nephilim are grounded to land."

"And if any of those bastards try to use the sea, my crew will take care of them," Atina says. "Those bastards won't make it far in my waters."

"I think I have a girl crush on her," Hettie whispers loudly to Rip's cousin, Tallie. Both women laugh as Rip glares at his wife. Atina only smirks.

"Lycan Forest and Dragon's Keep have both been free of Nephilim," Rip continues. "But we've heard reports that a great number are headed toward the Demon's Clan and Pixie Cove."

"Gadreel is not amongst them," Malix says, his voice deep and foreboding.

"Who is Gadreel?" I ask, not having heard the name before.

"He is the leader of the Nephilim. Arguably the most dangerous," Allarick explains.

"We believe he is sending his people out to keep us distracted so we don't attempt to locate him," Malix says. "I have sent word to the demon king, Oziel, to inform him of the invasion of his territory."

"Did he heed your warning?" Allarick asks.

Malix shrugs. "I don't know. Oziel is notorious for his lack of communication to outside kingdoms. He doesn't exactly play well with others."

"Neither do you, my love." Rose chuckles. Malix smiles down at his pregnant wife, so much love and adoration in his expression.

"What is needed from the merpeople?" Allarick asks the table.

"Stay vigilant. The war is far from over. And hope The Guardian can provide assistance once again," Malix says, tearing his eyes away from Rose.

Rip scoffs. "Yeah, he has his work cut out for him with Oziel. He's one cunning bastard and an asshole to boot."

"Uhm, you were the biggest asshole when we first met. You told me I smelled like a dog." Hettie narrows her eyes at Rip. "If The Guardian can find someone to love you, then I'm certain he can find someone for the demon king."

"He said you smelled like a dog?" I ask incredulously, unable to stifle my laugh.

Luckily Hettie isn't offended. She just smiles and nods. "Yup. Isn't that romantic?"

"You're going to have to tell me all about it." I smile, desperately wanting to know more about the lives of the two human queens from Grym Hollow.

"You know, unless we are needed for more of this meeting, I think it would be nice if the ladies have lunch together in the dining room while the menfolk grunt and glare at each other," Hettie says.

"We do not grunt and glare," Rip grunts while glaring.

"Sure you don't, babe." Hettie rolls her eyes.

"I think that's a lovely idea. I could use some girl time," Rose says. "What about you, Erin? Want to join us for lunch?"

Before I answer, I turn to my husband. He's smiling at me and leans down to press a gentle kiss to my lips. "Go, sweet girl. Have fun. I'll be here when you're ready to leave."

"It won't be for a while because we are going to get wasted." Hettie scoots her chair back and stands up, grabbing Tallie's hand.

"Not all of us are," Rose says, standing up with a hand over her belly. "But Erin will drink for me, won't you?"

"I don't drink," I admit, trying not to bring down the mood.

"Honestly, I don't either," Hettie says, "But we will get wasted with dessert."

"Oh, that I can get behind." I laugh and stand. Allarick lets go of my hand, and I wave goodbye to him. "Love you," I whisper.

"Love you, my queen." He winks at me.

Rose then hooks her arm through mine and leads me toward the door. "I have so much to ask you about living under the water. I can't even imagine."

True joy blooms in my chest. For the first time in my life, I have the ability to make true friendships. The three of us are bonded by our choice to leave Grym Hollow. For me, it was the best choice I've ever made for myself because I found purpose and the love of a man I didn't know I deserved. Along the way, I found myself again.

And I couldn't be happier.

# EPILOGUE
## ENDER

Pain is something I'm accustomed to. Always with me, creeping into every part of my life. I once thought I understood pain, but that was before my banishment to Grym Hollow. This is where I learned true suffering and that a lonely heart is the cruelest punishment of all.

My only escape from this pain is making amends and setting my wrongs right. With three successful matches, a newfound entity grows inside me. Something I haven't felt in a long time.

Hope.

Rose was the start to all of this. She's brave and a natural leader. No one enters a realm of dragons without fear, but Rose had no problems making Mescos her home.

Hettie came next—fierce and proud, someone hoping to fix her mistakes. I can empathize with her. Her sacrifice gave her mother and sister a better life.

And then there's Erin—the sweetest of the three and

the most selfless. There was no other pick for Allarick. It was always Erin. He would allow her the opportunity to grow and discover who she is. And that's exactly what she did.

All three women hold valuable traits Mescos needs. Leadership. Bravery. Selflessness.

All traits *she* had.

The traits I once vowed to uphold, too, until temptation got too strong and I too weak.

I see her everywhere and in everything I do. A reminder of what I lost and will hopefully one day gain back. But first I have to help the other three kings.

King Oziel is a challenging one indeed. In many ways, he reminds me of myself when I was younger. There's very little that fazes the demon and even less he cares about. He can be wicked when necessary and show mercy when there is mercy to be given. Usually. He's not a bad king; his kingdom thrives under his rule, but his ego and temper will cost him everything.

Unless I find his perfect match.

And I think I have.

I venture farther into the city than normal, but it's late, and many of the downtown shops are closed. A few bars remain open, but only a few patrons frequent them this late. I don't stop walking until I come to a set of stairs.

These stairs lead up to a brick building. Inside is sterile, cold, and dated with its meager furnishings. Although no lights are on, I know people are inside. A place like this doesn't close. Ever.

I take the stairs two at a time until I reach the

entrance. The customary *no weapons* sign is plastered to the front, which is ironic because everyone who works here carries numerous weapons on their person at all times.

I'm hit with harsh fluorescent lights as soon as I open the door. A low buzz from the ancient vending machine and the clicking of a keyboard drown out the shouts and cries coming from the back. It reeks of bodily fluids and bleach.

I approach the counter just as the man behind the barred window does a double take when he sees me. His already pale face drains of all color, and his body fidgets uncomfortably.

"Are you...The Guardian?" he whispers as if we aren't the only ones in the room.

"I'm here to post bail for an inmate." I ignore his question. It's idiotic. Who else looks like stone with their gray complexion and has horns protruding from their forehead?

"O-okay. Uh, can you tell me the name of the inmate?"

"Isabelle Sinclair."

The man stops what he's doing to peer over the computer at me. "Isabelle? You know what she's in for, right?"

"I do."

"And you still want to bail her out?"

I sigh, growing tired of this mundane conversation. "Is her bail not set?"

"It is for half a million dollars, but—"

"Then allow me to pay and bring the girl to me." My

command leaves no room for argument. Considering the man before me looks like he's about to piss his pants, I don't believe that to be a problem.

I hand him the cashier's check, and he inspects it. "I'm going to need to talk to my superiors about this. You good to wait, sir…The Guardian?"

"I have been waiting for years," I say.

The man just furrows his brow in confusion but nods. "Right. Going to check that for you. If she can be bailed out, I'll bring her to you. Honestly, your punishment is probably worse than what we have." He laughs, but when I don't join in, the man scrambles away.

I take a seat on the cheap plastic chair, crossing my right leg over my left, and place my folded-up hands in my lap.

And I wait for Isabelle Sinclair. The woman who murdered Erin's abuser. She took care of James for me, so posting bail is the least I can do.

Yes, Oziel will meet his match with this one.


To be continued…

# WANT MORE?

Allarick is planning something big for Erin's first birthday at the castle. Read the sweet—and spicy—scene in my newsletter.

Sign up for my newsletter here or head to Instagram and click the link in my bio.

# ALSO BY TATI B. ALVAREZ

### **<u>Dawn Of Dasos</u>**

1. The Ambrosia Throne

2. The Ambrosia Deception

### **<u>Grym Hollow</u>**

1. The Dragon's Rose

1.5 Tallie's Secret

2. The Wolf's Mate

3. The Kraken's Queen

4. *The Demon's Beauty - Coming Soon*

# THANK YOU FOR READING!

I can't thank you enough for picking up my book. I hope you enjoyed it as much as I enjoyed writing it! If you did and are willing please consider leaving a review on your favorite book sites. This helps out small authors like me so much. Thank you for your continued support!

# ABOUT THE AUTHOR

Tati B. Alvarez lives in Austin, Texas with her family. She spends most days lost in her own head, creating stories. When she is not writing, you can find her vacationing at Disney World.

www.ingramcontent.com/pod-product-compliance
Lightning Source LLC
Chambersburg PA
CBHW030117310726
48970CB00004B/1304